T0357078

Black Hamptons 2:

Gentrification

Black Hamptons 2:

Gentrification

Carl Weber

with

La Jill Hunt

www.urbanbooks.net

Urban Books, LLC
300 Farmingdale Road, NY-Route 109
Farmingdale, NY 11735

ISBN 13: 978-1-64556-716-5
EBOOK ISBN 13: 978-1-64556-717-2

First Hardcover Printing March 2025
Printed in the United States of America

10 9 8 7 6 5 4 3 2 1

Distributed by Kensington Publishing Corp.
Submit orders to:
Customer Service
400 Hahn Road
Westminster, MD 21157-4627
Phone: 1-800-733-3000
Fax: 1-800-659-2436

Black Hamptons 2:

Gentrification

Carl Weber

with

La Jill Hunt

Prologue

My mother's yacht was empty most of the time, so it was the perfect place to chill with Tania whenever she was able to sneak away from Peter's clingy ass. He might have been a fighter, but he obviously wasn't laying it down correctly, because Tania was hooking up with me every chance she got. Not that I was complaining, because I was starting to catch real feelings for her.

"So, I was wondering," I said hesitantly as we lay in bed in the master suite after another sweaty round of sex. She was snuggled up against me, and I ran my hand across her smooth skin.

"Wondering what?" she asked right before her phone started vibrating on the nightstand.

She reached over to pick up the phone and check the caller ID. When she shook her head and sighed, I didn't need to ask who was calling. I didn't care anyway.

She put the phone back, and I playfully pulled her into me, nibbling her ear. "Where are you going? You can't get away from me."

"I'm sorry, but I gotta go, Jesse."

"No." I wrapped my arms around her waist. "Stay with me, just for a little while longer. I gotta go to some party my grandma's giving in about an hour anyway."

"Seriously, Jesse, he's blowing up my phone." She picked up the phone and turned the screen toward me. "Look. He's calling again."

She wasn't lying. Dude was seriously trying to keep Verizon, AT&T, or whatever service he used in business. That had to be like the twentieth call in the last hour.

"He'll be all right. It's about time you kicked that clown to the curb anyway."

"You know I can't do that. And you also know I can't stay." She gently shoved me away, but I wouldn't give up. My finger traced her collar bone and across her chest, brushing against her nipples, now erect from my touch.

I smirked. "It's not cold in here, so it's pretty obvious you wanna stay."

Tania grinned and folded her arms across her chest. "You're devious. You know that, right? Erect nipples could mean a lot of things."

I lifted the sheet so she could see that I was aroused. "But I think we both know what this means, and you said you would never leave me unsatisfied."

"You don't play fair." She giggled, staring longingly under the sheets.

"Neither do you. Now, are you going to put that phone down and handle your business or what?"

She thought about it for a second. "Both."

"Both?"

"Both. I'm leaving." Tania hopped out of the bed before I could stop her. "But I'll meet you back here after your grandmother's party."

"You promise? Because I'm starting to feel something I never felt before."

"And what's that?" she asked.

"Love," I mumbled, barely able to get it out. I'm sure it sounded corny, but it was true. I was definitely falling in love with her.

"Are you serious?" Her face softened, and she looked like she wanted to say something but changed her mind. She picked up the rest of her clothes off the floor and got dressed. "We agreed this was a sneaky link, Jesse. We're not supposed to catch feelings."

"I know that," I replied. I'd fucked up. I shouldn't have opened my mouth. "I can't help how I feel. I think about you all the time. I'm lonely five minutes after you leave, and I can't stop smiling when you're here. I didn't mean for it to happen, but I'm in love with you. I just need you to know."

"You know what the most messed up thing is?" She lowered her head.

"What?"

"I'm in love with you too, but summer is over in two weeks, and you're leaving to go back to school. I'll still be here while you're doing God knows what with God knows who." She let out a sad breath before wrapping her arms around my neck. We shared a long kiss that left us both breathless, and when it ended, she touched my face. "I want you to prove me wrong. I really do."

"Good." I smiled and kissed her again. "'Cause I will."

A noise came from behind the stateroom door in the small hallway, catching us both off guard.

"Is that your parents?"

"I don't know. I guess it could be, but I told my mom we were coming here."

"You told her?" There was an uncomfortable look on Tania's face.

Someone on the other side of the door tried the handle, but ever since we'd been busted by Sergeant Lane the first night we were here, I always made sure to lock the door. Whoever it was started banging so loudly it made Tania jump. I threw the sheet off and put on my pants, then stepped beside her protectively.

"Who is it?"

There was no answer, but the knocking started again.

"Mom, that you?"

Still no response. Tania's eyes shifted uneasily to mine.

I was about to step to the door when something hit it with such force that I felt the boat move. The door and lock held, but a few more hits like that and it would come flying off the hinges.

"Shit! Who the fuck is that?" I shouted.

"Oh God, it has to be Peter," Tania said frantically, and I sensed that she was right.

He must have heard her voice because he started yelling "Tania!" over and over again as the door shook in its frame. I imagined him on the other side, throwing his massive body against it to force it open.

"He's going to break that door down!" she cried.

"What the fuck is he doing on my boat?" I looked around the room for a weapon, but everything in the cabin was nailed down. "Shit!"

"What I'm doing to this door ain't shit compared to what I'm gonna do to you, motherfucker!" he bellowed through the door.

He gave the door one more powerful kick, and it came crashing down, leaving Tania and me exposed and at his mercy.

Tania screamed. Instinctively, I pushed her behind me just as he rushed toward us.

"Noooooooo! Jesse, look out!"

I had nowhere to go in the 12-by-15 cabin, and her screams hit me the same moment he did. I was no weakling, but my strength was no match for a guy who trained in the boxing ring for hours every day. He snatched me up like a rag doll and threw me around the room a couple of times. I flew into the dresser headfirst, and as I got up on wobbly legs, I felt a slow trickle of blood down my face. The excruciating pain only got worse when Peter charged me again and connected his fist to my jaw. I was on the ground again, with no time to recuperate before he straddled me and delivered one blow after another to my face.

"Peter! Stop! Stop!" Tania cried, but he wasn't trying to hear none of that.

She jumped on Peter's back to try to stop him. He paused only long enough to push her away, tossing her tiny body onto the bed before resuming his brutal beatdown. I reached out for her, and as long as I lived to tell the tale, I would never forget the fearful look in her eyes. She looked at me through her tears, her lip trembling, before she jumped from the bed and ran out of the room.

"Help! Help! Someone, please! Please call the police!"

The sweat from Peter's menacing face dripped onto mine, and each blow he landed was accompanied by a loud, animalistic grunt. The blank look in his eyes told me that his humanity was on sabbatical. All that was left was the beast within. He was going to kill me.

Gasping for breath, I struggled to stay awake, but it was impossible. My body was telling me to stop fighting. Hoping to find some kind of relief, I gave in and succumbed to the numbing darkness.

1

Sergeant Tom Lane

I stood outside the back door of the police precinct, gasping for air and fighting the overwhelming feeling of nausea. I had rushed out of the building soon after the Brittons made their dramatic exit, still screaming about how my son should suffer just like their precious Jesse had.

My worst nightmare had come true, and I was living in the middle of it. Over the years, I worked hard to protect my son. Like a lot of boys, he had tons of energy and could be a bit wild at times, so I had introduced him to boxing to channel that energy in the gym. It kept him off the streets and out of trouble. He was a talented fighter, too, most likely headed for the Olympics someday—until now. Ever since he got together with that damn girl, he'd been slacking off on his workouts, always in a rush to finish so he could go see her. I knew she wasn't worth a damn, and I was hoping that Peter would figure that out one day and leave her alone. But he was hooked, and now, because Tania couldn't stay away from that spoiled son of a bitch, Jesse Britton, my son was locked up.

Chief Harrington had told me I couldn't talk to Peter until he was processed, so I didn't know the full details about what had happened between him and that Britton punk. What I did know was that there was no way my son was going to sit in jail. I would fight to get him released just as hard as Carolyn Britton planned to fight to keep him in there. Hell, if she had her way, Peter would be headed to death row without a trial.

The uneasy feeling came over me again, but I swallowed it. I didn't have time to be sick. I had to save my son.

"Fuck this." Taking my phone from my back pocket, I called the only person I could think of who might be able to help.

After a few rings, I was relieved to hear his voice on the other end.

"Hello?"

The voice belonged to a lawyer named Jeffrey Bowen. His wife, Vanessa, was the head of the Black Hamptons Homeowners Association. She was the woman who had convinced the Chief to hire me as the town's first Black police officer. I didn't really know Jeffrey that well, but I guess I was hoping that my position as the police liaison to the Black Hamptons community might mean something to him. Besides, he was the only lawyer I knew in Sag Harbor, and I was desperate. So desperate, in fact, that I called him even knowing that his wife was related to the Britton family, which complicated things, to say the least. Under normal circumstances, I might have just Googled someone else, but I was so stressed I wasn't really thinking straight.

"Jeffrey, it's Sergeant Tom Lane," I said. "I know it's late, but I'm dealing with an emergency."

He cleared his throat. "Uh, yes, I heard about what happened with your son."

It came as no surprise that Jeffrey was already aware of Peter's dilemma, but hearing him say so still caused me to feel deflated.

"I forgot how fast news travels around here." I sighed.

"Travels even faster when it's bad news."

"Indeed. Well, Peter's in need of an attorney. I'd like to hire you." The words tumbled out of my mouth without hesitation. The desperation in my voice was obvious, but I didn't care.

The moment of silence that followed was brief but ominous. I held my breath and closed my eyes, praying, *Dear God, please let him say yes. My son and I need him.*

He finally spoke. "Sergeant Lane, I can't do that. Representing your son would be a conflict of interest on both a personal and professional level."

I was silent as I struggled to process what he'd said. What the hell was I going to do now?

"Sergeant Lane, are you still here?"

"Uh, yeah. I knew it was a long shot, but I just thought . . ."

"I know it took a hell of a lot for you to call me, and this is a hell of a predicament for both your son and yourself." He paused, and for a moment, I thought the conversation was over. Then he said, "From what I understand, Peter is going to need a suitable attorney for the felony charges he's facing. That's not my specialty, so even if I wasn't involved with the family, I wouldn't agree to take the case. If he were my son, I'd find the best criminal defense attorney possible."

I sighed, feeling lost. "I understand. I'm sorry to have taken up your time."

"Hey, no need to apologize. I probably would've done the same thing if I were in your shoes. I hope it all works out for you guys."

"Thanks."

"And I do have one more piece of advice for you."

"What's that?" I asked.

"When you do hire an attorney, find someone outside the county. My wife's family has significant influence around here that could complicate things for your son's defense."

"Yeah, that makes sense," I said. "Carolyn's reach is far, and I'm sure she's going to do everything in her power to make my son pay. Don't get me wrong, I'm not saying he shouldn't be held accountable, but he's a good kid and he deserves to be treated fairly."

"I agree. And you're right about Carolyn. She's a beast on a mission. But honestly, that's not the person you need to be worried about."

"Then who?"

"Moses is home."

"Who the hell is Moses?"

"Her husband. He loves his family and will fight for them even harder than she will."

"Shit," I said aloud before I could stop myself.

"I'm just keeping it real with you. If it was my son, I'd want someone to tell me."

"Yeah. Well, thanks again, Jeffrey. I appreciate it."

"Good luck, Sergeant Lane."

I ended the call, feeling even more anxious. Not only was finding a suitable lawyer going to be a challenge, but we were going to be up against someone even more vicious than Carolyn Britton.

"You still here, Sergeant?"

The voice caught me off guard, and I turned around to see Officer Nugent exiting the back door. He was eyeing me with a look that I couldn't read. It was either concern or pity.

"Yeah, I'm still trying to wait around until they let me see Peter."

Nugent shook his head as he walked toward me. "I don't think that's gonna happen, Sarge. Chief Harrington isn't letting anyone see him."

"Fuck that. I'm seeing my—" I started to yell, but Nugent raised his hand to stop my growing anger.

"I know you're worried, but Peter's good. He's in a cell by himself, away from everyone else. I know it may seem like Chief is being an asshole about this, but he's not. He's really looking out for him, but he has to be careful so it doesn't look like he's giving him preferential treatment. The last thing anyone needs is for the Brittons to hear that Peter's being treated any different than anyone else in custody."

The word "custody" almost made me break. My son was in police custody and alone. I held back the tears that threatened to escape.

"We made sure he got some food and some bedding."

"Bedding?" I frowned.

"Come on now, Sarge. He's spending the night here, if not a couple more." Nugent shrugged. "Hopefully he will go before the magistrate tomorrow morning, but you heard what Carolyn Britton said."

"I don't give a damn what she said. My son isn't spending more than one night in jail," I snapped. "Tell Chief Harrington I'll be back in the morning, and I expect to be able to see Peter."

I walked off, leaving Nugent to watch as I got into my cruiser and drove off. I had no doubt that once I was out of the parking lot, he would be inside delivering my message to our boss. Undoubtedly, this entire ordeal would be the talk of the station, the community—hell, the entire town. The reality was my son had assaulted Jesse Britton, crown prince of the Black Hamptons and heir to the Britton throne, all because of Peter's cheating-ass girlfriend, Tania.

The more I thought about the situation, the more guilt I felt. Earlier in the summer, I'd been called to the marina to investigate a suspected break-in, only to find Jesse and Tania on his mother's yacht, butt-ass naked in the bed. I knew that girl wasn't shit, but I couldn't bring myself to tell Peter what I'd discovered. I was too worried that it would distract him from training for the upcoming Olympic boxing trials. Maybe I could have found a way to break it to him gently and prevented things from escalating to violence.

Going to an empty house seemed pointless, so instead, I drove around Sag Harbor. When Peter and I had first moved to the community, we would drive around to get familiar with the area. It was a quaint little village, nothing like the Brooklyn neighborhood where we'd lived before. He loved it when we drove past the wealthy communities with their immaculate lawns and huge homes.

"Look at that one, Dad," Peter would say as he admired yet another million-dollar mansion.

"Yeah, that one is nice." I agreed. "When you win that gold medal and then become Heavyweight Champion of the World, you can buy that one."

"And I'm gonna buy you the one next door, I promise."

"Next door? That's a little close, son. How about across the street?" I laughed.

"I'm gonna have so much money that I might buy the whole block and let you pick," Peter answered. "I owe you that, and I'm gonna make you proud."

The way Peter said it had made me proud and confirmed that accepting the job had been a good move for both of us. Now, I had to wonder if I'd made the right decision. My mind was all over the place, and the drive didn't seem to help. Exhaustion set in, so I headed home and went to bed without taking off my uniform.

2

Moses Britton

After seven long years, I was finally home, though no thanks to my wife, who hadn't even bothered to visit me while I was in hiding in Venezuela. The irony was that my escape had been orchestrated to protect her. It was Carolyn's financial mismanagement at Amistad Bank, the institution founded by my great-grandfather, that had brought my world crashing down in the first place, but the Feds set their sights on me. After I was indicted, it became clear that my only surefire defense would be to point a finger at Carolyn, and I couldn't bring myself to do that, so I fled. I was hiding out in South America until my lawyer, Jeffrey Bowen, could negotiate to get the charges against me dropped. It had taken years, but after a change in administration and a hefty donation, it was finally safe for me to go home.

One would think she'd show more support for my sacrifice, but in true Carolyn Britton fashion, she had seized my absence to her advantage, stepping into the role of CFO at Amistad Bank once it was released from government conservatorship. Carolyn had always been smart and beautiful, but she was also an opportunistic bitch, and that characteristic remained. Still, there was something about the tough woman that I admired, and once I'd sufficiently punished her for her disloyalty, I just might try to see if the flame between us could be rekindled.

When I had popped up unannounced, the look on my wife's face and her reaction to seeing me wasn't nearly as satisfying as I'd imagined, especially after our brief encounter was cut short. The news of my grandson's beating took precedence over our reunion. In what I assumed was an attempt to assert her dominance, she refused to let Malcolm and me get into the car with her. We had no choice but to accept a ride from Jeffrey, who offered to take us to the hospital.

"Dad, I can't believe you're really home," Malcolm said as we sat in the rear of Jeffrey's car.

"Believe it, son."

"But, how? Why didn't anyone say anything to us about it?"

"I didn't want anyone to know, especially your mother," I said, glancing at him. "I couldn't risk her taking any actions that might jeopardize my legal status."

"Oh." Malcolm's terse response confirmed what I already knew: Carolyn was the cause of the delays that Jeffrey had encountered.

"But I'm here now. That's all that matters."

"Damn right. This family needs you, Dad."

"I'm glad to hear you say that, son. I'm hoping your brother feels the same way. He didn't seem too thrilled to see me." Martin was in the car with his mother and didn't protest one bit when she kicked me and Malcolm out.

"I think he was just shocked, that's all." Malcolm defended his younger brother. "We all were."

I wasn't really surprised by Martin's reaction. He'd always been more partial to his mother. As my firstborn son, Malcom had always been close to me. I taught him everything from tying his shoe and riding a bike to selecting valuable timepieces and the proper way to hoist a sail. Our tight bond was probably the catalyst for Carolyn monopolizing our younger son, Martin. By the time he was a teenager, it was obvious that he preferred being around his mother, who spoiled him with toys and video games, rather than spending time with his older brother and me. Now that I'd returned home, I planned to change that and forge closer connections to both of my sons. I was going to need their support in rebuilding the life that I'd had before.

Malcom grew quiet beside me, and Jeffrey matched his silence with his hands clenched on the steering wheel. We all had a lot on our minds.

"What happened to Jesse?" I asked urgently. Things had been pretty chaotic when I showed up just as everyone was getting into the car to go to the hospital, and in the rush, no one had bothered to give me any details.

"It was Peter Lane," he said. "He attacked Jesse."

"Who?"

"A local kid. Recently moved here. From what I was told, Peter found Jesse with a girl named Tania. They were . . . together, and Peter snapped. He's a menace, Dad. An amateur boxer with a bad temper."

I winced at the thought of my grandson, who was just a preteen the last time I'd seen him, being beaten by a boxer. "How badly was he hurt?"

Malcolm's jaw clenched. "It's bad."

"I'm sorry, son. I truly am."

I was silent for the rest of the ride. This was certainly a terrible way to come home.

By the time we arrived at the hospital and Jeffrey pulled up by the front door, I was livid and ready to kill the man who'd attacked Jesse.

"Where is this punk at now?" I asked.

"He's in jail. That's why we were at the police precinct, to make sure he wasn't getting any special treatment since his father is on the force," Malcolm explained.

Malcolm and I got out of the car. "Thank you, Jeffrey, for the ride and everything else. We'll speak tomorrow."

"No problem, Moses. Welcome home." Jeffrey nodded toward me. "I hope Jesse's okay."

"He will be. I'd appreciate it if you would go to the DA's office first thing in the morning and make sure whoever this kid is, he doesn't get away with this. I know I've been gone a while, but the DA wouldn't have that position if it weren't for me. He owes me, and I haven't forgotten."

"Will do, Moses." Jeffrey pulled off.

"I see you're not wasting any time Dad," Malcolm commented. "You've only been back a few hours, and you're already taking charge."

"What can I say? I'm always going to be the head of this household. Now, let's go check on Jesse." I cupped Malcolm's shoulder, and we headed toward the entrance.

We were directed to the waiting room. The others had already beaten us there, and all eyes were on me once we entered. Vanessa, my daughter-in-law, stared at me in shock from where she sat with Carolyn and Martin.

"Moses, you're actually back," Vanessa said.

"I am." I nodded, ignoring the evil glare of my wife.

"How is Jesse? What are the doctors saying?" Malcolm asked, hurrying to Vanessa and hugging her.

"Nothing yet other than they needed to run some tests," Vanessa answered.

"Mr. and Mrs. Britton?"

"Yes?" Malcolm, Vanessa, Carolyn, and I all said simultaneously to the white-coated doctor who stepped into the waiting room.

He looked around briefly, then his eyes settled on Malcolm and Vanessa. "I'm Dr. Phillips. I'm the physician treating your son."

Carolyn rose to her feet. "I'm his grandmother. What's going on with Jesse, doctor?"

"Well, he still hasn't regained consciousness. We've done an MRI and CT scan to make sure there's no bleeding in his brain, and we are waiting on the results. His nose is broken. So are his ribs and his arm."

"My God." Vanessa cried into Malcolm's shoulder.

"He's going to be fine, Vanessa. The tests are routine for head injuries, baby," Malcolm reassured her.

"He's right," Dr. Phillips agreed. "Jesse is young and strong. It's likely he'll make a full recovery."

"I've already made a call to the top neurologist in the state to come and check on him. He'll be here later tonight," Carolyn announced. "And if he needs a plastic surgeon for his nose, we'll take care of that as well."

"Thanks, Mother," Malcolm whispered toward Carolyn.

"When can we see him?" Vanessa asked.

"He won't be back in his room for a little while. I would encourage you all to go home and get some sleep."

"I'm staying. I'm not going anywhere until I see my son," Vanessa said quickly.

"Neither am I," Carolyn agreed.

"That's fine. I'll have a nurse come and get you when he's ready," Dr. Phillips said. "I do need to let you know that visiting hours end in an hour."

"Like I said, I'm not leaving, and neither are his parents." Carolyn's voice was as rigid as the look on her face. It was a look I knew well.

"The rules are the rules, Mrs. Britton." Dr. Phillips shrugged.

"I don't give a damn if—"

"Dr. Phillips." I took a step forward to interrupt my wife. "Certainly, you can make an exception considering the extent of my grandson's injuries, in addition to the substantial amount of money the Britton Foundation has donated to this hospital."

Dr. Phillips inhaled slightly, then said, "I'll make sure they know that I've approved an additional hour. That's the best I can do for tonight."

"Thank you." Malcolm shook the doctor's hand before he exited.

"Well, I guess that's my cue to leave." Martin sighed. "I'm gonna head on home."

"I guess I will just ride home with you, son," I told him.

Martin looked caught off guard. He shot a glance toward his mother as if he needed to confirm her approval. "Uh, okay. I'll go get the car and meet you out front."

"We'll call you if there's any update with Jesse, Dad," Malcolm said before he gave me another hug.

I turned to Carolyn. "I'll see you at home."

She was silent. Although she was looking directly at me, it was as if her mind was somewhere else. She'd zoned out.

"Mom?" Malcolm said.

Carolyn pursed her lips and turned to Vanessa. "I have a phone call to make. A private one. I'll be right back."

Not caring to wait for her to return, I gave a small wave and went after Martin. As he said he would, he'd pulled the car to the front doors of the hospital and was waiting for me. I couldn't help but notice the uncomfortable expression on his face as I got in. There were no words to describe how that made me feel, being a stranger to my son. Not in the physical form, but in the mind. Hopefully we could change that.

He said nothing to me when he started driving. After fifteen minutes, I grew tired of hearing the sound of the outside air as we whizzed by.

"It's nice to see your brother and Vanessa getting along," I said to Martin, breaking the ice. "But I'm even more surprised that Vanessa and Carolyn seem to be cordial. I always thought they'd be sworn enemies forever." Carolyn had never thought any woman was good enough for her sons, so when Vanessa and Malcolm got married, she had made the woman's life a living hell. In the end, it led to the breakup of their marriage.

"Yeah, things changed after they got remarried, so everyone's cool," Martin responded, keeping his eyes on the road.

"Remarried? And your mother allowed it? Things certainly have changed since I've been gone."

"She was the one who orchestrated it." Martin turned onto our street.

Carolyn arranging my son's remarriage was just as shocking as it was troubling. She wasn't one to change her opinion about a person once she'd formed it. There had to be a calculated reason behind her apparent change of heart, but I couldn't imagine what that could be.

"Why would she—"

"Damn, why the hell are they here?" Martin interrupted, slowing his Maserati down as we turned into the driveway.

He leaned forward in his seat, and my gaze followed his to the police cruiser sitting in front of our house. Martin parked, and the two of us got out. The door of the cruiser opened, and Chief Samuel Harrington stepped out.

"Maybe they have more questions," I said as we walked over to the chief.

"We told them everything we knew while we were at the precinct," Martin responded.

The chief extended a hand to me in greeting.

"Sam, how you been?" I asked.

"Been good, Moses. I can only hope the same for you."

"What are you doing here this late, Chief?" Martin asked. "Have you upgraded the charges against that punk?"

"No, this is about something else." Sam glanced over at me, then back to Martin. The look of discomfort on his face let me know that whatever it was, it had to do with me.

"What's going on, Sam?" I asked.

"Well, Moses, I hate to tell you this, but you aren't allowed to enter the house."

"Are you crazy? It's my damn house," I said, now standing face to face with him.

"I know, but right now, we've been told to escort you from the premises."

"Escort him from his own property? That's crazy." Martin reached for his cell phone. "I'm calling Jeffrey. My father just got back in the United States. Legally. I don't know what kind of political games y'all are trying to play, but—"

Sam interrupted him. "This doesn't have anything to with politics or the legal issues."

In that moment, I knew what this was about. And as much as I admired the fact that my youngest son, who up until that moment had seemed quite indifferent about my return home, suddenly came to my defense, I couldn't let him get involved.

"It's fine, Martin," I said. "You don't need to call anyone."

"You know what? You're right. I don't need to call anyone because this is *my* house, and I can give permission to whoever the hell I want," Martin snapped. "You can leave, Chief."

Sam shook his head. "I can't do that, Martin. I'm sorry."

"Fine, stay." Martin turned to me. "Come on, Dad. Let's go inside."

"Moses." Sam and I locked eyes. I heard and heeded the warning in his voice.

"You know, I think I'll stay somewhere else tonight, son, until we get this situation taken care of," I said.

"What? You're staying here, Dad. No one can tell you that you can't come in," Martin insisted.

"No one but your mother," I said. "She made the call, but I'll sort it out. No one is going to stop me from coming home."

3

Sydney Johnson

After a night full of post-celebratory lovemaking with my husband, I was surprised to wake up to an empty bed. Flashes of his sexy body going to work on top of mine as his hands ravished my body brought back chills as I lay alone. I closed my eyes and relished the memory of my husband stroking deeply inside of me. I thought for sure that Anthony and I would spend the entire morning cuddled in each other's arms in between passionate rounds of sex. I needed it. Fucking had always been the strong point in our marriage. However, recently our intimacy had dwindled due to Anthony being stressed after almost losing Sydney Tech, the company he'd built from the ground up—with my help, of course.

Our company became a target for Carolyn Britton after we outbid her for the property adjacent to both of our homes in the Black Hamptons. The moment we learned it was for sale, I urged Anthony to do whatever it took to secure it. It was the ideal spot for us to expand and finally install a swimming pool—the one feature our dream home lacked. Unfortunately, Carolyn wanted that property just as fiercely, and she made her intentions clear.

The bidding war was intense, but I was relentless, and I made sure my husband understood that money should be no object. However, I quickly discovered that my determination was no match for Carolyn's stubbornness. She escalated the situation beyond anything we could have anticipated, sabotaging the largest contract Sydney Tech had ever secured. Using Amistad Bank as leverage, she put everything we had worked for at risk.

"When it's all said and done, we may have to sell this house in order to save the company," Anthony had confessed when it was obvious that our livelihood was in jeopardy.

"Sell this house?" I felt my heart crack.

"And possibly the house in Westchester, too. It's either that or sell Sydney Tech and all its patents. We're going to have to weigh all of our options."

Facing bankruptcy was a tremendous burden for my husband, but telling me about it had been even more difficult. The emotional toll on him was evident. Thankfully, hiring David Michaels as CFO proved to be one of his best decisions. He devised a strategy to outmaneuver Carolyn, and that ultimately saved Sydney Tech.

Since the business was safe now, one would think I'd be getting my back broken in every morning, noon, and night, but I guess I'd have to settle for what I got. For now, anyway,

"Welp, looks like I won't be getting any wakeup sex," I murmured as I climbed out of bed.

I headed to my closet to figure out what I wanted to look like that day. I loved everything about being beautiful and dressing myself like I used to do my Barbie dolls back when I was a girl. I had no idea what the day had in store, so being ready for anything seemed like the best move. I opted for a gray plaid blazer dress and a pair of pumps. After brushing my teeth and taking a quick shower, I got dressed and ventured downstairs to get my day started.

"Morning, Mom." My daughter, Gabrielle, greeted me when I entered the kitchen.

I walked over and kissed her cheek, catching a whiff of the green liquid she was pouring out of the blender into a travel mug. "Morning, sweetie. I see you're back on your green juice kick."

"I am. I guess that look on your face means you don't want any." She laughed.

"No, thanks. I'm good with coffee," I answered. "Have you seen your dad?"

"He's in the back yard talking to the new lawn guy, I think," Gabby replied. "Did you hear about Jesse Britton?"

"Your father told me last night. Sad." I shook my head as I poured myself a cup of coffee.

"I know. He's still in the hospital. Listen, I know you don't like the Brittons, but—"

"Gabrielle Johnson, don't do that."

"Do what?" Gabby asked. "You don't."

"That doesn't mean I don't have sympathy for Jesse. You act like I'm heartless, which I'm not, by the way."

"Not what?" My younger sister, Karrin, asked as she walked into the kitchen wearing a cute athleisure set that clung to her physique.

Gabby answered for me. "Heartless. She's not heartless."

"Oh." Karrin said. "Well, you can be a little mean, but I wouldn't call you heartless. Why are y'all looking at me like that?"

"Because it's not even eight o'clock and you're dressed and downstairs," I told her. "Wait. Did you stay out all night? Are you just getting home?"

"No, heifer. I was home all night," Karrin replied. "But instead of sleeping in, I decided to go for an early run, that's all."

"That's great, Auntie." Gabby hugged Karrin. "Early morning cardio is the best."

"I guess," Karrin said. "But I'd prefer some early morning breakfast. You cooking, Syd?"

"Well, I hadn't planned on it."

"Hmmm, after the loud night you and Anthony had, I figured both of you would be starving." Karrin raised an eyebrow.

"And on that note, I'm off to yoga." Gabby waved as she rushed out of the kitchen.

"Karrin," I scolded. "What the hell?"

"What? That girl's practically grown. And besides, it's not like she didn't hear you and Anthony. We all did." Karrin reached into the bread box and took out a bag of bagels. "Y'all were hella loud. You always are. Not as loud as that lawn mower this morning, but still."

"I can't believe you sometimes." I shook my head, questioning for the hundredth time my decision to allow my sister to stay with us. I was glad to have her around, but sometimes, her vulgar mouth was a bit much to handle.

I decided to give her a pass this time because I was in a good mood and wasn't going to let her ruin it.

"Fine, I'm sorry." Karrin sighed. "And why the hell is the grass getting cut so early this morning?"

"I don't know. I guess Anthony hired a new landscaper," I said, taking a pack of bacon and a carton of eggs out of the fridge.

Karrin popped her bagel into the toaster and walked over to the window facing the back yard. "Well, damn. I ain't even mad about that loud-ass lawnmower anymore. The man riding it is *fine,*" she said.

"Oh, hell no," Anthony said when he entered the kitchen. "Don't start."

Karrin and I both turned to look at him. He was giving my sister one of his knowing looks, and she grinned innocently back at him.

"Start what? I'm just stating the obvious. The man *is* fine."

Anthony shook his head at her as he strolled over to me and gave me a hug and a kiss. "Good morning, baby."

"I thought it was gonna be," I whispered into his ear, giggling as I wrapped my free arm around his waist. "But you weren't in bed when I woke up."

"Aw, I can't say I didn't think about it." Anthony smiled. "But I remembered the landscaper was coming, so I had to get ready to meet with him."

"Oh, the landscaper coming was more important than me com—" I stopped myself and flirtatiously looked Anthony up and down. Even in his cargo shorts and Polo shirt, he was the sexiest man on earth in my eyes.

"Syd." He laughed, pulling away from me.

"And since when do we have a landscaper? I mean, what happened to Tyler doing the yard?" I asked, taking a sip of my coffee.

"Honestly, I forgot that I'd reached out. Ty does a decent job, but when we were considering selling the house, I figured I'd have the front and back professionally done to add some curb appeal," Anthony explained.

"And now? I mean, we won't be selling our house anytime soon, thank God."

"I figured he was here, so there was no point in sending him home. Besides, he's cool as hell. I really like the guy." Anthony took the cup from my hand and took a swallow. "God, it needs sweetener and cream."

"I like my coffee like I like my men: strong and dark."

"Well, I for one am glad that you hired the new yard man," Karrin announced. "He's doing an amazing job. You gotta see him, Syd. He's all muscular and sweaty. He even took his shirt off."

"Get away from that damn window, Karrin," Anthony warned. "And he's not a yard man. He's a landscape architect, the best in the Hamptons. We're lucky I was able to get him."

"Yeah, we definitely are lucky." Karrin laughed.

"Sis, stop it before you get the man fired. You know how Anthony is." I yanked my sister from the window back into the kitchen.

"Where the hell is my bagel?" she asked, looking into the now empty toaster.

Anthony took a big bite and said, "Oops, my bad. Was this yours?"

"Yes, it was mine," Karrin yelped.

"Guess you gotta make another one." Anthony shrugged and exited the kitchen.

I couldn't help but laugh at the dumbfounded look on Karrin's face. I was relieved that my husband and sister were getting along. It was no secret that he didn't care for Karrin, and for good reason. Over the past few years, my sister had become a financial drain, relying solely on her looks while failing to hold down a job, an apartment, or even a car. Despite her shortcomings, she was still my sister, which was why I continued to bail her out, even against Anthony's insistence that I stop. Unlike him, I believed she would eventually get her life together; she just hadn't found her way yet.

When Karrin had arrived unannounced at our home this summer, Anthony was far from welcoming. He made it clear that her stay would have a two-week limit. What he didn't realize was that it wasn't just a visit. Karrin had been evicted, and she didn't have a car, despite me sending her money for both every month for the past two years. I advised her to keep a low profile and avoid drawing Anthony's attention, and she had followed that advice. In fact, some days we barely saw her. I knew her frequent absence from the house could only be because of one thing: a man. My beautiful sister had never had a problem finding a man, although most of them didn't seem to stick around for too long.

Maybe out here she'd snag a rich one so he could support her instead of me.

"Your husband irks." Karrin went back to staring out the window. "Good Lord, he is sexy."

"Stay away from the yard man," I told her. "Besides, don't think I don't know about your secret boo that you've been seeing. You still haven't told me who it is yet, but you will."

A strange look came across my sister's face. "Secret boo? You know me better than that, Syd. I have several options, not just one. I'll try not to add your sexy new yard man to the roster, but I won't make any promises."

"Hey, babe, can you come out here for a minute?" Anthony called from the front of the house.

"I'll be right there."

"I'll come with you," Karrin volunteered.

"You stay here," I hissed.

"Syd, I want you to meet our new landscape architect, Rashid Logan." He stepped out of the door frame, and I got a glimpse of the man standing on the front steps. "Rashid, this is my wife, and the one who runs things around here, Sydney."

I had to struggle to keep my composure as Rashid eye's connected with mine. He was every bit as fine as Karrin said, and he was also someone from my past that I had never expected to see again. Standing well over six feet tall, with smooth skin the color of dark chocolate, teeth just as perfect as his muscular physique, and thick, wavy hair, he was what Gabby and her friends would refer to as a "zaddy" with his gray-sprinkled goatee. He'd aged since the last time I saw him, but time had treated him well.

There was a slight flicker of something across his face when he recognized me, but fortunately, he played it off as if we were meeting for the first time. "Pleasure to meet you, Mrs. Johnson," he said.

"Uh, nice to meet you too, Mr. Logan," I responded, grateful for his discretion.

Anthony seemed oblivious to any tension in the air. "So, I told Rashid how we tried to get the land to add a pool to the back yard. He did some measurements and came up with an awesome idea for our existing space. He's gonna redesign it for us."

One thing my husband prided himself on was making me happy. I should've known that despite losing the property to Carolyn Britton, he would find a way to make our yard the great entertaining space I'd wanted. I loved the way he catered to me.

"You won't be able to get a swimming pool, but I can design an outdoor space to include a nice Jacuzzi and a water wall feature. I promise it will be just as nice," Rashid said.

"A hot tub? Do we really need one of those?" I asked, not because I didn't want a hot tub, but because it might be best if I convinced Anthony that we didn't need Rashid's services. "I think the yard we have now is fine."

Anthony looked confused and a little deflated. I'm sure he had been expecting an enthusiastic response from me. "Syd, come on. Don't be like that. I know you wanted the backyard redone, and this is the guy who can make that happen. Right, Rashid?"

"Oh, no doubt. I can make that space a beautiful, romantic oasis of your dreams. You won't even miss a swimming pool." Rashid winked at me, and I narrowed my eyes at him as a warning.

"My man, that's what's up. So when can you get started?" Anthony asked.

"Don't you need to discuss this with your boss first?" I asked. "I mean, maybe we should find out the price before we commit to anything."

"I'm the owner." He pointed to the logo on his shirt that read: *Logan Landscape Design*. "I like to get in the trenches with my guys from time to time, especially when it comes to VIP clients like you."

"I knew I liked you, Rashid." Anthony clapped his hand on Rashid's muscular shoulder.

"Likewise. I can go ahead and take some measurements while I'm here, then get some design plans done and get them over to you by the first of next week. Will that work?" Rashid asked.

"Sounds great to me. I've got an important meeting I've gotta get to, but if you have any questions, Sydney can answer. Like I said, she runs things around here anyway, and she'll be in charge. Right, babe?" Anthony put his arm around me and kissed my cheek.

"I . . . Anthony, babe, I . . ." I stammered, trying to hide the anxiety blossoming in my stomach. Not only was Rashid at my home, but Anthony planned to hire him and put me in charge. There would be no way of avoiding contact.

I couldn't allow that to happen without at least making one last effort to stop it. "I think this is something we should talk about first, Anthony."

"Nonsense, Syd. This is something you've been wanting, and now you're gonna get it. I gotta go meet Michael." Anthony kissed me again and stepped outside.

"I'll be in touch, Mrs. Johnson." Rashid smiled at me, then followed Anthony into the driveway.

I stood alone in the doorway, unable to move for a moment while my mind tried to comprehend what had just happened.

"Syd, I told you that man was fine, didn't I?" Karrin said with a laugh, gliding into the foyer and peeking out of one of the smaller windows near the front door. "Lawd, he's sexy as fuck."

I was too caught up in my emotions to respond.

"Syd, you good?" Karrin's hand on my shoulder brought me back to reality.

"What? Yeah."

"Why you look like you just saw a ghost?"

I shook my head to clear it. "I . . . I was just thinking about something."

"Must've been something deep." Karrin gave me a strange look. "You sure you're okay?"

"I'm fine," I lied.

"Fine is that man that's out there talking to your husband." Karrin laughed. "Girl, you know I was listening. He's really gonna be hanging around here for a while redoing the back?"

"It appears that way."

"Good. We need some eye candy around here."

"Eye candy is the last thing we need around here," I mumbled. "Anyway, enough about the lawn guy. Did you hear what happened to Jesse Britton? I hope he's okay."

Karrin stepped away from the window. "What happened?"

"He was attacked yesterday. Beaten so bad that he's in ICU."

"Oh my God." Karrin covered her mouth with her hand.

"I know. The Brittons aren't my favorite people, but it's still sad. You still want me to make your breakfast?"

Karrin shook her head. "I'm not hungry. I'm just gonna go out. I'll be back later."

She rushed up the stairs, leaving me alone, and my mind went right back to Rashid. I eased in front of the window, unable to resist the urge to look out at the driveway. There was Anthony with Rashid. They were standing in front of a large box truck with the Logan Landscape logo and phone number in big, bright lettering.

God damn, I thought. *How is this even happening?*

Rashid was fine as hell, always had been, and he still had that perfect smile that I had tried so hard to forget over the years. What were the odds that the last man I slept with before I married Anthony would be standing in my driveway all these years later?

4

Sergeant Tom Lane

Thoughts of Peter behind bars had plagued my dreams, causing me to toss and turn for most of the night. I had just barely fallen asleep when my doorbell rang just after sunrise and startled me awake. I sat up and grabbed my phone from the nightstand to check for any missed calls about my son. Nothing.

The same thoughts that had kept me awake came rushing back now. Peter was in jail. How was I going to get him out? The doorbell rang again, so I got out of bed to see who it was. The sun peeking through the blinds reflected off my badge, reminding me that I was still wearing my uniform. I ran my hand quickly over my hair as I made my way to the front door.

"How you doing, Mr. Lane?"

There was no love lost between me and Bobby "The Beast" Boyd, yet there he was, dressed in a black sweatsuit with his signature blinged-out *BTB* pendant around his neck. Light heavyweight champion Bobby Boyd was the highest-paid boxer in the game, boasting an undefeated record and more than ten championship belts. He was the creator of the most elite boxing promotional firm: Team BTB. He was also Peter's personal hero. While I admired Bobby's athletic prowess and remarkable success, I couldn't overlook his questionable business dealings hidden behind a flashy, glamorous lifestyle.

When Bobby and his manager, Cornelius, had popped up at the house to talk to Peter and offer him a contract to sign with BTB, I was concerned, to say the least. They praised Peter for his skills and talents in the ring, but it was nothing I hadn't already been telling Peter since he started working the heavy bag: Peter was a champion. My son was so star-struck and excited about being signed to Team BTB that he was willing to abandon another dream: joining the USA Olympic Boxing Team. I wouldn't let that happen. I refused to allow Peter to sign the contract Bobby presented.

"I know what this is about, Dad. You want me to be stuck out here with you," Peter had said to me.

"I'd never hold you back, son. I just don't want you under Bobby. You have to trust that I'm making the right call here. I've never led you astray. I know what I'm doing."

That contract had driven a wedge between me and my son, and there I was, face to face with the man who'd offered it.

"How can I help you, Mr. Boyd? Peter isn't here."

"Call me Bobby. And I know. That's why I'm here." He raised one of his pointy eyebrows at me. "I heard Peter got himself into a little legal trouble. I'm here to help."

I glared past him at the Bugatti in the driveway parked behind my police cruiser. That car probably cost enough to pay for a lawyer a few times over. I couldn't stand this dude, but something told me that I should try to hear what he had to say. For Peter. I stepped aside and motioned for him to come in, leading him into the living room. Wanting to stand face to face for the discussion, I purposely didn't offer him a seat.

"Okay, so you're here to help?" I asked.

"Look, I really like Peter. He reminds me of myself in a lot of ways, including this shit." Bobby sighed. "Unfortunately, I got into a little trouble myself a time or two. Hell, if it wasn't for the grace of the good Lord and Cornelius looking out for me, I'd be behind bars right now."

"Look, Mr. Boyd—"

"Bobby, please." He reached into his pocket then handed me a business card. "Here you go."

I stared at the card in his hand. "What is this?"

"It's the contact information for Christopher Johnson, Peter's attorney," Bobby said assertively. "He's already on his way to the courthouse to talk to the city prosecutor and make sure Peter's bail hearing is first thing on the docket this morning."

"Wha—how?" I shook my head.

"Does Peter have a suit and tie?" Bobby asked, ignoring my question.

"He . . . yeah."

"Good. You may wanna grab it and take it to the precinct for him. It'll make a better impression on the judge instead of that ugly-ass orange jumpsuit they would have him in."

"Listen, I get that you're trying to help, but this Christopher Johnson guy—"

"Is a friend of mine. He's one of the top defense attorneys on the East Coast, and his success record for violent offenses is the highest in the state of New York. The guy's no joke."

"He sounds expensive. I appreciate it, but I don't know if I'll be able to afford him." I tried to hand the business card back to him, but he just forged ahead like he hadn't heard a thing I said.

"Let me go ahead and let you get outta here so you can get to Peter," Bobby said before heading toward the door. "Oh, and Mr. Lane?"

"Yeah?"

"Don't worry. Christopher's retainer has already been paid. I took care of it."

My jaw dropped. "Why?"

"Like I said, I like Peter. He's got a bright future, and he's family." Bobby grinned and walked out.

The word "family" lingered inside the room. I heard the front door open and close as I stood there dumbfounded. Finally, there was a glimmer of hope in my chest that my son could still get his future back on track.

5

Carolyn Britton

As I sat on the four-thousand-dollar sofa and sipped my morning tea, I finally had a few moments of peace to really think about what it meant to have Moses back in town. It wasn't that I hated him. After all, he had left the country rather than implicate me in all those messy legal issues that were hanging over his head. We had always had a tumultuous relationship, and sometimes it seemed like we were business partners more than we were husband and wife, yet deep down, there was still some fondness between us. That didn't mean I wanted him here, though. Moses wasn't a stupid man, so undoubtedly, he had figured out by now that I had something to do with the delays in getting his indictment dropped. I had accomplished what I set out to do, which was get myself installed at the head of the bank in his absence, but I had wanted some time to cement my power and earn the loyalty of our employees before he could return. Now that he was here, I had to worry about what type of retribution he might have in mind for my disloyalty.

"Mother, we need to talk."

Recognizing the voice of my son, I looked up from my cup and stared at Martin. The tone of voice he was taking with me was unsettling, but the stern look on his face was even more unexpected. I set my cup down on the table so I could give him my undivided attention.

"Whatever has you so riled up this early in the morning to speak to me like that? Lose it, because—"

"You'll have Chief Harrington come remove me from our home too?" Martin asked boldly. "I can't believe you did that."

"I made that call to the chief to make sure my place of residence was safe."

"Safe from what?" Martin asked. "I understand Dad's arrival was a bit unexpected for everyone, including me, but do you think that was necessary? This is his home."

"I'm not going to have this discussion with you, Martin. Now is not the time. I did what I thought was best for everyone. I'm leaving it at that."

In truth, I was doing what was best for me. My sons had no idea that it was my risky trades that had brought the bank under scrutiny in the first place, and I wanted to keep it that way. I needed to keep Moses away from the boys as much as possible so he wouldn't reveal the truth. Maybe someday I would tell them, but not now.

"Martin, now is not the time for this discussion. The thing we need to be focused on this morning is being at the courthouse for that monster's bail hearing. That's what I care about, and you should too."

"I do care about that, but I also care about what's going on with Dad."

We were interrupted by Malcom coming into the room. I let out a long breath, preparing for his attitude, because Malcom was team Moses all the way. Quite frankly, I was shocked that it was Martin who'd come to me first. Maybe Martin was becoming the man his father had always wanted him to be.

"Dad? What's going on with him, and where is he?" Malcolm asked, looking from me to his brother.

Martin looked at me with raised eyebrows as if to say it was my responsibility to answer.

"Your father's not here," I politely replied.

Malcolm looked surprised. "Do you know where he went? I thought we'd all go to the courtroom together this morning."

"I have no idea where he is." When I saw Martin open his mouth to speak, I quickly interjected. "How's Jesse?"

"He's still not awake. Vanessa is still there, and her sister Alyssa came to sit with them until I get back. The good news is the tests didn't show any signs of brain damage," Malcolm told us. "He'll make a full recovery."

"Thank God." I sighed. "That's good to know. We're still gonna make sure they throw the book at the boy who did this."

"Damn right we are," Malcolm agreed.

"Which is why we need to get ready to get to the courthouse," I told them. "We leave in ten minutes."

While Malcolm quickly exited, Martin remained. "Mother, you know—"

I held up my hand, signaling that the conversation was over. "Not now, Martin. I told you. While you're worried about your father, your nephew and brother need us."

Luckily, he didn't fight it. "Fine," he huffed and then made his exit.

I got up and went to my office to gather my briefcase, making a stop in front of the floor-length mirror in the corner to take a good look at myself. Of course, my outfit looked impeccable. I never allowed myself to look anything less than spectacular. However, my eyes revealed just how tired I felt. I was a fighter, and that day would be full of fighting just like every other. It had only just begun, and it already had so much weight on it.

I brushed my hair with my fingers and grabbed my briefcase from my desk. When I turned to walk out of the room, I almost ran right into my trusted assistant. "Kimberly! I wasn't expecting you right now."

"Good morning, Carolyn. I was just stopping by to check on you. Malcom just gave me the update about Jesse. I'm sure he'll be better soon."

"From your mouth to God's ears. Oh, before I forget, I am going to need you to get in contact with Dr. Hayes Taylor, the neurologist from Mount Sinai that was supposed to come and check on Jesse last night. I need to know his findings," I instructed her. "And then there's another pressing matter. It seems that my husband has returned."

"I heard that as well."

"Then you know we have to get a jump start on preserving everything we've gained over the past few years."

For years, Moses had given me various vanity titles with little authority, but now I wielded real power as Chairman of the Board of Amistad Bank. I had worked tirelessly to transform our financial institution into a powerhouse, securing additional corporate accounts, expanding our asset and wealth management services, and enhancing our offerings in financial products like insurance and mutual funds.

I had heeded Malcolm's advice to build Amistad's digital banking and FinTech partnerships, and it paid off. Our client base had tripled. Meanwhile, the Britton Foundation, previously dismissed as unimportant by Moses, had ramped up its philanthropic efforts and outreach programs, elevating the family name in the community, thanks to Martin, who served as the director. My most recent triumph was landing the accounts of Singh Corporation and facilitating its acquisition of Entech Freight, marking one of the largest business moves in our bank's history.

My leadership strategies had earned the respect of the Board of Trustees, and I was honored to be named one of the top women in business by *Forbes* magazine. I had worked too hard over the past seven years to be sidelined while Moses stepped back into the spotlight.

"Um, I guess there was another reason I was stopping by as well." Kimberly stepped forward and handed me a white envelope.

"What's this?" I asked, taking it from her. I removed the letter inside, expecting it to be some inside information, possibly pertaining to Moses's return. Kimberly was always on top of things and would have anticipated that I needed such information. But it wasn't that.

As I read the words on the paper my mouth opened wider in surprise. "You're quitting?"

"Yes, I am."

"Why the hell would you do that now, with everything we're dealing with?"

Kimberly had started as an intern at Amistad Bank during her college years and quickly became one of my mentees through the Britton Foundation. After graduation, she transitioned to my assistant, proving to be both instrumental and insightful as I took on a leadership role. Her education, intuition, and business acumen were invaluable, guiding me through strategic decisions in both my professional and personal life, especially when it came to family. She was my eyes and ears in all the places I couldn't reach. Most importantly, she was fiercely loyal. I trusted Kimberly, and now, more than ever, I would need her support. There was no way I was going to let her leave.

"I did, and I know that the timing is inconvenient, but unfortunately, this is necessary," Kimberly said.

"No, you can't quit, Kimberly. I won't let you. You're too valuable an asset to this family to even consider not having you here."

"I don't have a choice. I do appreciate everything you've taught me, but it's time for me to move on."

What did she mean that she didn't have a choice? Before I could ask, Malcolm came into the office. "Mother, the car is here."

"Kimberly, I have to get to the courthouse and meet with the DA before this bail hearing. I'm asking that you give me some time—no, you take some time to think about this before giving it to me." I held the letter back out to her. "Then we can talk about it."

Kimberly hesitated briefly before finally taking back her resignation letter. "Okay, but the decision has already been made."

"Forty-eight hours, please."

At the word "please," Kimberly's eyes widened. It wasn't a word I used often. Begging was something I never did, but this was a time of desperation.

"I'll give it another day, but I'm sure I won't change my mind," she said.

"Thank you." I was relieved that I'd bought at least a little time to try to convince her to stay. "We'll talk then."

"Okay, and good luck in court today."

I touched her shoulder affectionately before I left the room. Truth be told, Kimberly was more than an employee. She was the closest thing I had to a daughter. She had always seemed content with her position both with the company and in the family. For her to want to leave, something major had to be driving her to do so. I was determined to figure out who or what it was, and then convince her to stay.

As I went down the steps, I heard my phone ringing inside of my messenger briefcase. I pulled it out and answered it.

"Hello?"

"Good morning, Carolyn. I hope you slept well."

The moment I heard Moses's voice on the other end, I stopped. "What do you want? I have somewhere to be and no time to talk."

"I'm sure. My time is limited as well. Jeffrey and I are heading to meet with the district attorney as we speak."

"What? You don't need to do that, Moses. The boys and I are on the way to his office," I snapped.

"Good. We will be finished when you arrive, and then we can all walk into the courtroom together, as a family. I'll see you when you get here." The way he said it inflamed my already-on-edge nerves.

Before I could respond, he ended the call. All I could do was groan. The man had been back less than twenty-four hours and was already acting like he was in charge. I wasn't going to allow him to be in control of anything, not again.

I made my way out of the house to where my sons were waiting for me.

"Mother, are you ready?" Malcolm asked as he held the door of the Rolls Royce open. Martin stood on the opposite side of the car, waiting.

I took a moment, admiring both of my handsome creations. They were my pride and joy. Well groomed, educated, and successful, standing there in their perfectly fitted custom designer suits. All of the hard work that I'd put into them paid off. We were a tight unit, and the last thing I would allow was Moses waltzing back in and disrupting our lives, especially now. I finally had the power and both of my sons by my side. There was no way I was going to lose it to him or anyone else.

6

Karrin Wilkes

There was something about the sun, sand, and water that could bring me serenity and peace I didn't feel anywhere else. It confirmed that I had made the right decision to escape the hustle and bustle of the city in search of something better. Life in Brooklyn, where I had been living before I showed up on my sister's doorstep with everything I could fit in the Louis Vuitton luggage set she gifted me a couple of Christmases ago, had become a total disaster. In just two days, I had managed to get fired, been evicted, and had my car repossessed. It all seemed absurd in the grand scheme of things, especially since Sydney sent me a monthly household stipend that was more than enough to cover most of my expenses, and I was sleeping with my landlord to get a discount on my rent.

Unfortunately, my spending habits had spiraled out of control, and I blew most of my money on designer clothes and shoes, facials, manicures, and the finest quality weaves. Then Fred's wife found out about our arrangement, and he put me out on my ass with nowhere to go and no money for a down payment on another place. Determined to find a silver lining, I convinced myself that losing everything was a sign I needed a fresh start. So, despite my brother-in-law's disdain for me, I decided to visit my family in Sag Harbor and regroup.

The beach had become my happy place. It was also where I met the man I thought would change my life for the better. Martin Britton was everything I had ever dreamed of and more: fine as hell, college-educated, impeccably dressed, and funny, all qualities I desired in a man. But more importantly, he met my biggest requirement: he was wealthy, and very much so. I figured it couldn't get any better than that.

Beyond his surface qualities, Martin made me feel valued for more than just my looks. With him, I felt safe and truly seen, which was why I eventually opened up about my secret passion for drawing. To my surprise, he genuinely believed I was talented and encouraged me to pursue my art. That support felt like the icing on the cake, and I knew I had found a winner, someone I was determined to keep.

Too bad his mother didn't think I was good enough for her son and decided to freeze me out. Once Martin made it clear that he had chosen me, Carolyn retaliated by cutting off access to all his accounts. She even called the police to have me removed from the family yacht then filed a restraining order against me.

As quickly as Martin and I started, we were over. He bent to his mother's will and blocked my number without so much as a goodbye. Now I had nobody and nothing to show for the time we spent together. In a matter of days, I felt like I was right back where I'd started the summer—at rock bottom.

I was angry at Martin and his family, but I was still sad to hear about Jesse. He seemed like an okay kid, and I was sure the family was devastated. I found myself wondering if Martin was okay.

I still hadn't told Sydney the full story of me and Martin, because I didn't want to tell her about Carolyn Britton's crusade against me. At the time it happened, Syd and Anthony had enough going on with their own feud with the Brittons. They almost lost their house and their business behind that mess. The last thing I wanted to do was add fuel to the already blazing inferno, especially when I had no place to go.

"Ouch!" I yelped as an object bounced off the top of my head. I looked beside the towel I was sitting on and saw a football land in the sand. "Damn kids need to watch where the hell they're playing."

"My bad, beautiful."

I put my hands over my eyes to shield them from the sun so I could see the owner of the sexy baritone voice. It belonged to a man with a chiseled physique who stood before me, sunlight gleaming off the light layer of sweat on his chest. I forced my eyes to tear themselves away from his shirtless torso and move up to his handsome face. His presence was magnetic.

"Oh, shit. You're The Beast."

"Well, you can call me Bobby, but yeah." He smiled, displaying the whitest teeth I'd ever seen.

"Wow, it really is you." I blinked, staring at the huge *BTB* medallion displayed on his chest.

My shitty day instantly turned to sunshine as the highest-ranking athlete in *Forbes* magazine plopped down beside me without an invite. Everything around me faded into the background.

"Yep, it's me, and I can't believe someone as fine as you is out here by yourself," he said, flashing those pearly whites again. "Where's your man at?"

"I don't have a man," I said, then added, "right now."

"That's what I was hoping you'd say."

"What are you doing here?" I asked, thankful that I'd chosen the high-cut, plunging Versace one-piece swimsuit that showed off everything I wanted to show off. Bobby's eyes were all over me, and I could see that he was enjoying the view.

"I'm here with my team. Doing a little scouting and getting some R and R at the same time."

"Business and pleasure," I said. "I hear ya."

"Speaking of pleasure, I'd love to take you to dinner tonight," he said, looking at my breasts before finally moving his eyes up to my face.

"Dinner? You haven't even asked my name."

"I was just going to call you Beauty, but you're right, that's rude of me. What's your name, sweetheart?"

"I'm Karrin."

"Karrin. I like that. But I still like Beauty better. What do you think about having dinner with a beast like me?"

I shrugged. "Maybe. I mean, I can try to make it."

My pulse quickened, a mix of excitement and nerves. I was thrilled about the prospect of having dinner with Bobby Boyd. Still, I had to play it cool. I didn't want to come off like I was just another groupie. I kept my demeanor relaxed, as if being asked out by a boxing champion was a routine occurrence for me.

"Nah, I'm gonna need you to make sure you make it. It's gonna be a good time. I promise." He ran his fingers along my arm.

"Well then, how can I possibly turn down a good time with Bobby Boyd?" I winked, enjoying the attention.

"You can't," he said, then stood after we exchanged numbers. "See you later, Beauty."

"I'm looking forward to it."

He picked up his football and walked away. I waited before reacting, knowing he would turn back around to look again. And sure enough, he did, looking happy, like a kid let loose in his favorite store. I gave a cute little wave, and he flashed his white teeth at me again; then, he jogged toward the group of guys that I hadn't noticed before. When they were out of sight, I finally stood and let out a little excited squeak. There I'd been thinking Martin Britton was some kind of jackpot that I'd lost. He quickly became an afterthought the moment I met Bobby "The Beast" Boyd.

7

Jeffrey Bowen

Instead of waking up to the warmth of my wife beside me in bed, I was jolted awake by the sharp pain of a pinched nerve in my back, a result of the uncomfortable mattress in the guest room where I'd slept. I had anticipated coming home to a nice dinner and a relaxing evening, but that was far from what I experienced.

"Have you lost your fucking mind?" Leslie had asked as soon as I arrived home after taking Moses and Malcolm to the hospital. "You helped bring Uncle Moses home from Venezuela and you didn't say shit to me about it?"

"Hello to you too, Leslie," I said, loosening my tie and taking off my suit jacket. "My day was fine. How was yours?"

"Jeffrey, my God, do you know what this means?" she yelled.

"It means that you're going to show me your appreciation for helping your uncle, who's been out of the country for the past seven years, come home legally where he can now live as a free man?" I leaned over to try to kiss her, but she pushed me away.

"Don't fucking play with me. This isn't a joking matter," Leslie warned.

"I wasn't joking. I thought you'd be happy that he's home." I frowned. "Hell, when he left, you were devastated. You wouldn't let up about finding a way to get his ass back in the US."

"I know, and I'm ecstatic that he's back," Leslie admitted. "But still, the news should've come from you and not Everett Simpson of all people."

I should have known that Everett wouldn't waste any time broadcasting Moses's return. The man thrived on being the center of attention, especially when it came to gossip. I had hesitated to involve him in our plans, but I felt I had no choice. At this point, I could only hope he hadn't divulged any specific details about the deal we made. It would only complicate matters, and the last thing Moses, Anthony Johnson, or I needed was complications.

"You're right, Les," I agreed. "I should've told you. But we couldn't risk—"

"Risk what?" Leslie frowned.

I hesitated, knowing that we both already knew the answer. Hoping to defuse the situation, I simply said, "Risk ruining the surprise, baby."

"Liar," she snapped. "You thought I would tell Aunt Carolyn. That's why you didn't say anything."

It was a true statement. The relationship between my wife and her aunt was arduous, at best. They shared a love-hate relationship that was both toxic and codependent, but their bond was as tight as mother and daughter. When things were good between them, they were enamored with one another, but when things were bad, Carolyn didn't hesitate to remind Leslie who was boss. Like a wounded lover trying to get back into good graces, my wife would do whatever it took. I hated it, which was one of the main reasons I had worked diligently to devise a plan to bring Moses back where he belonged. Carolyn's power had gone to her head, and her controlling nature had been even more unbearable lately. In some ways, I saw bringing Moses back as a way to take some pressure off my wife.

"The important thing is Moses is home, Leslie. We should be celebrating, not arguing." I reached for her. This time, she didn't pull away and allowed me to kiss her. Now that I'd done my job and gone above and beyond to make shit happen, I was in the mood for some good loving. From the way Leslie was responding, I could tell she was too. She wrapped her arms around my neck, and I quickly untied the robe she wore, revealing her sexy curves. I cupped her breasts, and my thumbs quickly found her hardened nipples that seemed to be waiting to be touched.

"Ummmm, Jeffrey." She moaned as I kissed her neck. The way she called my name made my already stiffened manhood even harder. I moved her hand to my crotch so she could see just how excited I was.

"You feel that?" I whispered into her ear.

"Damn right. I wanna feel it somewhere else, though," she murmured as she massaged my dick in her hand.

Instead of leading her into the bedroom, I pulled her into the den, laying her back onto the sofa. I got onto my knees and slipped off her lace panties, excited to taste her sweet nectar.

Just as my tongue made contact with her warm center, my cell phone rang, and like a trained dog, I couldn't help myself. I flinched like I was about to reach for the phone.

"You'd better not answer that," she warned, placing her hand on the top of my head.

"I'm not," I said as I kissed her mound. At the same time, I reached into my pants pocket and silenced my phone. Unfortunately, it began ringing again immediately. Whoever was trying to reach me had something important to say.

"Jeffrey, turn the damn phone off."

I sat back on my haunches and removed the phone from my pants pocket. I made the mistake of looking at the screen and saw that the caller was Moses. Something had to be wrong if he was calling me, especially back-to-back. I had to answer.

"I'm sorry, babe," I said to Leslie. "They're gonna keep calling until I answer."

Before she could protest, I accepted the call.

"Hello."

"I hate to bother you, but my wife has called the police and had me escorted from our home."

I stood to my feet. "What?"

"Don't worry, it's fine. But I need your legal expertise before I have Chief Harrington take me to my next destination," Moses said. "Can you meet me at the dock?"

"I'm on my way."

"What?" Leslie hissed. "You've gotta be kidding."

"Oh, and Jeffrey, let's keep this between you and me." Moses ended the call.

"Oh, hell no. Who the fuck is that?" Leslie's voice was an octave higher than usual, letting me know that she was beyond livid.

"Baby, I'm sorry. I gotta go handle something right quick, but I'll be right back, I promise. It won't take long," I said as I adjusted my pants.

"You're leaving? Now?"

"I have to, but I told you I'll be right back. It's an emergency."

"What could be more important than this?" Leslie spread her legs even wider to make her point.

"You know I wouldn't leave if I didn't have to." I kissed her forehead then turned to walk out of the den.

"Jeffrey Bowen, if you leave this house, don't bother coming back," Leslie threatened. "I mean it."

"Right back, Les. I love you," I called over my shoulder, grabbing my discarded shirt as I walked out the front door.

When I arrived at the dock fifteen minutes later, there was Moses, leaning against Chief Harrington's car.

"What the hell is going on?" I asked.

"Carolyn, that's all." Moses shrugged.

"She won't let him in the house. Said he's not allowed," Chief Harrington explained.

"So, I told him to bring me here." Moses pointed to the USS Carolyn sitting in the water behind him. "I mean, it's just as much mine as hers, right?"

"It is." Now I realized why Moses had made the call to me. He needed me to confirm his right to be on the yacht for the police chief. "Mr. Britton has every right to the yacht, along with several other properties."

Chief Harrington sighed. I was sure he didn't want to be involved in a marital dispute between two uppity rich people. "Well, the only thing she mentioned was the house. She didn't say anything about the boat. Now that your lawyer has confirmed it, I'm leaving. I got more important shit to deal with."

"I appreciate the ride, Sam." Moses shook Chief Harrington's hand. "I suppose I'll see you in the morning in court."

When the chief was gone, I turned to Moses and said, "I can't believe her."

Moses laughed. "I can."

"So, how the hell are you gonna get inside?" I asked.

At that moment, another set of headlights pulled up, and Moses and I stared at the Mercedes sedan parking beside my car. Kimberly, Carolyn's assistant, opened the door and stepped out.

"Uncle Moses!" She rushed over and threw her arms around his neck.

"Thank you for coming."

"Welcome home." Kimberly smiled. "And you don't have to thank me."

"Hey, Kimberly," I greeted her.

"Jeffrey," she said, "I hear you're the one who made this happen."

"It was a group effort, but I'm just glad it all worked out," I answered. "Well, I'm sure you can take it from here. Moses, you're in good hands. I'm going to get going. My wife was not happy when I left."

"I appreciate you, Jeffrey," Moses told me.

I shook his hand, gave Kimberly a brief hug, then left.

I was glad I had been able to come, but no good deed went unpunished. When I returned home, I was expecting to pick up where I'd left off with my wife, but that was the wrong thing to assume. Our bedroom door was locked, and I knew it would be pointless to ask her to open it. In an effort to avoid another argument, I accepted my punishment and found another room to lay my head. That was the decision that had led me to the guestroom with the terrible mattress.

As uncomfortable as I was, I didn't get up until I heard the whirring of the espresso machine in the kitchen. Leslie was a coffee aficionado with barista-level skills, and I never needed to leave home for the perfect cappuccino. My wife prepared one for me every morning, a comforting ritual that I looked forward to. However, I had enough sense to know that being in the doghouse meant I probably wouldn't be getting a glass of water, let alone a cup of coffee. Still, there was no point in avoiding her.

Leslie was sitting at the table, scrolling on her phone while sipping from her favorite coffee mug. My own mug was sitting empty on the counter.

I sat across from her. "Good morning."

"Morning," she mumbled, barely looking up at me.

I took a deep breath, preparing myself for the conversation.

"Leslie, I want to apologize for withholding information from you," I began, trying to find the right words. "The reason I do it is to protect you and the clients I work with."

Leslie crossed her arms, finally looking up and raising an eyebrow at me. "Protect me? Or protect your interests? You know how much I value transparency, Jeffrey. This isn't the first time you've kept me in the dark."

"I understand your frustration," I replied, keeping my tone even. "But you have to remember the times when you shared sensitive information with certain individuals. It's not just about what I can or can't disclose. It's about the potential fallout for everyone involved."

Leslie knew exactly what I was talking about. She couldn't deny that on more than one occasion, Carolyn had convinced her to share sensitive information that I told my wife in confidentiality. If Carolyn had heard about what I was doing, Moses might still be in Venezuela wondering why the deal to drop charges had fallen through again.

Leslie's phone buzzed, and she glanced at the screen. A frown came over her face.

"What?" she snapped into the phone, clearly annoyed.

I watched her, sensing her becoming more irritated as she listened.

"Again? This is the third one this week," she said. "I'll check it out and let you know."

"Was that Carolyn?" I asked when she ended the call.

"What? No, it wasn't. It was Denise Cole, another realtor," Leslie replied curtly, rolling her eyes. "Not that I should be sharing my business with you, since clearly you don't feel the need to share with me. But honestly, it's getting ridiculous. For the past week, we've been up against white realtors who I believe are working for white developers trying to muscle in on the Black Hamptons."

This was concerning news. "What? I hope that's not what's happening. One or two white families buying homes here is one thing, but sudden interest in the Black Hamptons from developers could mean trouble. Before we know it, they could displace us from the community our parents and grandparents built."

Leslie leaned back in her chair, her voice full of sarcasm. "Well, maybe you can confide in your clients and figure out what's really going on, since you seem to have all the inside information," she shot back, her frustration palpable.

"Leslie, I'm not trying to undermine you or your work," I said, hoping to bridge the growing gap between us. "I just want to keep everyone safe."

She shook her head and stood up, picking up her phone and coffee mug. “I appreciate your intentions, but I need more than just vague reassurances. I need you to be honest with me, Jeffrey.”

“I promise I’ll do better,” I replied, but I could see that my words weren’t enough to soothe her anger. As she strolled out of the kitchen, leaving me sitting alone at the table, the distance between us felt wider than ever.

8

Malcolm Britton

The ride to the Sag Harbor Municipal Center only took ten minutes, but because my nerves were on edge, it seemed much longer. When we arrived, there were several news reporters and paparazzi already waiting, indicating that news about my son's assault had made headlines.

"Damn it," my mother said from the back seat. "The circus has already begun."

I looked over at Martin. "Maybe you should drive around to the back and let Mother and I out before you park."

"That's a good idea, Malcolm," Mother agreed.

"Okay, I'll meet you all inside." Martin eased through the parking lot to the rear of the building. Luckily, there were no signs of any reporters and no cameras present back there.

"Do not make any statements to anybody," Mother instructed. "I'll write a statement on behalf of the family and release it later."

"You want me to call Kimberly and have her do it?" Martin offered.

"No," Mother replied quickly. "I'll do it myself."

I got out of the car, adjusted my suit jacket, then opened the rear door so my mother could exit. She ran her hands down the front of her blazer and straightened the diamond-encrusted brooch on her lapel. Then, she linked her arm into mine, and we made our way to the building together. Martin waited until we made it to the rear entrance before he drove off. I opened the door, and instead of allowing Mother to enter first, I stepped inside and made sure the coast was clear.

"We need to go speak with DA Byron Griggs before we do anything," Mother whispered, looking around the area where we stood, although no one was paying any attention to us. “I want to make sure he’s handling this thing and not trying to pass it off to anyone else. I meant what I said to Harrington last night. I want the maximum charges filed.”

“I know, Mother. I feel the same way.”

Mother turned to me and placed her hands firmly on my shoulders, looking up into my eyes. “I’m going to tell you the same thing I told your brother earlier. Now isn’t the time for us to be distracted by your father’s sudden return. We have to be on our toes and prepared for what we’re about to face as a family.”

“Mother, he’s not a distraction. He’s just as concerned about Jesse’s well-being as we are. As a matter of fact, he told Jeffrey when we were on the way to the hospital to reach out to the DA on our behalf.”

“We didn’t need him to do that. I am perfectly capable of handling things when it comes to this family.” Mother raised an eyebrow. “Haven’t I been doing it while he was gone?”

“Yes, you have. No one is disputing that fact,” I said. “But he’s here, and at the end of the day, Dad is family.”

“I don’t have time to argue with you about this.” Mother sighed and let me go. She started to walk to the elevator, but I stopped her.

“We have to wait on Martin,” I reminded her.

She pressed the button anyway. “We don’t have time to wait,” she said, visibly frustrated. “We need to meet with Griggs before the bail hearing, and we don’t even know what time that will be.”

“Excuse me. Is DA Griggs’s office on this floor?” I asked a well-dressed man as he walked toward the elevators.

“Two floors up,” the man answered. “That’s where I’m headed.”

“Oh, okay.” I resumed my position at my mother’s side. The doors opened, and he and I allowed Mother to enter before we did. As we rode up in silence, I couldn’t help staring at the man on the elevator with us. There was something familiar about him. I was certain I’d seen him before. He was a handsome man, and I took inventory of his Armani Exchange suit, Gucci loafers, Creed Aventus cologne, and the Italian leather messenger bag on his shoulder. Whoever he was, he was a man of importance. I glanced over at Mother to see if she noticed, but her eyes remained forward.

"Here we are," he said, politely holding the elevator door open for us when we arrived at the second floor.

"Thanks, man."

"You're welcome." He nodded, and we began walking down the hall toward the DA's office.

"You look kinda familiar," I told him. "Do I know you from somewhere?"

"I get that all the time." The guy laughed. "People see me from time to time on TV. I think I have one of those faces folks never forget."

"Are you an actor?" I asked.

"No, I'm an attorney," he answered as we arrived at the office door. As he reached for the handle, the door opened, and Jeffrey and my father walked out.

"You made it." Dad greeted me with a smile.

"Dad, you're here," I said, surprised to see him.

"Yes, I told your mother this morning when we spoke on the phone that Jeffrey and I were here meeting with Griggs." He glanced over at Mother, then back at me. "She didn't tell you?"

"No, she didn't." I shot a look at my mother.

"For good reason," Mother stated as she stared at my father.

"Excuse me." The tall stranger from the elevator maneuvered past us to enter the office.

"What the hell is he doing here?" Jeffrey mumbled.

"You know him?" I asked. "I'm trying to figure out where I know him from."

"Hell yeah, I know him. That's Christopher Johnson, the guy who defended that rapper Shiloh and won the fucking murder trial last year," Jeffrey answered.

Suddenly, I remembered where I knew Christopher's face from. Shiloh's case had made headlines, especially when, despite the overwhelming evidence including a gun with his fingerprints, Shiloh was found not guilty. All thanks to Christopher Johnson.

"You don't think . . ." Mother looked panicked.

"Nah, he can't be here for Peter. That man's retainer starts at five hundred grand," Jeffrey insisted. "There's no way his father could come up with that much money."

"Well, what exactly did Griggs have to say?" Mother directed her question to Jeffrey.

"He said that the investigation is still pending, but—"

"Pending?" I interrupted. "What the hell do they need to investigate? That goddamn kid attacked Jessie and nearly killed him. Charges need to be filed for aggravated assault, trespassing, attempted murder, and that's just to start."

I turned to enter the office but was stopped by my father's hand on my arm.

"Hey, son, I know this is upsetting, but we're going to do everything we can to make sure this thing is handled the right way. This initial hearing this morning is just the beginning, and Griggs said that additional charges can be filed and upgraded as the investigation continues. For now, we know that Peter will be charged with trespassing and assault. From what Jeffrey told me, that's a good start, especially since his father doesn't have the means to bail him out anyway."

It was odd but comforting having my father by my side, offering words of encouragement. His absence over the past few years had created a void in my life, particularly because we had been so close. Due to the circumstances of his departure and the associated legal ramifications, we were instructed not to contact him—no phone calls, no emails, no letters, and no visits. Initially, Mom assured us that this was best for the bank and for everyone involved. She promised to do everything in her power to help bring him back to the United States. Unfortunately, that never happened. Her focus had quickly shifted to herself and the business.

She might not have been happy about it, but I for one was grateful that he was with us. Her negativity about him couldn't overshadow my love for him. Deep down, I knew that as angry as she seemed, she still loved him in her own way. They had been married for nearly forty years, and throughout my father's absence, my mother had never once mentioned divorce. It would have been the perfect time for her to leave him, yet she didn't. I was convinced that her aversion to his sudden return stemmed more from pride and the fear that he would reclaim his position as head of the bank, reducing her to a lesser role. That was my assumption anyway.

"What time does this thing start?" I asked.

“In about twenty minutes,” Jeffrey answered. “We should probably head down to the courtroom.”

“Here you all are. I’ve been looking for you,” Martin called out as he approached from the opposite end of the hallway.

“What on earth took you so long?” Mother asked.

“The reporters out front were like vultures, and I couldn’t park out back because it was permit parking only.”

“We probably should’ve warned you about the media,” Dad commented.

“There’s a hell of a lot more you should’ve told me about, but I won’t go there.” Mother cut her eyes at him.

“Carolyn, I believe I speak for all of us when I say you’ve made your point. You aren’t pleased by my presence. But I’m here, and there’s nothing you can do about it,” Dad shot back at my mother. “Now, can we please move past this? There’s enough going on this morning, and your attitude isn’t helping.”

Mother’s eyes widened, and she opened her mouth to respond, but I quickly interrupted.

“You didn’t give a statement, did you?” I asked Martin.

Martin shook his head. “Of course I didn’t.”

“The media being here should be expected,” Jeffrey said. “Jesse is a Britton, and this will most likely be a high-profile case. This also gives us more reason to have it moved from this jurisdiction, if need be. A jury in Sag Harbor may be sympathetic toward Peter, especially considering he’s now considered somewhat of a local celebrity.”

“The thing is, they weren’t asking me questions about Jesse or the fight.” Martin shook his head. “They wanted to know about Dad being back.”

9

Martin Britton

Nothing could have prepared me to see Attorney Christopher Johnson sitting beside Peter at the defendant's table. Malcom, Mother, Dad, Jeffrey, and I were making our way to our seats when I noticed him. Back when Christopher handled Shiloh's murder case, I had to give him his props. He was one hell of an attorney. However, seeing him seated by Peter, who looked like a prep school student in his suit and tie instead of a brutal attacker, made my stomach go to my ass.

"Why the hell is he there with him?" I hissed, disbelief washing over me.

"I thought you said he was a big-time lawyer that Peter Lane could never afford," Malcom said to Jeffrey.

"He is," Jeffrey replied, his expression mirroring my surprise. "I'm just as taken aback as you are."

"I don't care if that boy's lawyer is Alan Dershowitz. He's going to jail for a long time." My mother's voice was firm as we took our seats. "Jeffrey, I hope you spoke with the DA to ensure the proper charges are filed."

"I did, Carolyn," Jeffrey assured her. "The DA is fully aware that we expect Peter to be held accountable for the damages he's caused. But keep in mind, the investigation is still pending."

"I'm more concerned about how Peter Lane can afford Christopher Johnson," I said, shaking my head in disbelief.

"This case is open and shut," Malcolm insisted, his tone unwavering. "We shouldn't have anything to worry about. Hopefully, he'll make it easier on everyone and just enter a guilty plea so this can all be over."

"I doubt that will happen," Jeffrey replied. "Christopher Johnson doesn't back down without a fight, and he rarely loses."

Either he just knew the job well or he could tell the future, but Jeffrey was spot on. Just as he predicted, once the hearing started, Christopher Johnson not only entered a plea of not guilty but also contested the bail amount requested by the DA.

"Your Honor, unlike most of the people in this courtroom today, Peter Lane doesn't come from wealth. His father is a servant of the people in Sag Harbor. Three hundred and fifty thousand dollars is overly excessive," Christopher Johnson argued confidently.

"Peter Lane's lineage has nothing to do with the bail amount we are requesting," DA Griggs countered, his voice steady. "The nature of the crimes he's charged with should be the determining factor. These are truly serious offenses."

"I hear and understand both of your arguments. I'm going to set bail at two hundred thousand dollars," the judge announced, leaving me in stunned silence.

"What?" my mother gasped incredulously.

"And I'm also going to grant your motion to have your client placed on house arrest, Mr. Johnson," the judge added, his tone final.

"Thank you, Your Honor." A satisfied smile crept onto Christopher's face.

"Trial date will be set for November seventeenth. Until then, court is adjourned." The judge struck his gavel and disappeared into his chambers before I could process what had just happened.

We jumped up and stormed out of the courtroom. I didn't know whose steam was blowing the hottest, but I was pretty ticked off. I wanted to hit one of the walls outside of the courtroom, but I contained myself. The injustice of it all was swirling around in the pit of my gut.

"That's it? They're not even going to keep that monster locked up?" I asked in anguish.

"I can't believe this. Jeffrey, you need to do something," Mother insisted.

"There's nothing I can do," Jeffrey told her. "Charges have been filed, and the bail has been set. But the investigation is still pending, so maybe more charges will be filed later."

"I wouldn't worry too much, Mother," I offered, trying to find some small shred of hope. "I doubt that Peter's father can post that bail amount."

"Yeah, the same way we doubted he could afford Christopher Johnson as his lawyer?" Malcolm said, shaking his head. "This is bullshit! Fucking bullshit."

"I'm going to talk to him," Mother announced as Chief Harrington exited the courtroom and entered the hallway where we were gathered.

"And say what?" Dad asked.

"Don't worry about that," Mother told him, then before walking off, added, "How about you focus your energy on dealing with the questions from the media waiting downstairs? After all, you're the one they seem to be concerned about, instead of justice for our grandson."

When she was gone, I noticed that the unbothered expression was gone from his face, replaced with deep worry lines.

"She didn't mean that," I told him.

"She did, and she does make a good point." Dad sighed. "But we're going to get through all of this, son, I promise."

"Moses?" Jeffrey interrupted. "We have another meeting to get to."

"Meeting with who?" Malcolm asked.

"Nothing to concern yourself with," Dad answered. "I have some business I need to take care of so things can start getting back to normal, that's all."

"You really think that's possible, Dad?" I asked.

"I have no doubt." Dad nodded. "I'll catch you two boys later. We have a lot to discuss." Dad hugged each of us, then left with Jeffrey.

"What do you think that's about?" I asked my brother.

"I don't know." Malcolm shrugged. "Like he said, he has some things to take care of. I mean, he's been gone for seven years. That's a long time."

Because of Jesse's attack, I really hadn't talked to Malcolm about our father's return. When it came to matters dealing with Dad, Malcolm had a tendency to become very emotional, and not in a good way. Not too long ago, he'd sucker-punched Anthony Johnson for making an innocent joke during a game of tennis.

"Yeah! Who's your daddy now?" Anthony had taunted after he served the winning point that whizzed right by Malcolm. That little joke earned Anthony a bloody nose courtesy of my hot-headed brother.

That day, Anthony learned a lesson I'd understood for a long time: tread lightly when discussing Moses Britton. But now wasn't the time for me to tiptoe around the subject.

"Malcolm, did you even hear what Jeffrey said last night when about how he got Dad back home?" I reminded him. "That didn't seem odd to you?"

"What do you mean?" Malcolm frowned.

"The fact that Anthony and Everett Simpson were the ones who helped bring Dad home. And him being home. What does that mean for your position as CEO of Amistad Bank?" Mother had just handed the role to him after his wedding, and I would have thought he'd be more concerned with keeping it.

Malcom stared at me with a blank look on his face as if he had no idea what I was talking about. I suppose it's possible he was so overwhelmed by what had happened to Jesse, and then seeing Dad a few moments later, that he really hadn't heard Jeffrey.

"You'll be pleased to know that Anthony, with the help of Everett Simpson, took care of that situation down in Venezuela, so you don't have to," Jeffrey had said to Mother as we came face to face with them outside the police station. The smirk on his face told me he enjoyed delivering this shocking news to my mother, but I didn't really understand why.

My need to understand what had led to my father's return was slowly but surely becoming a pressing concern. How had Anthony and Everett learned about the situation in Venezuela? More importantly, why had Jeffrey allowed them to get involved? The feud between our family and the Johnsons was well-known, and it was no secret that Everett and my brother didn't get along, one of the reasons being that Everett's current fiancé was Malcolm's ex. That alone should have raised red flags for him, yet he appeared completely unfazed by it all.

I stood there studying my brother's expression as he pondered my question.

"Honestly?" Malcom sighed. "I'm happy he's home. But I'd be lying if I said I wasn't a little concerned. I've spent years building my role here, and Mother entrusted me with these responsibilities while he was gone. This is my life we're talking about, so it's a lot to consider."

"So, what are you going to do? Fight for your position, or be the loyal son and let him take it back?" I challenged.

"That's a hard question to answer. On one hand, I support Mother. She's worked so hard to keep things running smoothly. But on the other hand, Dad's been the one leading this family and the bank for decades. And then, there's an invisible hand. Me. What do I want? I can't just ignore that."

"I'm assuming you haven't talked to her about it?" I asked.

"No, not yet. I think she's in denial about it all, honestly," Malcolm replied, frustration creeping into his voice. "I've seen how much she loves being in charge. She might not want to acknowledge it, but him reclaiming his position as CEO isn't what she wants."

"Do you think he'll just walk back in and take over without expecting a fight?"

"I don't know. Dad has always been assertive, but this is different. He might not understand how much has changed in his absence. He knows he can't just slide back into the top spot without considering what Mom and I have built."

"Whatever you decide, you have my support. Family is important, but the balance within the family is what makes everything work," I reassured him.

He looked down at his vibrating phone. "This is Vanessa. I have to take this."

"I'll go get the car and meet you around back," I told him, rushing toward the elevator before it could close.

The day had already taken a toll on me, so I was glad for the few moments of alone time. I leaned back and took my phone out to call the one person I wanted to talk to. Karrin. I just wanted to hear her voice. As I was about to hit CALL, I remembered that I couldn't. After what my mother had done to her, I was probably the last person she wanted to hear from. I felt horrible about the entire ordeal, but I'd had no choice.

I'd fallen hard for Karrin, captivated by her beauty, vivacious spirit, and the way she effortlessly lit up a room. There was also the fact that her body was as perfect as her smile, and she was sexy as hell. But to Mother, she was simply unacceptable. My mother believed that any woman dating her son needed to embody a certain pedigree and have an education that reflected our family's status. In other words, the kind of refined upbringing that Karrin simply didn't have. She dismissed Karrin as lacking the class and sophistication that, in her eyes, were essential for anyone hoping to be part of the Britton family. It didn't matter that she had a lot of qualities that made up for any lack. My mother refused to see her for who she truly was. Instead, she fixated on the superficial: Karrin's provocative looks, off-the-rack clothing, modest background, and lack of social connections.

When I stood my ground and refused to end my relationship with Karrin, my mother responded with something I never expected. She cut me off financially, leaving me in a position where I had to choose: Karrin or the Britton legacy, the family name, the financial security, and the privileges that came with it.

"Do you think I'm going to allow you to keep wining and dining here on my dime? Now that I think about it, not only are you irresponsible and erratic, but you're delusional as well. All over a piece of ass. My, my, my, how pussy whipped can you be?" She'd asked when I confronted her about my relationship with Karrin. "Either you can go be with your broke Brooklyn boo and live your best broke life, or you can remain in your current position as vice president and help me continue to build the Britton legacy. Now, what are you going to do? Sit in that chair or walk out that door?"

I was truly conflicted. I loved Karrin, but the weight of my family's expectations wasn't something I took lightly. The fear of losing everything I'd known, everything I'd been raised to value, made the decision even more difficult. Ultimately, I chose my family. Letting Karrin go felt like losing a piece of my heart, but it was the price I had to pay for family loyalty.

I hated my mother's controlling ways. It was like we were all pieces on her personal chess board. And it wasn't just *my* love life that she pulled the strings to. It was Malcom's, too. She was the driving force behind Malcolm's divorce and then, in a bizarre twist, his recent remarriage to Vanessa. It was funny because she deemed Vanessa a gold digger, even though she had also come from wealth. Shortly after Jesse was born, my mother insisted that Malcolm leave Vanessa, orchestrating a scheme that secured him full custody of their son in exchange for a hefty alimony settlement. Vanessa's acceptance of the offer, although under duress, only reinforced my mother's gold-digger accusations.

When it came to our romantic entanglements, she was ruthless, always seeking to direct the narrative, but there was one relationship that seemed to slip beyond her grasp, Malcom and Morgan. Mother hated the fact that Malcolm also liked men. She worried about what the community would have to say if it ever became public knowledge. So, she formed an unlikely alliance with Vanessa and then offered Malcolm the role of CEO if he would cut Morgan loose and remarry Vanessa. It wasn't an easy decision for him, but in the end, he caved to the pressure, just like I had with Karrin.

"You're Jesse's uncle Martin?"

The question caught me off guard when I stepped off the elevator. I'd been so consumed with my thoughts I almost didn't see the young lady standing in front of the elevator. I didn't recognize her at first, but her pretty face soon came back to me.

"I am," I said. "And you're Tania."

"Yes, sir," she said. "H–how is Jesse?"

"He's alive . . . barely. No thanks to your boyfriend."

"I'm sorry all of this happened. I never meant . . . Peter, he . . ." she mumbled.

"We don't need to discuss it," I said. "What happened in court was enough."

"Oh, I wasn't in there," Tania said.

"Isn't that why you're here?"

"No, my mom had some business to take care of, and I tagged along," she explained. "She told me it was best that I didn't go to the hearing."

"That was wise," I agreed. I didn't know her personally, but despite the circumstances, she seemed to be nice enough, and more importantly, remorseful.

"I'm praying for Jesse," she told me as she stepped onto the elevator and the doors closed.

Thankfully, I didn't have to fight off the media as I exited the building because Jeffrey and my father were speaking with them. I eased past and walked into the parking lot. As I got into the car and drove to the rear of the building, once again, my mind turned to Karrin. It had only been two days since we'd spoken. I needed to hear her voice, even if it meant I was being cussed out. I missed her that much. Deciding to risk it, I took out my phone to call her but stopped again when I saw my mother and brother exiting the building. The timing of everything was horrible, but somehow, I was going to get back the woman I loved.

10

Sergeant Tom Lane

"Okay, Peter," the officer said as he adjusted the ankle monitor. "You're required to wear this at all times."

"How am I supposed to shower?" Peter asked.

"You can shower and bathe. You just can't have it under water for an extended period of time. Now, as part of your bail agreement, you'll have to abstain from drugs and alcohol, and you can't leave your home unless it's for medical care, approved employment hours, and required activities."

He looked over at me as he asked, "So, I can still train?"

"That's something we'll have to discuss with the district attorney," Christopher answered.

"All right, you're good to go." The officer motioned for Peter to stand. "Just remember everything I told you. Oh, and one more thing."

"Yeah?" Peter asked.

"You must adhere to any and all restraining orders presented against you."

"Restraining orders? I don't have any restraining orders."

The rules he had to follow beat the hell out of being in jail, and soon, he would understand that. I'd been hesitant when Bobby Boyd insisted on hiring Christopher Johnson, but the man had been a godsend. He had worked wonders in the courtroom and secured Peter's bond. I hated that Peter had to endure the whole ordeal, but I was grateful for the powerhouse attorney defending him.

"My client has no problem complying with the guidelines of the agreement," Christopher told the officer. "Where does he need to sign?"

The officer slid a clipboard over to Peter. "Sign here, and then you guys are free to go."

"Thank you," Peter said quietly.

As we headed to the door, I put my arm around Peter's shoulder. "You're gonna be all right, son. We just need to get you home."

"I'm definitely ready to get there," Peter said. "I'm starving."

I laughed. "That doesn't surprise me You're always starving. I'll whip you up some eggs and bacon when we get there."

"I'll come to the house a little later this afternoon so we can chat. We still have to go over your statement that you've gotta give to the police," Christopher told us.

"Thank you again, Mr. Johnson." Peter extended his hand.

"Hey, I keep telling you, it's Chris. And your dad's right. You're gonna be all right. We've got a long road ahead, but I'll be with you every step of the way."

"Appreciate that, Chris." I shook his hand, then asked, "You ready, son?"

"Yes, sir." Peter nodded.

Just before we stepped outside, I heard my name.

"Sergeant Lane."

I turned around to see Chief Harrington walking in our direction. I couldn't read the expression on his face.

"I need to speak with you before you leave," he told me. "Alone, if possible."

"Go ahead and go to the car," I instructed Peter, and he didn't hesitate to go. I looked at my boss. "Chief, I know Peter still needs to give a statement for the investigation. His attorney is already working on it."

"That's good to know, Lane, but this isn't about Peter. This is about you."

"What about me?"

"I think now might be the time for you to take a leave of absence for a while."

His words didn't just catch me off guard; they stunned me. I don't know how long I stood there looking at his serious face before I caught my breath. A leave of absence in the midst of everything going on?

"Chief, you've gotta know that's not a good idea. Especially right now."

"I don't want you to think I'm not sympathetic to your situation, because I am. But I think it would be best."

"Best for who? It sure as hell isn't for me or my son!" The anger surged through me like wildfire, igniting every nerve in my body. "This trial is going to be costly, and we need money. I'm the only real source of income as it is, and now you want me to just stop working? That ain't happening."

I could feel my heart racing, each pulse echoing my growing agitation. The heat radiated from my core, spreading through my limbs.

"I hear you, but right now, tensions are running high, and folks are on edge," he explained. "Some of whom feel that you shouldn't even be allowed to remain on the force."

There was something about the way he said it and raised a brow at me that made a light switch go off in my head. It became very clear what he was saying.

"The Brittons are gunning for my job. Is that what this is about, Chief?"

"This is about keeping the peace and looking at the bigger picture, Lane." He danced around my question. "Look, you have some vacation time built up, and if need be, I'll even sign off on you borrowing from future vacation days or sick leave if you'd like. It's just until this thing quiets down."

"*This thing* is my son's life and his freedom. I'm the only person he's got. My family is in jeopardy, and you want me to stop working because Carolyn Britton is in your ear."

"Your son made a choice that not only affected his life, but it affected yours. Unfortunately, my hands are tied on this thing. I want you to take some time and help Peter through this, damn it," Chief Harrington said with a commanding bass in his voice. "You think you're gonna be any good to the community or the force while this is going on? Hell, it's already the talk of the town. I'm trying to be supportive here."

"I don't give a damn about what anyone has to say, including those folks in the Black Hamptons. They've been talking about me since I got here," I snapped back, frustration boiling over. "And let's be real—Carolyn Britton's influence is still hanging over this community like a dark cloud. But you're right. I do need to be with my son right now, Chief. I'll be taking a couple of weeks to do that, and it'll be with pay."

Chief Harrington looked relieved. “Good decision, Sergeant.”

“And for the record, this ain’t got shit to do with Carolyn or any other Britton. She doesn’t control me,” I told him. “I have no problem with Peter being held accountable for what he did, but that isn’t up to her. It’s the district attorney’s job.”

“I hear you, Lane, and I’m praying this all works out . . . for everyone,” Chief Harrington said.

I was a walking ball of fire when I left the building and went to the car. I could see my son sitting there in the front seat with a happy look on his face. Despite the troubles ahead, I knew he was just happy to feel some real outside air on his face. Knowing I had to be his rock, I fixed my face and demeanor the best I could.

“What was that about?” Peter asked when I sat in the driver’s seat.

“I put in for some time off. He just wanted to let me know it was approved, that’s all.” I started the car.

“Dad, I’m sorry about all of this. It’s just, I was so mad in the moment. I didn’t deserve to get done like that, but I also didn’t mean to hurt Jesse so bad. God, I hope he’s okay.”

The remorseful look on his face was heartbreaking, and all I wanted to do was make all of it go away. He’d barely been on earth for twenty-one years and had already been through so much. Between his mother’s death and being bullied for having a cop as a father, I couldn’t imagine what was going on in his head. Boxing was his saving grace and his future. Now, his freedom was on the line. I wasn’t sure how to help him, but I knew I couldn’t do it alone.

With his mother gone, I was my son’s only protector, and for the longest time, it had just been the two of us against the world. I had to put my ego aside and, despite my lingering distrust, accepted help from Bobby Boyd. It was a difficult pill to swallow, but I understood that sometimes strength was in embracing support, even from unexpected places.

“I know you didn’t, Peter.” I sighed. “Let’s just get home so you can get showered and a good meal, then get some rest before Christopher comes.”

“Sounds like a plan. But you’re forgetting one thing.”

“What’s that?” I asked.

"I need to work out," he said. "That's the only thing that's gonna keep me sane right about now, Dad."

"Hey, that's why we built a home gym, right?" I told him. "We still got goals. And I still ain't letting up on your training."

We arrived home, and while Peter went to handle his business, I headed to the kitchen to make the breakfast I had promised. When he was done, he looked more like the kid I knew. He had changed into a simple pair of sweats and a T-shirt. No more words really needed to be said between us. He just sat down in front of his plate, and we dug into the food.

I hadn't even taken four bites before we were interrupted by the ringing of the doorbell.

"I'll get it," Peter offered and went to stand.

"No, you stay," I told him, wiping my mouth with a napkin before getting up and venturing down the hallway.

It was Bobby Boyd. Of course, he was dressed in another flashy ensemble, same as always, and he had a beaming smile on his face. I wasn't happy to see him, especially since he was interrupting my meal, but I couldn't turn him away. Not after what he'd done for my son.

"Hey there, Sergeant," he greeted me. "You remember my manager Cornelius, right?"

"I do," I replied, forcing myself to nod at Cornelius, the older gentleman standing beside him. "Nice to see you again."

"Likewise," Cornelius said.

"So, listen," Bobby said. "Chris called and told me how everything went in court. I stopped by to check on my man, Peter."

"Uh, yeah, he's eating right now," I said, running my hand over my head, trying to shake off my discomfort.

"That's good, that's good." Bobby pushed past me and entered the house with Cornelius on his heels. "Powerhouse Pete! Where you at, man?"

"In the kitchen!" Peter yelled back.

As I closed the door behind me, I felt a surge of irritation. Bobby was trying to claim territory that wasn't his, and I could feel the tension coiling in my chest. But as I stepped into the kitchen and saw Peter jump to his feet, excitement lighting up his face at Bobby's arrival, I decided against protesting. In that moment, Peter's happiness outweighed my discomfort, and I knew that maintaining a positive atmosphere for him was more important than my pride.

"What's up, Double P!" Bobby dapped Peter and gave him a brief hug. "I'm glad you're home."

"I'm glad to be home, man. It's been crazy, but I really appreciate you helping me out and getting me a lawyer."

"Hey, when I met you, I told you we was fam, Pete," Bobby said.

I waited for Peter to correct Bobby. He hated to be called Pete and always made sure to let people know that. To my surprise, he didn't say anything about the nickname.

I cleared my throat loudly. "We appreciate you guys coming by and checking on Peter," I said, "but he's gotta finish eating, and then he wants to hit the bag. Tryna stay in the swing of things, you know."

"That's good to hear. Pretty much why we're here," Bobby told me. "But I did want to talk to you about something right quick."

"You know what? Where are my manners?" Peter pulled out the two empty chairs at the table. "You guys, please sit. You want some breakfast? Coffee? Water?"

"Nah, we're good." Bobby remained standing. "Appreciate the offer, though."

"So, you said you wanted to talk to us about something." I spoke up in an effort to move things along so they could leave.

"Yes, sir. I want Pete to come and stay with me at my crib while he's dealing with all of this."

"You want what?" A rush of disbelief surged through me, tightening my chest as I stared at him, my expression hardening.

The words came out sharper than I had intended, the shock mixing with a swell of protectiveness. My pulse quickened, and I felt a heat rising in my cheeks. *How could he even consider this?* I had to fight the urge to let my frustration spill over, reminding myself to keep my composure for Peter's sake.

"I want him to come and hang out at my mansion while he's under house arrest. I have plenty of space, a fully equipped gym and spa, pool, chef, and he can train with me every day." Bobby bragged, "It's right on the beach and not far from here. You can visit whenever you want. He won't want for anything, and most of all, he'll be safe."

"What makes you think he's not safe right here at home?" I folded my arms.

"Hey, I didn't mean to offend you. I know you're an officer of the law." Bobby smirked, tossing his hands up and taking a step back with a flourish, his movements almost theatrical.

The arrogance in his posture made my blood boil, and I felt a wave of heat rush to my face, my fists clenching at my sides as I struggled to contain my rising anger. It was infuriating to see him act so nonchalant, as if my authority was nothing more than a joke.

"No offense taken." I sat down in my seat, glancing at my now cold eggs and pancakes.

"I just thought it would be a great opportunity for the young man," Bobby said.

"Dad, I mean, if I go stay with Bobby, you won't need to take any time from work," Peter said. "You can hold onto your vacation."

"Peter's right, Mr. Lane." Cornelius apparently had decided that it was the right time to add his two cents. "All Team BTB wants to do is help alleviate any type of hardship on you and Pete. Hence why we hired Christopher, arranged bail, and—"

"Wait, you paid my bail?" Peter's head snapped up, and he looked over at Bobby. "I knew about the lawyer thing, but I didn't know you took care of the bail. Wow, that's big of you, Bobby."

"Hey, I'm just trying to help, that's all. I explained to your father that I've been in your shoes, and I know how it is. And I believe without a doubt that you're gonna beat this thing with a plan in place." Bobby put his arm around Peter.

"You really think that?" Peter asked, his voice full of hope.

"Hell yeah. Right now, it's your word against Jesse's, and neither of you has given a statement yet. Sure, self-defense seems like a stretch, especially since you don't have any injuries and Jesse is unconscious, but it's still a possibility. The charges against you are solely based on his injuries, nothing more. Trust me, Christopher is going to work his magic, and before you know it, all of this shit will be a bad memory. We just have to find a way to keep you out of jail at any cost."

The way Bobby presented it made me not only nearly buy into the absurdity of Peter's defense but also hope that it might actually work. Despite his facade as some hero on a rescue mission, I couldn't shake the feeling that there was an underlying motive. My instincts told me it had to do with the contract Peter had yet to sign.

"I appreciate your vote of confidence and all that you've done to help my son, Bobby. And I'm going to pay you back every dime for all of it . . ." I started.

"You don't have to do that," Bobby interjected. "Like I said—"

"I know, Peter's family. Well, in this family, we pay our debts, and you'll get every dime back," I told him. "And as far as Peter staying with you, we're gonna have to decline the offer. He's just been placed on house arrest, and the judge has already decided that the best place for him is right here. The paperwork has been filed, the monitor is on, and this is where he'll be staying."

"You do know all it takes is a phone call to have the address changed, right?" Cornelius asked. "Christopher can take care of that today."

"No need for anyone to do anything else. Now, if you'll excuse us, we'd like to finish our breakfast, and I'm sure a busy man like yourself has other things to take care of." I stood up.

Bobby shrugged. "I guess that's our cue to exit, Cornelius."

"It is." Cornelius nodded.

"Powerhouse Pete, you got my number. I know you can't leave the crib, but call if you need anything or want me to come through and work out with you." Bobby dapped Peter again.

I watched Peter's eyes as they remained on the flashy *BTB* chain hanging around Bobby's neck. "Thank you, fellas, for stopping by. I'll walk you out."

"Nah, you sit and enjoy your meal. We can lock the door on our way out. Wouldn't want anything to happen to you guys, right, Pete?" Bobby laughed.

"You definitely don't have to worry about that," I said, clenching my jaw, "And for the record, my son's name is Peter."

11

Anthony Johnson

"What time is this thing supposed to start?" Everett Simpson asked as we sat in the conference room at Jeffrey Bowen's office. We'd only been waiting for about five minutes, but he was fidgety and anxious.

"Mr. Bowen has called and said that he's right around the corner," Jeffrey's administrative assistant told him. "Can I get you gentlemen anything while you wait?"

"I'm fine. Thanks, Gina," I said.

"So am I," David, my second in command at Sydney Tech, said.

"Do you have any wine?" Everett asked. "Preferably something white."

"We have coffee, tea, and water. Sparkling or spring."

"That's it?" Everett responded. "I've known Jeffrey Bowen for years. I'm sure he's got some liquor around here somewhere."

"Well, if he does, it's someplace where I can't get to it." Gina laughed. "I'll bring you a bottle of Pellegrino to tide you over until he gets here."

"I guess that'll have to suffice." Everett shrugged. Like David and I, he was casually dressed in slacks and a collared polo shirt, but his pants were floral, and his shirt was bright yellow, the same color as the nail polish he wore.

"Everett, you're crazy." David laughed. "Always have been."

"Man, I'm just me, and you know that," Everett told him. "You and I both know Jeffrey got some hard stuff around here. He's married to Leslie and probably takes a drink before going home to deal with Carolyn Junior's ass."

"Ha!" I couldn't help but laugh. "Come on. Leslie's not that bad."

"Fine. She's not as much of a dragon as Carolyn. That was a stretch," Everett conceded. "I do like her, though, at least when she's not trying to prove something to her aunt."

"You make a good point," David agreed.

"And based on the power move that we just made, I'd say it's more of a call for champagne than cognac. I don't know about you guys, but I'm quite excited about what's to come." Everett smirked.

I didn't know how to react. The truth of the matter was that I really didn't know what I'd even gotten myself into. What I did know was that Jeffrey had approached David and me with a way to save the multimillion-dollar deal that had almost cost me everything. The only thing we needed to do was partner with Everett and come up with four million dollars.

"Mr. Singh never wanted to kill the deal with us, Anthony," David had explained to me when our deal with Singh fell apart. "Carolyn and Malcolm made him do it as a stipulation for Amistad to finance the Entech deal."

"I knew it," I said bitterly. My wife and I were locked in a feud with Carolyn Britton over a piece of land that we both wanted to purchase, and she played dirty. If she could kill the Singh deal and bankrupt my company, then I would not have the money to compete for that land.

"The only person who can supersede her is in Venezuela. It will cost you four million dollars to help bring him back to the States, but, then again, it might save you fifty."

Hell, it didn't take rocket science to see that it was the only chance I had. Too much pride coursed through my body to approach the many wealthy businessmen in my line of work to ask for help. Especially given the fact I only had forty-eight hours to do so. It would have felt too much like begging. But learning that my only option involved the name Britton gave me cause for concern. I was wary to wire the money, but I trusted David with both my life and my company, so when he insisted that the Hail Mary of a deal would work in our favor in more ways than one, I sent the money. It worked. Hours later, we received word that Moses Britton had arrived from Venezuela via private jet, and we went to meet him.

Now, here we were again, waiting to meet for a follow-up, and hopefully, a solid plan to secure the future of Sydney Tech.

"Gentlemen, sorry for our tardiness." Jeffrey breezed into the conference room with Moses Britton right behind him. We all shook hands before they took their seats at the table.

"Mr. Johnson, nice to see you again. You too, David. Everett," Moses greeted us.

"Good to see you too." I nodded. "How is Jesse?"

"He's slowly improving. Thank you for asking."

"I'm sure Malcolm is devastated behind all of this," Everett said. "I'm glad he has Vanessa by his side to comfort him."

Moses nodded. "Yes, I'm glad they have each other right now. She hasn't even left the hospital. She stayed while we went to court this morning for the bail hearing."

"I guess they got remarried just in time," Everett commented, and I detected some kind of insincerity in his voice. "That's sweet."

"Your water, Mr. Simpson." Gina entered with a bottle of Perrier and a glass, placing them in front of Everett. "Can I get anyone anything else?"

"No, we're fine, Gina. Thank you," Jeffrey answered on everyone's behalf, then waited for Gina to walk out before speaking. "Well, the past few days have been quite eventful. And I'm sure you all are wondering what our next steps are."

"That would be correct," I said. "I know your family has a crisis that you're dealing with, Moses, but right now, there is a major deal pending that will greatly affect us. The purchase of Entech by the Singh Corporation, which is pending funds from Amistad Bank."

"And from what I've been told, my wife has threatened to pull the loan for Singh because of the deal with Singh-Sydney Tech, correct?" Moses asked.

"That's right." I nodded. "Which complicated things tremendously."

"Not anymore," Jeffrey said. "Now that Moses is back, he can override that decision and ensure the funding of the Entech deal."

"How? Didn't Carolyn go before a federal judge to be granted the position as head of Amistad?" Everett volunteered as he took a sip of his water.

"She did," Jeffrey answered. "But there is a way, and we have a plan in place. The loan will go through."

"And you're sure about this?" I asked.

Despite David, Jeffrey, and Everett being certain about Moses and his ability to get things done, I wasn't so sure. It seemed a little too late to be doubtful, though. I was four million dollars in now.

"I owe you gentlemen a great deal for your assistance." Moses looked at each of us around the table. "I want you to know that the financial compensation will be great, but the non-tangible reward you will receive is priceless. Just wait and see."

"I'm looking forward to it." Everett raised his glass. "I can't wait to receive my invitation to dinner parties at the Britton mansion and sunset cruises on the yacht."

"Anthony, I know that my wife has been a thorn in your side for the past few months," Moses said to me.

"That's an understatement," David murmured.

"You don't have to worry about her anymore. I promise." He extended his hand. "You have Amistad Bank at your disposal."

"Thank you for that, Moses, but for now, I'll just stick with the financial institution we already have." I shook his hand. "You just make sure this Entech deal goes through, and we're good."

We said our goodbyes, and I headed back home to spend time with my wife. Things were finally looking up for us, thanks to Moses Britton. Hell, with the Singh deal being finalized, things would be settled soon, and then I wouldn't mind going on a month-long vacation. We damn sure needed it. We hadn't been on a couples' trip in decades. Now that the kids were grown and almost on their own, it was time. I couldn't wait to tell her, especially after the lackluster excitement she had shown about me hiring the new landscaper to design the back yard and install the spa.

When I arrived at the house, the landscaping truck was gone, but there was another car parked near the driveway that I didn't recognize. I parked my car and got out. As I walked toward the front door, I noticed an older white guy in a suit, talking to a middle-aged white woman as they walked from the side of our home.

"Excuse me. Can I help you?" I asked.

"Oh, how are you, sir?" The man smiled. "You must be Mr. Johnson. I'm Eli Bradshaw, and this is my assistant, Sharon."

"And how can I help you, Mr. Bradshaw?" I'd seen him in passing and knew that he was one of the few non-Black residents in the Black Hamptons, but we hadn't formally met. "Why exactly are you lurking around my property?"

"I'm actually interested in purchasing it. We were just taking a look around." Eli didn't seem embarrassed at all to have been caught snooping. This was one arrogant prick, I decided.

"Well, I'm sorry, but my home isn't for sale."

"Really? I was told that you were placing it on the market for a short sale. Something about your business being in trouble."

The doubtful look he gave me made me even more irritated. Not only was the man trespassing with his assistant, but he had the nerve to be insinuating that I was lying.

"You were told wrong, and I'd appreciate it if you and your assistant would get off my property, sir," I said forcefully.

"No problem. We can do that," Sharon said as she hurried off.

Unfortunately, her boss didn't seem to be in any type of rush. He slowly sauntered, then turned around and held out a business card. "I know you said that you're not selling, but I want you to know that I'm willing to make an offer on your property that's more than fair, Mr. Johnson. I really want to buy this house."

"Like I said, Mr. Bradshaw, my house isn't for sale." I stared at the card without taking it.

"Honey, is everything okay?" Sydney walked out onto the front porch.

"Yeah, Syd. Everything's fine, baby," I yelled back at her. "This man's lost, but he's leaving."

"Nice meeting you, Mr. Johnson," Eli said. "See you soon."

As he strutted off toward the car where Sharon was waiting, he paused to look at the house across the street.

Sydney walked over and asked, "What was that about?"

"I don't know. He claims he heard the house was for sale."

"What? Who would tell him that?" Sydney frowned. "Leslie never even listed it."

My eyes remained on Eli and Sharon until they got into the car and drove away. "It's something up with him for sure, and whatever it is, I don't like it."

12

Carolyn Britton

I instructed Martin to drop me off at the bank before taking his brother to the hospital. Usually, I'd work at home, but now wasn't the time to work in comfort. It was time to prepare for battle. I'd been blindsided by Moses once, but it wasn't going to happen again. Next time, I would be ready.

Once I was in the privacy of my office I placed a phone call.

"Hudson and Hud—"

"Lamont Hudson, please."

"He's in a meeting right now. Would you like his voicemail?" the receptionist asked.

"No, I would not. What I'd like is for you to let him know Carolyn Britton needs to speak with him now."

"Okay, Mrs. Britton. I'll relay the message as soon as his meeting is over."

"I don't think you understand what I'm saying," I told her. "I want you to go and tell him now while I'm on the phone. I'll wait."

"Uh, I don't think—"

"I don't care what you think. The monthly retainer I give that law firm is double your salary. I would hate for you to lose it for being insubordinate to one of the most valuable clients your employer has," I said tersely.

There was a brief pause, until finally she said, "One moment, Mrs. Britton."

She placed me on a brief hold, and I took a seat at my desk while I waited for Lamont to pick up the phone. Although his father, Bradley Hudson, was the head of the firm, Lamont was less resistant to my demands and easier to deal with than the elder Hudson. Plus, I needed someone who would be more of a risk taker.

"Carolyn." Lamont's voice came through the phone.

"Hello, Lamont. I've been trying to reach you directly on your cell, but for some reason, you haven't responded to my calls or texts. Hence the reason why I had to resort to calling your office."

"That's because I've been in a client meeting for the past couple of hours. The same meeting that you're interrupting, I might add," he responded. "I have every intention of returning your call—or should I say calls."

"I'm a client as well, and I'm in the middle of a legal crisis," I said.

"And this crisis couldn't wait until after my meeting ended? Have you been arrested, or is your life in danger?"

"No, neither of those."

"Then whatever it is, Carolyn, it can wait."

I exhaled deeply. "Moses is back, Lamont."

There was a brief pause. He was stunned, just as I had expected. "When you say *back* . . ."

"Back as in here in Sag Harbor." I sighed. "Now do you understand my sense of urgency?"

"My meeting will be over in ten minutes, and I'll be on my way," Lamont said, now sounding alert.

"I'm not home. I'm at the bank."

"I'll meet you in your office," he said before hanging up.

Knowing Lamont was on his way gave me a bit of relief. I had a lot to do and a short time to get it done. In addition to my already tight schedule, I still needed to prepare an official statement from Amistad Bank about Moses's return and one from the family regarding Jesse and his attack.

I turned on my computer and decided to get started on my lengthy to do list for the day.

"Aunt Carolyn?"

I glanced up from the computer screen to see my niece, Leslie, standing in the doorway. I couldn't believe her audacity to show up in person, clearly eager to receive the verbal lashing she knew was coming. Our relationship was a complicated one, marked by an emotional rollercoaster. I loved her deeply and found her to be lovely and intelligent, yet her lack of business acumen and her failure to leverage her position in both business and marriage left me frustrated. Despite her best efforts to prove her worth,

I often felt as if she were an irritating puppy, always seeking approval but never quite grasping the nuances of the game. For example, the fact that it was her husband who had helped Moses arrange his great return, while she remained completely in the dark. It infuriated me. Her pillow talk skills were nonexistent, and she'd failed on more than one occasion to use them to her benefit and mine.

"What the hell do you want?" I asked in a tone that was just as stern as the look I gave her.

"I stopped by the house to talk to you, but you weren't there. I thought you would've come home after court this morning." Leslie entered the office without being invited.

"You thought wrong," I told her. "The same way it's wrong for you to assume that I have anything to say to you. Because I don't."

"You don't have to talk, but I would like for you to hear me out." She came to stand directly in front of my desk and faced me. "I know you're upset with me because you think—"

"Before you even start trying to explain how you had no knowledge of your uncle returning, you can stop. The whole goddamn thing was orchestrated by your husband. The same husband that announced the Simpson property being for sale without your knowledge. Are you seeing a pattern here? Because I am." I shook my head. "Either you're a liar, or your marriage is in trouble."

"Aunt Carolyn, neither one of those are true. I'm telling the truth, and my marriage is most definitely solid," Leslie protested.

I couldn't help but roll my eyes. It baffled me that she remained completely in the dark about Jeffrey's dealings and significant business moves. She was always oblivious.

"That has yet to be determined." I exhaled. "And right now, I don't have the time, nor do I care to discuss it."

"I'm sure," Leslie relented. "I just wanted to let you know that I was as surprised about it as you were."

"And I'm certain that you were elated when you did get the news." I leaned forward and waited for her response.

She paused for a moment, then started, "I . . . I really . . . I . . ."

"Save it. For God's sake, you can't be honest about anything." I tossed my hand in the air, preparing to unleash the admonishment that I'd been reserving until the right moment. Before I could start, my attention was drawn to my cell phone chiming at the same time that Leslie's let out a loud alert. We both looked at our phones.

"Shit," she murmured.

"You've got to be kidding." I stared at the screen, shocked by the words that I read. I slammed the phone on my desk and stood. "What the hell is this about?"

"I don't know." Leslie shrugged helplessly.

"Why not? Your husband is the one who just sent the email announcing the emergency meeting for Amistad board members, isn't he?" I folded my arms and shook my head. "Wait, don't tell me. He didn't mention anything about this to you either, did he?"

"He didn't. I had no idea. I got the email at the same time you did, Aunt Carolyn." Leslie had the nerve to look downright embarrassed, and I almost felt sorry for her.

"Here's a little advice for you," I said, gathering my items from my desk and putting them into my leather attaché case. "You may want to have a real discussion with your husband and find out why there's all this secrecy between you. There's no telling what else he's been hiding."

"Yes, ma'am." Leslie nodded, then turned to leave.

"Oh, and Leslie," I called out.

"Yes?" She paused, looking back over her shoulder at me.

"It would be in your best interest to find out what the hell this emergency board meeting is about."

"Yes, I will." Leslie scurried out of my office.

When she was gone, I immediately picked up my phone and dialed Lamont's cell number. This time, he was gracious enough to answer.

"Yes, Carolyn."

"Change of plans. Meet me at the house," I told him. "And clear your schedule for the rest of the day."

"I already have."

"Good."

Rather than waiting for Martin to return to the bank and pick me up, I called a car service to drive me home. In less than thirty minutes, I was stepping out of the rear of the Lamborghini truck and heading toward my front door.

"Carolyn, do you have a moment?"

I turned around to see one of my neighbors, Valencia Burnett, walking in my direction. "I really don't. I have an important meeting I need to prepare for."

"I know your time is valuable, but I need to talk to you about something important." She continued approaching.

I'd known Valencia for decades, and in addition to us both being residents of the Black Hamptons, we were members of the same church and belonged to the same bridge club. We had shared laughter and light moments, but we were friendly acquaintances: familiar yet not particularly close. In light of the events of the past few days, that would no longer be the case.

"Valencia . . ."

"Carolyn, please, just one moment," she pleaded. "Things have been really hard for my daughter and me for the past few months. I thought moving in with her after her divorce would help both of us, but we got notice that the taxes on the house are past due, and we're facing some serious trouble. I really need to see if I can take out a loan from Amistad before things get to the point of no return."

"Is that why you rushed over here to see me?" I frowned. "Really?"

"Yes. I know it's not customary and these things are handled at the bank, but I wanted to personally come and talk to you."

Normally, I would have been pleased to see her and talk with her. I'd even go so far as to say I would have considered helping her. That was no longer the case.

"I must say, I'm at a loss for words," I told her. "For you to stroll over and stop me just to explain that you're in financial dire straits and ask me for help."

Valencia lowered her eyes. "I know, and I hate to have to come to you with this, Carolyn. Really, I do."

"It's unfortunate," I told her. "To think that you would come to me with this without even acknowledging what happened to Jesse."

Valencia's eyes met mine. She was breathing so hard that I could see the rise and fall of her chest. "Oh, I'm sor—"

"Save your apology, Valencia, because if you think for one minute that I'd loan you one cent after the danger that tramp granddaughter of yours caused, you are mistaken. Jesse was almost killed because of her." I was shouting now.

"I know, and it was unfortunate, but Tania—"

"Instead of coming and asking for money, you should be thanking me for not pressing charges against her. She could be sitting in jail beside that boyfriend of hers," I pointed out.

Valencia gasped. "Tania didn't do anything illegal."

"She didn't have permission to be on that boat," I said. "It would be best if both you and her stay the hell away from my family."

Valencia slowly took in air as tears filled her eyes. For a brief second, I felt a twinge of sadness. Then, I thought about Jesse lying in the ICU, battered and bruised, connected to IVs and monitors. Tania might not have been the one who put hands on him, but she was the cause.

"Point taken," Valencia said sadly.

Without saying another word, I walked past her and entered the house.

13

Vanessa Britton

"Well, I'm mad they even gave that bastard bail, but I'm glad they filed charges against him." I sighed, leaning my head against Malcolm's shoulder as we sat at Jesse's bedside.

"Yeah, plus the DA said if Jesse wakes up and gives a statement, more charges can be filed," he said.

"*When* he wakes up," I whispered, staring at my son's sleeping body. Despite the positive prognosis from the doctors, I was still worried because he hadn't regained consciousness.

Malcolm took my hand into his. "He's going to wake up soon, baby."

"Malcolm's right," my sister Alyssa agreed. "You know how much Jesse has always loved a good nap. Today's no different."

I couldn't help but smile. She was right. Jesse had loved napping ever since he was a baby. To think that was all that he was doing right now brought me a little comfort.

"You're probably right," I said, wishing I felt more confident about it.

"Thanks for being here, Lys," Malcolm said to Alyssa.

"You know you don't have to thank me," she said. "Jesse is my favorite nephew. Where else would I be?"

"He's your only nephew." Malcolm laughed. "But I get what you're saying."

"Now that you're here, I'm going to go down and grab some more coffee." Alyssa stood. "You guys want anything?"

"No, I'm good," I answered.

"So am I," Malcolm said.

Alyssa rubbed our shoulders, then walked out of the room. I turned and looked at Malcolm, who stared at the floor, his face full of worry. I couldn't remember the last time I'd seen him so troubled. There was something bothering him, and it was more than just our son.

"Malcolm? What's going on?"

"Huh?" Malcolm looked over at me.

"Talk to me. I know this is about more than Jesse."

"I've just got a lot on my mind." Malcolm gave me a semi-smile. "Nothing you need to be worried about. You have enough you're dealing with right now with this."

"We're both dealing with this." I pointed to Jesse. "But we're a team. Always have been, even when we were divorced. Now that I'm your wife again, that hasn't changed. Does this have anything to do with Moses?"

"Yeah, it does."

"I thought you were happy that he was home. What's going on?"

"I am happy about him being home," Malcolm said. "But the people who helped him get back home is what's odd to me."

"I thought Jeffrey was behind all of this."

"He was, but he didn't act alone."

"Who helped him?" I asked.

"Anthony Johnson and Everett Simpson."

I sat up in my chair. "Wait, why those two? That doesn't make any sense. The two of them barely know one another, and I didn't think they ran in the same circles."

Anthony was a married tech guru who rarely got out and about, mainly because his wife kept him on a very short leash. Everett was a gay socialite and trust fund baby who thrived on being the center of attention. Neither one of them had any association with Moses.

"Now you see why I'm confused," Malcolm told me. "This entire situation is getting weirder and weirder."

"Does your mother know that Anthony was the one who helped Moses?" I voiced my main concern.

Of course his phone would ring right before I could find out the most important detail. If Carolyn knew that Anthony was behind anything pertaining to her husband, everything around us might burn.

He gave me an apologetic look before pulling it out and looking at the screen. “Hey, Martin,” he answered.

I watched his eyebrows crinkle as he listened to whatever his brother was saying.

“Hold on, wait. When? No, I haven’t looked at my email. Give me a second. I’ll call you back.”

Malcolm disconnected the call and stood up. He paced back and forth a few steps as he scrolled through his phone. There was a look of uncertainty on his face, and I didn’t like it.

“What happened?” I asked.

“Something’s going on. Jeffrey called an emergency board meeting.” Malcolm shook his head. “I need to go and find my father. I’m sorry, baby. I know I just got here, but—”

“Malcolm, it’s fine,” I reassured him, standing so that I faced him. “Go and take care of whatever it is you need to. We’ll be fine. I’ll call you if Jesse wakes up.”

“When he wakes up,” Malcolm corrected me and kissed me softly.

When he pulled away, I pulled him back in again for another one. His lips were a source of comfort for me, and I needed it right then. No matter how brief. I was so grateful that we’d reconciled and remarried, even if our nuptials were part of one of Carolyn’s schemes. My mother-in-law was relentless in her pursuit of what she wanted, and nothing or no one else mattered to her. The only thing more dangerous than her determination was her capacity for vengeance, which was why knowing that Anthony Johnson was part of Moses’s great return had my nerves on edge. I couldn’t shake the feeling that a storm was brewing.

When he left, I busied myself by fluffing my son’s pillow and making sure he wasn’t too cold or warm. His eyes were closed, and he was still unconscious, but I wondered if a part of him knew that I was there. I hoped so. I needed him to know he had a reason to fight. We were all there for him.

I heard footsteps entering the room and thought it was his nurse, but it was just Alyssa returning.

“Where’d Malcolm go?” she asked.

“He had to run out, but he’ll be back. I need to talk to you about something, though.”

She sat in the chair left empty by my husband. "Okay, what?" Alyssa took a sip of her coffee.

"I might have a problem, and I'm going to need your help." I gave her a look that only my sister could understand, one that transferred my feelings with no words.

"What kind of problem, and why are the hairs on the back of my neck standing up suddenly? What did you do?"

"The problem is a big one," I answered, suddenly feeling ashamed. "I have a debt I owe, and I have a feeling I'll have to pay it back soon."

Alyssa's eyes widened. "I'ma be honest, Vanessa. I got a little money saved, but you've always been the one with all the coin. But whatever you need, I got you."

"I wish it were as simple as a monetary debt." I stood up and started pacing.

"You're making me nervous. What the hell is going on? Who do you owe this debt to?" Alyssa asked as she watched me walk back and forth.

I stopped and looked at her. "Carolyn."

"Shit. You owe Carolyn Britton of all people?" Alyssa's voice raised an octave.

"Shhhhh." I placed a finger over my lips and glanced over at Jesse, still sleeping peacefully.

"What the hell do you owe her? And why?" she whispered.

"I made a promise a few months back," I explained. "I agreed to take care of something in exchange for something bigger."

Alyssa shook her head. "You're talking in circles, and I don't understand."

"I know. Looking back, I know that it was a mistake, and I shouldn't have agreed. But it was an offer I couldn't refuse, and so I agreed. Then, next thing you know, Carolyn bought the property she was trying to get, and things worked out. Malcolm and I got married, I moved back into the house, and I thought this whole thing was over," I rambled. "But now, here we are again, and I know she's going to come back to me."

"Vanessa, please calm down."

"I can't calm down," I said. "I love Malcolm, and I don't want to do anything to hurt him. I don't want to risk losing him again. I can't."

Alyssa put her coffee down and grabbed me by the shoulders. "Vanessa, what is it that Carolyn wants you to do?"

"It's not just what. It's who."

"Okay, who?"

"Anthony Johnson."

"What about him?"

"I promised to seduce him in exchange for Carolyn supporting—no, insisting that Malcolm and I remarry," I admitted.

It was one time I hadn't minded being used as a pawn. I had wanted my husband back ever since our divorce. Now, I had him, but I would have to keep Carolyn appeased, or else she might interfere with our marriage just like she had the first time.

"Why would she want you to do that?" Alyssa asked.

"To get back at his wife. The two of them were going at it over the piece of property that separates their two homes. Sydney Johnson wanted that property just as much as Carolyn did and was quite vocal about it. It got ugly between them, and you know how Carolyn is."

"Vengeance should be that woman's middle name," Alyssa commented.

"You're right. She made me an offer I couldn't refuse, and I accepted. Now, are you going to help me or not?"

Alyssa stared at me in silence.

"Say something, please."

"I–I don't know what to say," Alyssa whispered.

"Say—"

"Mom?"

"Jesse?" I gasped and pushed past my sister to get to his bed. "Jesse!"

Jesse's eyes opened slightly, and he winced in pain as he called out to me again. I wanted to grab his hand, but I was afraid to hurt him. So instead, I gripped his bedding as I peered down into his face. He began to blink feverishly.

"He's awake! I'll get the doctor." Alyssa rushed out of the room.

"I'm here, baby. Mommy's right here." My eyesight was blurring, and I didn't even try to keep my tears at bay. "I'm right here."

"My head. It hurts so bad," Jesse told me in a raspy voice. "And my arm."

"I know, but the doctors are on the way. Aunt Alyssa went to get them," I whispered. "You're going to be okay."

Jesse stared at me with a confused look. "What happened to me?"

I blinked. "You don't remember?"

Jesse looked like he was deep in thought for a moment, then he slowly shook his head. "No, Mom, I don't."

14

Reverend Chauncey

The weather was perfect for fishing, despite the late hour. Usually, I was at the dunes before sunset, but I'd decided to sleep in a little. When I emerged from my house, I went to cast my rod and reel from the pier instead of the beach for a change.

I'd found the ideal spot, tossed my line into the water, and was about to get settled in my beach chair when I spotted movement in my peripheral vision. I turned and saw a man walking toward me.

"Good afternoon, Reverend Chauncey."

"Afternoon, Eli." I nodded toward Eli Bradshaw, one of the only two white men who resided in the Black Hamptons. I could count on one hand the number of times I'd seen him. Each of those times, he'd barely looked in my direction, which led me to question why he had felt the need to buy a home in an all-Black community, especially when he seemed to never be in the house he'd purchased. It was as odd as he was.

He looked somewhat out of place. While everyone else, including myself, wore shorts, bathing suits, and other summertime attire, he was dressed in a business suit with a traditional Kippah sitting on his head.

"It's good to see you, Reverend." Eli extended his hand.

"Likewise."

"You know, I've owned a house in this community for two years, and this is actually my first time being out here on the pier. It's very nice." Eli stared out into the water.

"It's one of my favorite places to fish. You should try it sometime."

"I appreciate the invitation, Reverend." Eli leaned forward, his elbows on the wooden planks. "How long have you been over the church?"

"About twenty years now," I answered, feeling my brow rise slightly. It was an odd question considering I was fairly certain he wasn't interested in becoming a member. I had the sense there was some underlying motive.

"Hey, Reverend Chauncey!" a group of teens yelled as they passed by in a speedboat.

"Hey there!" I waved back and then went back to wondering why a man who'd barely said hello now felt the need to have a full conversation.

"Wow, that's a pretty long time. I bet you know every single family in the community, huh?"

"Maybe not all of them, but at least ninety-five percent of 'em. I'm kind of a community ambassador." I chuckled.

Eli continued his interrogation. "And that building where you all worship, that's the original building, right?"

"Yes, it is. Still standing after all these years. Lots of history in that building."

"You haven't had any problems with it at all?"

I shrugged. "Oh, the roof leaks every now and then, and we may have a plumbing issue with the baptismal pool from time to time. But it's holding up just fine, thanks to the good Lord."

"That's a blessing."

"Why all the questions, Eli?" I asked bluntly.

"Well, Reverend, what if I told you I had a proposition that could help you pay for a new roof and update that baptismal pool, plus put a few thousand dollars in your pocket? What would you say?" Eli smiled at me.

I leaned my fishing pole against the rail, then folded my arms as I turned toward Eli. "I'd say what's the catch? You don't get something for nothing these days. And you don't appear to be a looking-for-salvation type of guy."

"You're right about that on both accounts. This world is all about giving and receiving. And no, I'm not looking for salvation." Eli smirked. "But if you were willing to talk to a few of your parishioners who've fallen on hard times and maybe suggest that they sell their homes to me, I'd be more than happy to not only give you a finder's fee, but send some of my guys over to put on a new roof and install a new pool."

"Hmmmm, interesting." My head tilted to the side, and I was grateful that I had enough discernment to recognize that the smile Eli gave me was just as insincere and fake as the concern in his voice.

"So, do you think this proposition is one you'd like to accept now, or you need some time to mull it over?" Eli stood up straight.

"No, Eli, I don't need time at all." I smiled back at him.

"Great! We can get started on repairs as soon as you'd like," Eli said with anticipation.

"No. My answer would be hell-to-the-no," I told him.

The shocked look on Eli's face almost made me laugh out loud, but I kept my composure.

"Excuse me?" Eli looked around to see if anyone else had heard what I said.

"You didn't hear me? Maybe I wasn't clear enough. I said *hell no*! Respectfully, of course. After all, I am a man of God."

"Reverend, I don't think you understand how much money there is to be made. You do realize that there are congregants who have property taxes owed and other debts. I'm trying to be proactive and be a good neighbor by offering folks an alternative they can profit from."

At this point, my patience was nearly gone, and I no longer tried to mask the anger rising within me. The man had insulted me, my parishioners, the church, and the community. After that, he *still* had the audacity to try to justify what he was attempting to do.

"What you're doing is trying to infiltrate the community that we have built and dismantle it for your own personal gain. And I'll be damned if I allow it, let alone help you to do it. As a matter of fact, I'm wondering where you got the audacity to even ask me. As if I'm too gullible to know what you're up to." I put down my fishing rod and took a step toward him.

Eli's face was beet red as he stammered. "No, I . . . that's not . . ."

"Or maybe you thought I was greedy enough to sell out my people. Or that I was desperate. Either way, I'm not any of those things, in case you don't know," I said through clenched teeth.

Eli's demeanor changed. He stiffened, and his eyes became dark. "Reverend, what I thought was that you were a man who was smart enough to understand that times have changed, and soon, so will this community. I guess I was mistaken that you would be wise enough to be a part of the progress and reap the benefits of doing so. I see that I was wrong on all accounts."

Unintimidated, I replied. "You were definitely wrong, but you'll soon learn that if you're looking for a fight, you got the right one. I promise you that. Now, get the hell away from me. You're scaring away the fish."

"Have a good day, Reverend," Eli said curtly, taking a step back then turning to walk away.

I put my hat back onto my head and composed myself, glancing up at the sky. "Sorry about that foul language, Lord, but we both know it was well deserved. I know I'm forgiven."

Trouble was coming to the Black Hamptons, and I understood it was going to take more than me, my prayers, and faith to combat it. It was going to take money, power, and teamwork. I took out my phone and made the first call.

15

Kimberly

I waved at Reverend Chauncey as I strolled down the pier. As usual, he was fishing. The day was gorgeous, and I would have rather spent my "day off" enjoying the beach, but even though I technically wasn't working, I still had plenty of tasks to complete. It didn't surprise me that Carolyn didn't take the news of my resignation too well, but it was time for me to move on to bigger and better, starting now.

"Hell of a first day back, huh?" I laughed as I stepped onto the yacht and walked toward Moses, who was standing on the deck, drink in hand. He'd taken off his suit jacket and tie, and the top buttons of his shirt were undone. He looked worn out, as if he'd worked a double shift.

He turned around and asked, "How can you tell?"

"Dark liquor in the daytime." I pointed at the glass he was holding. "You usually reserve bourbon or brandy for after sunset."

"I forget how well you know me, Kimberly." He raised his glass and took a sip, then hugged me. "But it's been a day, for sure. What about yours?"

"Mine was quite interesting too."

He motioned toward two deck chairs, and we went to take seats. "How so?"

"I quit my job this morning," I told him. "Well, at least I tried to quit. Carolyn is refusing to accept my resignation. She doesn't realize she doesn't have a choice."

"That doesn't come as a surprise to me. You're quite valuable to my wife." Moses smiled. "Everyone knows that."

"Was valuable, past tense," I corrected him.

"What I don't understand is why you quit."

His question surprised me considering the circumstances. "Huh? You of all people should know why. For God's sake, the woman wouldn't even let you sleep in your own house. She's an abhorrent bitch who relentlessly tries to ruin anybody's life if the don't agree with her. Carolyn is evil."

"She's set in her ways, that's for sure. You've always known that about her. We all have, but that doesn't stop us from loving her."

Unfortunately, as much as I hated to admit it, Moses was right. Carolyn was all the things I said and more, but I did have a level of both love and respect for her. However, I also had my own level of self-respect and morality. The lessons on strategy, banking, politics, and business I'd learned over the years were oftentimes overshadowed by the manipulation, corruption, backbiting, and dishonesty I witnessed firsthand. I'd played my position alongside Carolyn long enough. Now that Uncle Moses was back, the time had finally come for me to release myself from the tangled web of Carolyn Britton.

"It's time for me to leave," I insisted. "My skills and talents are needed elsewhere."

"I know where this is going, and I appreciate your loyalty." He looked at me fondly. "Which is why I need you to stay exactly where you are."

My eyes widened. "What? Why? Like you said, I know you very well. I probably know her even better. You do realize how beneficial that makes me, right? Your new organization needs me."

"What new organization is that?" He raised an eyebrow.

"You don't think I know you have a master plan in place? I'm sure this emergency meeting of the Amistad Board of Trustees is your doing," I responded. "Jeffrey, Anthony Johnson, Everett Simpson, they're just a few pieces of the puzzle. Now, you have me."

It just made sense. To me, it seemed like a no-brainer. Make sure every corner was secured.

"Touché. Without question, I have a plan, and you have always been a major part of it. Kimberly, your father was my best friend, and you're like a daughter to me. You're smart, amicable, and most importantly, reliable. Hell, I don't understand why that foolish-ass youngest son of mine hasn't opened his eyes and swept you off your feet, but that's a discussion for another time." Moses laughed. "But please know, you are very valuable."

"So, all there's left to do is tell me. What do you need from me?"

"In addition to being at the emergency board meeting tomorrow, I need you to continue working for Carolyn," he stated. "I need someone on the inside to watch her and watch out for me."

"But that's what Malcom is for," I reminded him.

Moses shook his head. "You're the safest bet. My son is loyal, but that's also still his mother."

"I don't know." I sighed.

"What's there to know? You'll be doing what you've always done. You'll be Carolyn's right hand. Only now, you'll also be looking out for my best interests."

The twinge of guilt that had been plaguing me suddenly became overwhelming, and I began to cry. Moses stood and grabbed a napkin from the bar, then handed it to me.

"What's wrong?" he asked.

"I'm sorry, Moses. I really am." I sobbed.

"Why are you apologizing?"

I dabbed at my tears. "I knew what she was doing and didn't say anything. I should've spoken up when the SEC started their investigation, and I never did. If I had, none of this—"

"Hey, this isn't on you, Kimberly. It's on Carolyn. I took the fall for her. It was a mutual decision we made for the family and the bank," he reassured me. "There's no reason for you to feel bad."

"I know, but I do. I feel horrible, and now that's she's treating you this way, I just want to get away from her," I told him. "You should be able to enjoy your home."

"And I will. Carolyn will welcome me back with open arms sooner than you think. Trust me," Moses said. "Whatever plan she's working on now is destined to fail."

"Right." I nodded, wishing I shared his confidence.

"So, you'll stay, right?"

"Yes," I agreed. "There's something you need to know, though."

"What?"

"She has a lover."

Instead of shock as my words settled on him, I saw a look of intrigue pass over his features. "Who is it?" he finally asked.

"I'm not sure. But I have an idea."

16

Martin Britton

A good, stiff drink was calling my name. Too much was going on, and I needed a buzz. Usually, I'd just retreat to the USS Carolyn, but since Dad had already claimed it as his temporary residence, I needed somewhere else to get some peace and quiet. I still could have gone to the yacht, but I wasn't in the space yet to divulge my heart's woes to my father. So instead, I chose to find solace at Fusions, a low-key local bar and restaurant. They had pretty good food and drinks strong enough to numb the things I needed to not feel at the moment.

The hostess seated me at a table in the back and handed me a menu. "What can I get you to drink?" she asked.

"A double Hennessy on the rocks and a water for now. I'll take a look at your menu while you're gone."

"Sounds good to me, honey," she said with a wink.

While she was gone, I looked over the food choices. I didn't know how many drinks I was about to consume, so greasy was the way to go. A burger and some wings would do me just fine. I set the menu aside.

"Ahem."

I heard someone clearing their throat. I looked up and saw Kimberly standing there with a hand on her hip and a fake attitude.

"I know you're not eating alone," she said.

"I was, but you're here now. Have a seat."

She sat across from me.

"And where the hell have you been, actually? I haven't seen you all day. You didn't even come to court today," I said.

Kimberly may not have shared the same bloodline, but to us, she was family, and I enjoyed her company. It was nice to see her casually dressed in jeans that fit her perfectly, by the way.

"I planned to be there, but shit got complicated."

"Complicated, how?" I frowned, then motioned for the waiter to bring two drinks instead of one.

"Honestly, I was considering resigning, but I changed my mind," she said.

"What? Why?" I asked, relieved that she hadn't actually done it.

"Like I said, it's complicated. But I thought about it, so I'm gonna stay."

"I'm glad to hear that. Mother wouldn't know what to do without you." The last thing the family needed was to be without Kimberly, especially now.

"Trust me, she almost did when I tried giving her my resignation. I've never seen that side of Carolyn before. She almost looked desperate," Kimberly said, cringing a little at the memory.

"Damn, she didn't even say shit about it." I shook my head.

"Probably because she refused to accept it. I'm sure she won't ever mention it, especially now that I'm not quitting. And it's probably best if you don't say anything about it either. Let's just keep it between us."

"Hey, my lips are sealed." I pretended to lock my lips and throw away the key.

With that settled, she picked up the menu. My eyes lingered on her maybe a little too long, but it was all right, because she was too preoccupied with the menu to notice. It felt special to have a secret with her, especially since she was closest to Malcolm. Kimberly was a trusted ally in any delicate situation. Malcom's relationship with Morgan, for example. She played a vital role in keeping that under wraps. Malcom being in a same sex relationship could have caused drama none of us wanted to face. We weren't necessarily homophobic, per se, but keeping our family out of the mouths of the local gossips would always be in our best interests. Kimberly understood the stakes, and her discretion allowed Malcolm to maintain his connection with Morgan without risking the family's reputation. To Kimberly, it wasn't just about keeping secrets. It was about preserving a fragile balance that protected both Malcolm's heart and the family's legacy. I respected her for that.

"I do have to ask. What made you stay?"

"Your mother is willing to do anything to keep me, and I'm going to take advantage of that. Shit, I'm not crazy," she said with a laugh.

I completely understood. There wasn't a point in going somewhere else if she could set her own terms with Mother. The waiter brought our drinks to the table.

"To job security." I raised my glass.

Kimberly tapped her glass against mine. "To job security. And since this has turned into a celebration, dinner will be your treat, right?"

"What? You're the one who's getting the huge raise," I said. "Remember, I barely just got back into Mother's good graces and got access to my accounts again. I have to make sure that any future potential partners meet Mother's standards if I want to be able to afford a decent meal once in a while."

Kinberly nodded. "This is true."

For a moment, I became engrossed in my own thoughts, thinking about the decision my mother had forced me to make. Love or money. As much as I missed Karrin, I suspected that without money, I might not have been attractive to her anyway.

"Oh my God, Martin. Look who just walked in," Kimberly whispered. "That's Bobby 'The Beast' Boyd."

"What? Where?" I turned to look toward the entrance.

Sure enough, making his way through the crowd was the boxing champ, surrounded by his entourage. News of his arrival quickly spread throughout the room, and people began taking out their cell phones to get a quick pic. While everyone else's attention was on Bobby's, mine was drawn somewhere else. I stood to get a better look.

"I'll be right back," I told Kimberly.

"Martin, where are you going?"

I didn't answer as I headed toward the gathering crowd. As I got closer, my eyes remained fixed on the stunning woman on Bobby's arm.

One of the security guards with Bobby announced, "All right, all right, we're gonna need everyone to move back."

"It's cool, Max. They're just tryna get a glimpse of the champ in person. Can you blame them?" Bobby laughed and smiled for the cameras.

As if she felt her eyes on me, the woman beside him turned, and gazed back at me. We stared at each other for a long moment, neither one wanting to look away first. Dressed in a form-fitting black dress that hugged her curves and left nothing to the imagination, she looked as amazing as the last time I'd seen her. That was saying something, because she'd been naked and lying in the center of my bed on the yacht.

"Martin." Kimberly's voice came from behind me, and I felt her hand on my shoulder.

"Yeah," I answered just as Bobby noticed me.

"What's up, man? You want a pic with the champ?" Bobby grinned at me.

"Nah, I'm good," I said, my eyes remaining on Karrin.

"Bobby, come on, let's go," she urged him, tugging his arm.

"A'ight, baby. I know you're hungry." Bobby leaned over and kissed her cheek before they continued to their table.

"Martin, let's go back to our table." Kimberly tugged at my arm, bringing me back to reality and diminishing any thoughts of making a public spectacle of myself. My family was already in the spotlight enough.

My heart sank as I watched the two of them engage so closely. I could tell by the way she looked at him that she liked him. That sparkle, I'd wanted it to only be for me. My entire body tensed, and for a moment, I considered snatching her away from him, ignoring the fact that he was a professional boxer. It had barely been seventy-two hours since Karrin had been in my arms. Now, she was hugged up with Bobby Boyd. I wanted to knock him out in front of everyone.

I turned and followed Kimberly back to our table, fighting the urge to search the dining room to see where Bobby and Karrin had gone.

"Are you okay?" Kimberly asked when we returned to our seats.

"I'm fine," I lied, ignoring the whirlwind of jealousy, confusion, and anger in my head.

"You're not fine," she said softly. "And that's understandable. Maybe we should leave."

"I'm not leaving. Why should I?" I asked, my voice a little louder than I intended as I looked over at her. Kimberly winced slightly, and I apologized. "I'm sorry. I didn't mean for that to come out like that."

"It's cool," she said. "I think we definitely need another round, though."

"You're right." I smiled slightly. "A few rounds."

We ordered another round of drinks, along with appetizers and food. The night was young, and I wanted to make sure I had something on my stomach to absorb the enormous amount of alcohol I knew I'd be consuming.

"You think she's really with that dude?" I asked after a while.

"I don't know. Maybe, or it could be just for show. You know how Bobby Boyd moves when it comes to women. He doesn't seem like the commitment type, so it's probably just a fling," Kimberly answered. "I'm sure it's nothing serious."

That didn't really make me feel any better. "Still, ain't this kinda fast? It hasn't even been that long, and—"

"Martin, you all broke up. She moved on, clearly. Look at it this way. I know the way Carolyn handled things may not have been the most orthodox, but she might have been right about this one," Kimberly stated. "You barely knew her, and your nose was wide open. You were ready to risk it all for a chick who clearly doesn't waste time."

"Fuck that," I snapped without meaning to and then quickly regained my composure, softening my tone. "I'm sorry. I mean, I know you're trying to help, but pointing out that Mother was right doesn't make me feel any better. But I guess I should be grateful."

"You should," Kimberly agreed. "And don't worry. You'll move on too."

I understood what she was saying, and I appreciated her trying to make me feel better, but the truth was, I wasn't sure that I wanted to move on. The truth was, I still wanted Karrin.

"I'll be back." I stood up again.

"God, Martin, where are you going?" Kimberly asked with a panicked look.

"Relax. I'm going to the bathroom before they bring our food. That's all." I smirked. "What did you think? That I was gonna go pick a fight with Bobby 'The Beast' Boyd over my ex?"

"I wasn't sure, but I'm glad to know that you're not. We got one Britton in the hospital. We don't need another one."

As I headed toward the restroom, my eyes remained forward, resisting the urge to search for Karrin. It didn't matter, though, because when I exited the restroom, I bumped right into the person I was hoping to avoid.

"Hello, Martin." Karrin spoke first.

"Karrin." I tried to hide the emotional turmoil I was feeling inside.

"How've you been?" she asked casually, as if we hadn't just shared a bed a few days before. "My sister told me about your nephew being hurt. How is he?"

"Which question would you like me to answer first? The one about me or him?"

"Whichever you prefer," Karrin answered.

"He's improving, and I'm fine."

"That's good to hear about both of you."

"I see you're doing extremely well." I motioned toward the dining area.

"I'm making it."

"I bet you are."

Karrin narrowed her eyes, letting me know that my words stung. "I mean, considering the way the last guy ended things, I deserve an upgrade, don't you think?"

I was so blindsided by her response that I couldn't think of a comeback. I didn't need one, though, because within seconds, Bobby appeared, along with one of his entourage members.

"Baby, you good?" he asked, pulling Karrin close and looking me up and down.

"I'm fine," Karrin answered. "There was a line for the bathroom. I'm going in now."

Karrin touched his cheek before she slipped into the women's bathroom.

"I don't think we've met," Bobby said, staring at me. "You a friend of Karrin's?"

"We know one another," I said. "I'm sure if you ask her, she'll tell you who I am."

"Nah, I'm asking you."

"I'm her neighbor, Martin Britton."

"Martin Britton," Bobby repeated. "You related to Jesse Britton?"

His question seemed odd. "That's my nephew."

Bobby grinned and nudged his boy. "Oh, okay, cool."

"Is something funny?"

"Nah, not funny. Just that you trying to act all tough with me. Too bad you weren't around to keep your nephew from getting his ass whooped."

Before I could stop myself, I lunged toward Bobby, only to be stopped by the guy with him. He grabbed me and pushed me back.

"Get the fuck off me!" I yelled.

"Man, you need to chill. That man probably just saved your damn life." Bobby shook his head. "You don't want no parts of this."

I went to lunge at Bobby again. He pushed me back, and I landed against the wall.

"Bobby!" Karrin ran out of the bathroom and jumped in between us.

"You better tell your *neighbor* to calm the fuck down," Bobby warned her.

"No, you need to calm down." I straightened my shirt.

"Bobby, we need to get back to the table, man. Come on," his boy said.

"Yeah, you do that," I said.

"Come on, Bobby." Karrin put her arm around Bobby's waist. He glared at me as they walked away.

"Fuck!" I cursed out loud to no one.

I waited a few moments before returning to my table.

"What's wrong?" Kimberly asked, seeing the outrage on my face.

"I'm leaving."

"Leaving? Now?" She pointed to the plates in front of her. "Our food just got here."

"I'm not hungry." I took out my wallet and placed three hundred-dollar bills on the table. "I just got into it with Bobby Boyd."

Kimberly stood and grabbed her purse. "Let's go."

"You don't have to leave. Stay and eat."

"You know that's not happening, Martin Britton," she told me. "Now, come on, let's go. The sooner we get away from trouble, the better."

I wasn't sure if she meant Bobby or Karrin, but either way, she was right. The way I felt, I didn't need to be near either one.

17

Carolyn Britton

I entered the conference room at Amistad Bank and Trust like the queen bitch I was. In addition to Malcolm and Martin by my side, I also had Kimberly, who had arrived at the house bright and early, ready to work.

"What brought about this sudden change of heart?" I asked when she walked into my office, where I'd been working damn near all night.

"I re-evaluated my priorities, in addition to taking everything you said into consideration," Kimberly replied. "So, I'm here."

"That's all that matters." I placed my hands on her shoulders. "I'm glad that you're here." Soon enough, I would learn just how much her change of heart was going to cost me, but for now, I was relieved that she'd come back.

"Now, first order of business is to get over to the bank and get this meeting over with," I said.

"So, you have no idea what this is about?"

"Not specifically, but I have a pretty good idea," I said. "I'm sure you already know that Moses is back. I expect he's going to attempt to get his title back as CEO."

"Do you really think he'd do that?"

"Of course. You know how power-hungry your Moses is. But I spoke with my attorney, and I've already been advised that he can't do that. At least not without petitioning the SEC, and they aren't going to be inclined to do that, considering the previous circumstances," I explained. "He doesn't understand that yet, but he will after today."

"Is he here?" Kimberly looked back toward the door.

"Absolutely not." I shook my head. "He's not allowed back into this house until I have had time to process and deal with this surprise resurgence of his."

Kimberly raised an eyebrow but didn't comment.

"Now, let's get the boys and get to this meeting," I told her.

When we got there, most of the members of the board were already seated and chatting. I took my place at the head of the table. I couldn't help but notice my husband's absence, which surprised me.

"Good afternoon, everyone," I said as Martin, Malcolm, and Kimberly settled into their seats.

"Carolyn, great to see you."

"Hello, Carolyn."

"Good afternoon."

After the cordial pleasantries were exchanged, I went straight to business. "In the interest of time, I think we should go ahead and call this meeting to order."

Jeffrey sat up in his chair and looked at his watch. "Carolyn, there's still four minutes left until we're scheduled to begin."

"True, but I don't see a need to delay." I looked around the table. "Everyone's here. Considering you're the one who called this meeting, I'd think you'd be anxious to go ahead and start."

"Carolyn's right," Margeaux Raymond agreed. She was a board member and also an avid golfer and LPGA member. "I have a tee time in an hour."

"Is there a reason we need to wait, Jeffrey?" I peered at him.

Jeffrey glanced down at his phone, then back at me. "Actually, no. We can begin. Since I am the one who requested the meeting, I motion for it to be called to order."

"I second the motion," Margeaux said matter-of-factly.

"Fine, let's begin," I stated. "Now, can you please explain why you gathered us here with such urgency?"

Jeffrey nodded. "It's regarding the funding of the Singh Corporation loan."

I had quietly scuttled that deal during the height of my feud with the Johnsons, and now Jeffrey was calling attention to it in front of the entire board.

"That has already been decided. There's no need to discuss it."

"I beg to differ," Jeffrey retorted. "The decision not to fund the deal was not in the best interest of Amistad. Singh Corporation is a successful international business, and their portfolio is strong, especially with their diversification. There's no reason not to fund this deal. I make a motion that we reconsider."

"How do you make a motion to reconsider something that was never presented?" Malcolm spoke up, and they eyed each other for a few moments.

"Fine. I move that the board consider financing the Singh loan," Jeffrey said.

"Like I said, the decision has already been made to deny the loan application," I reminded him.

"Which is also concerning, Carolyn. A decision of this magnitude should have been brought before the board. As a matter of fact, the bylaws state—"

"I know what the bylaws state," I snapped.

Martin reached over and touched my hand. "Mother, it's okay," he said in a low tone.

"It's not okay. What he's proposing is preposterous."

"Carolyn, I think I speak for all of us when I say we trust your judgement," Margeaux offered, "but maybe this *is* something we should bring to a vote."

Leslie, who'd been sitting quiet as a church mouse, finally spoke up. "I'm sure Carolyn reviewed the application and verified it thoroughly before making her decision."

"I most certainly did. And based on my findings, financing this deal would be a massive risk that I don't believe would benefit Amistad at this time."

"Then I'm wondering why the offer to finance the deal to Singh was made in the first place," Jeffrey said. There was some murmuring among the board members, and I worried that his comments were starting to pique their interest.

"Pardon my tardiness. I was making some last-minute preparations for the meeting." For the second time that week, Moses decided to make a grand entrance.

"What are you doing here?" I demanded to know, staring at the folders in his hand.

"I'm here for the meeting," he answered as he began passing out the folders. "I am still a voting member of this board, late or not. And I'm excited to be back."

"And we're very happy to have you back, Moses," Jeffrey stated.

"What is this that you're passing out? We're in the middle of a discussion," I said.

"Copies of the Singh Corp application that I prepared for the board's review," Moses answered. "When I heard about the loan denial, I immediately contacted Mr. Singh and had him send over a copy of his application."

My heart raced with fear as I watched the seated members start flipping through the thick stack of paperwork they had just received. It wouldn't take long for them to realize that my decision to deny the application was a grave mistake. There was no way I could admit that I had done it out of spite for Anthony Johnson, especially now that they had signed the contract with Sydney Tech. I was on the verge of looking like a fool.

"Moses . . ." I started.

"Now, while I'm certain that my wife did her due diligence in reviewing the application and made her decision in good faith, I felt that it does deserve a closer look," Moses said. "And a financial endeavor of this magnitude deserves the consideration from all of us, in the interest of our shareholders."

"That's quite considerate of you, Moses." Hugh Turner, another board member, said as he opened the folder.

Martin whispered, "Mother, do you want me—"

"No, everything is fine," I replied, waiting patiently as Moses distributed the folders. When he got to me, I smiled politely at him. "Can I speak to you outside for a moment?"

"In the middle of the meeting? Can't this wait?"

"It can't." I shook my head and stood, announcing to the table. "Excuse us."

"I'll come with you." Martin went to stand, but I stopped him.

"No, you stay," I told him. "We'll be fine."

"Don't worry, son." Moses gave him a reassuring smile. "We'll be back shortly. You stay and answer any questions anyone may have about the application."

I strolled out of the conference room, and Moses continued behind me. We entered my office at the end of the hallway, and I closed the door.

"What the hell kind of game are you playing, Moses?"

"Game? What makes you think I'm playing some kind of game?" he asked mockingly.

"Let me tell you this right now. This little show that you're putting on to try to get your position back as CEO isn't going to work. I've already spoken with my legal counsel and determined that fact. So, I advise you—"

"I don't want to be CEO of Amistad, Carolyn, or CFO either."

I blinked, stunned. "What? You're lying."

"No, I'm not." He shrugged. "You and Malcolm are already doing a fine job, minus the asinine decision not to fund the Singh Corp deal. But that's about to be reversed momentarily."

"I am the head of Amistad Bank. You don't get to just stroll in and reverse decisions that I've already made," I told him.

"Oh, yes I do, and I am." He took a step toward me. "You see, you may be the CFO, but with my current forty percent stock, I'm still the majority shareholder of Amistad, and my vote carries the most weight. Or have you forgotten about that?"

I inhaled slowly, realizing that he was right. He held a forty percent ownership stake, while I had just twenty, and our sons each owned ten. The remaining twenty percent was divided among board members and minority shareholders. He didn't need a title to have power. He had more than enough of it.

"I was certain that the bank was in good hands when I left, and you did an excellent job being at the helm. But you and I both know that denying that fucking loan was a mistake. The only reason you denied it was because of your little personal vendetta against Anthony Johnson." He slowly shook his head. "What I should've said back there was that your personal desire to win caused you to turn down a business deal that would've earned this bank over fifty million dollars. Honestly, Carolyn, in a way, I'm about to save your ass. Again."

"What the fuck do you want, Moses?"

"What I want is for you to stop acting like I'm the damn enemy, because I'm not. I was the one who took the fall for you, not the other way around." Moses stared at me. "To save face, we're both going to go back into that board meeting as the team that we've always been and agree to approve this loan."

As I listened to Moses, a mix of frustration and reluctant acceptance churned within me. *He thinks he can just waltz back in and dictate terms?* But deep down, I knew he had a point. My desire to maintain my position of power clashed with the reality of our situation. The board meeting loomed ahead, and I couldn't afford to appear divided. I thought about how hard I'd fought to keep Amistad Bank afloat during his absence, the way I'd earned the respect of the board and solidified my role as president. But the tension was evident, and the stakes were higher than my pride. If we didn't present a united front, I risked everything I had built in his absence, and the possibility of losing my influence was unbearable.

This isn't just about him. It's about us, I reminded myself. Keeping up the façade of solidarity was essential, especially now that we needed to navigate the media and public reaction to his return and the impending scrutiny from the board. Agreeing to Moses's demands might mean sacrificing a bit of my authority, but it was a calculated move. In the grand scheme of things, it was better to bend than to break. I could always reclaim my power later, once the dust settled. So, I took a deep breath and steeled myself. *For now, we're in this together.*

"Fine, let's go," I acquiesced. I turned to leave, but he grabbed my arm to stop me.

"I'm not done."

When I opened my mouth to protest, he pulled me closer. For the first time since his return, our bodies touched, and in that instant, I became breathless. It was the wildest thing how naturally my body melted into his. The intensity of his stare was magnetic, and I felt the same energy pulling me toward him that had captivated me all those years ago.

How did we end up here? I thought, caught in a crazy flashback of memories. I recalled the early days of our marriage, filled with ambition and dreams of building Amistad Bank together. We were a force to be reckoned with, thriving off each other's energy and passion. But over the years, the pressures of work and the fallout from my illegal business decisions had driven a wedge between us.

The night he left for Venezuela still haunted me. I could hear how he had assured me it was just temporary and that he would return stronger than ever. Instead, it was his name that became synonymous with scandal when the SEC launched an investigation and federal charges were filed against him. I remained behind while the walls of our empire began to crumble. I agreed to do whatever was necessary to keep the bank afloat during his absence, but my commitment to our shared dreams had quickly soured into resentment when I uncovered the truth about his decades-long affair with a woman I would never have expected.

That revelation shattered me, igniting a fire of revenge within. If he thought I would wait patiently for his return as the dutiful wife of an unfaithful husband, he was sorely mistaken. Instead, I seized the opportunity to solidify my own power and influence while he was gone, determined to show him that I was more than just a shadow. I could thrive without him.

Yet here we are, I thought, feeling the warmth of his body and a familiar affection. It was frustrating how quickly the memories of our love could resurface, how the heart had a way of clinging to what once was, even when the reality was so much more complicated.

His absence had led to my independence, which had eventually morphed into something closer to pride. I had felt abandoned, and in response, I built a wall around my heart, convincing myself that I didn't need him anymore. But now, standing so close to him, I couldn't help but wonder if the love we once shared could survive the cracks that had formed over the years.

Was it too late for us? I felt a glimmer of hope mixed with dread. If we were to rebuild, it would require a delicate balance of trust and vulnerability, something that felt almost impossible after everything we had been through. But in this moment, standing close enough to feel the heat of his body, I couldn't help but feel that maybe, just maybe, there was still a chance.

"What?" I said, my voice barely above a whisper.

"I'm coming home, and when I say that, I don't just mean the house. I mean the bed, too. Agreed?"

"Do I have a choice?" I shrugged, gently pulling away. This time, when I went to walk past him, he didn't stop me.

"Oh, and Carolyn, one more thing."

"What is it?" I glanced back at him.

"Tell that lover of yours that you won't be needing him anymore. Your husband is home, and he isn't leaving again."

I saved myself the discomfort of responding by quickly walking out the door. It was too much to process at one time. I knew Moses was going to cause a disruption, but I wasn't expecting total chaos.

18

Leslie Bowen

I wasn't sure what Uncle Moses had said to Aunt Carolyn, but whatever it was, it proved to be beneficial. When they returned to the conference room, Aunt Carolyn's demeanor was polite and damn near pleasant. She didn't protest when Jeffrey motioned that the loan for Singh Corp be approved, and after a unanimous vote, she even welcomed my uncle back to Amistad. By the time the meeting ended and we walked out of the bank, it was as if the Brittons were one big, happy family.

"Well, that was interesting," I commented to Jeffrey as we stood in the parking lot.

"I knew things were gonna be a little intense at first, but Moses told me he had everything under control," Jeffrey marveled. "And as you can see, he did."

"At least you had someone to give you a heads up," I commented. "Once again, I was blindsided."

"Come on, Leslie." Jeffrey put his arm around my shoulder. "Look at it this way. You weren't the only one blindsided. The look on Carolyn's face when he walked in was priceless. And like I keep telling you, your uncle is the one insisting he wanted to keep things under wraps. He didn't want you to be caught up in any drama if things had gone left. You being out of the loop was his way of protecting you."

"That's bullshit, and we both know it," I said, shaking my head.

Just as I was about to tear into him, I spotted Uncle Moses waving to us. I lowered my voice and said, "We'll talk about this later."

"Leslie, my favorite niece." Uncle Moses strolled over and greeted me with a smile and a hug.

"Uncle Moses, it's so good to see you." I returned his warm embrace. "I'm so glad you're home."

"So am I, and I owe it all to this brilliant husband of yours." He slapped Jeffrey on the back. "He made it happen."

"I heard," I said tartly.

"Listen, I'd like to have you both over to the house tonight for family dinner," Uncle Moses told us. "A little family celebration of sorts."

"We'll be there," I said.

"Great. We're about to head over to the hospital to check on Jesse."

"How is he?" I asked.

"He's finally awake. Vanessa said they might even let him come home tonight. Another reason for us to celebrate."

I breathed a sigh of relief. "I'm so glad to hear that."

"Jeffrey, we'll talk later." Uncle Moses extended his hand.

"That we will," Jeffrey said.

After their handshake, Uncle Moses gave me one final hug before returning to where Aunt Carolyn and the boys stood with Kimberly. Jeffrey and I got into our car and headed home.

We'd just pulled into the driveway when his phone rang.

"This is Jeffrey," he answered. As he listened, he looked over at me and whispered, "Go ahead inside while I take this, babe."

I didn't hide my irritation as I exited the car.

As soon as I stepped into the house, my own phone rang.

"Leslie Bowen, please." The baritone voice was so deep that I swear it sent a chill down my spine.

"This is Leslie," I said. "To whom am I speaking?"

"My name is Aries Cora. My father and I are vacationing in the area, and I happened to come across a home for sale on Harbor Way. I'm interested in purchasing it, but I don't have an agent. You were suggested."

"Okay, Mr. Cora. I'm familiar with that listing, and I'd love to assist."

"Please, call me Aries."

"Okay, Aries," I repeated. "That's a lovely property. I assume you'd like to take a tour?"

"I would. Are you available today to show it?"

Jeffrey and I had made plans to spend the afternoon on our sailboat. After being kicked out of our bedroom, he was making good on his promise to make up for lost time. Little did he know that I missed having him beside me and had already planned on welcoming him back in the bed.

"My schedule is full for today, but maybe tomorrow?" I offered. "We can meet at around ten in the morning at the house."

"Ten it is. I look forward to it."

"See you then." I ended the call as I walked into the kitchen.

I reached into the wine chiller and took out a bottle of rosé. Having a new potential buyer instantly put me into a good mood. The house Aries was interested in was listed at over eight million, and the commission would be enough to cover the new Lexus SUV I'd been eying for the past two months. Every time I mentioned wanting a bigger vehicle, Jeffrey refused. He thought it was frivolous to spend that money when it was just the two of us. Now, I could buy it myself, and it wouldn't cost him a dime.

"Honey?" Jeffrey called out.

"In here." I poured a glass of wine for him as well. When he entered the kitchen, I held it out to him. "Now we can relax for the rest of the day."

Jeffrey shook his head. "You can. I gotta run out for a while. I have a couple of things I need to take care of."

"What? Why?" I whined. "Uncle Moses is home now. Remember you said that's what was keeping you so busy."

"It was and still is." He sighed. "There are some loose ends I still need to tie up for him."

"What kind of loose ends?" I asked. "And why can't he tie them up himself?"

"For starters, he's not an attorney. And also because you know the family is over at the hospital dealing with Jesse."

"You have to go now? Today? It can't wait until tomorrow?"

"No, Les. We already have dinner plans tonight, and I want to have an update for Moses when we get there," Jeffrey replied. "I know you're frustrated, but—"

"Damn right I'm frustrated," I snapped. "You're the one who said we'd spend quality time once we got through the board meeting today."

"And that was the plan before I got that phone call."

"You're not the only one who works around here, you know." I frowned. "I just rescheduled with a client because I wanted to make spending time with my husband a priority. But you know what? It's fine."

"You are my priority, Leslie." He reached for my hand.

"It's fine," I told him. "Go ahead and go."

"I'll be back in time for us to head to dinner."

"No, I'll just meet you there. I have some important matters of my own to take care of." I removed my hand from his, picked up my wine glass, and walked off. I would call my new client to let him know my schedule was now open and I was free for the afternoon.

"Leslie, so nice to meet you."

Nothing had prepared me for Aries Cora to look just as fine as he sounded over the phone. I had to force myself to blink *and* breathe when he parked behind me and stepped out of his McLaren. We'd decided to meet at the home he was interested in. I barely remembered seeing him walk toward me I was so transfixed by his sexy face.

I cleared my throat, and as I shook his outstretched hand, I took in his muscular physique and magnetic smile. He had dimples deep enough to take a dive in, and his brown eyes glistened under the sunlight. I wasn't sure what line of work he was in, but based on his looks, he could've easily been a model or actor. He was that damn hot.

"Aries, likewise," I managed to say without stuttering. I got a whiff of his cologne, instantly recognizing the scent of Creed Aventus, a scent I loved but Jeffrey didn't.

"Wow, you're even more beautiful in person."

"In person?" I tilted my head to the side.

"The picture on your website," he said. "But don't worry. I'm not a stalker. I just did a little research before calling you."

Damn, he was charming.

"Well, that was smart," I said with a smile. "Now I know you're not a stalker, and you know that I'm not a catfish."

His laughter was deep and hearty. "I like you already, Leslie."

"Shall we go inside?" I asked, motioning toward the house.

I turned and began walking so that he wouldn't see the corners of my mouth twitching as I fought to hold back my grin. Yes, I was a married woman, but there was nothing wrong with admiring what was still on the menu, was there? I could feel his eyes boring into me as I walked, but I didn't mind, hoping he enjoyed the spectacular view.

I unlocked the door with a code, and he followed me inside the massive home. I heard a satisfied sigh come out of his mouth.

"I love it," he said, turning around and admiring the open floor plan.

"And you'll love me once I get you the best deal on it," I told him with a wink.

"Okay, confidence. I see why they say you're the best of the best," he said as he followed me. "This is a beautiful community. I can't believe it's all ours. Black excellence for sure."

"Well, we do have a few non-Black neighbors, but they're cool for the most part, and they don't really live here full time. But you're right. It's beautiful. And this house is by far the nicest of the homes that are not on the beach. You have a cabana and a pool to enjoy."

"I do like to relax poolside, and I love to swim, so that works," Aries said.

He took some time to admire the architecture of the foyer, and I could see that he was truly impressed. He smiled at the high crystal chandeliers, but his eyes lingered on the details in the walls and flooring.

"Wow, look at the archway. Are the marble floors throughout?" he asked.

"Yes, they are. If you like this, you're going to love the rest. This is just the beginning." I continued with the tour.

"What's the square footage?"

"Around six thousand. Six bedrooms, six and a half baths, and it sits on about three acres."

"Nice."

After I showed him the main floor, we continued up the stairs and eventually entered the bathroom in the master suite.

Aries let out a low whistle. "Damn. Now this is nice."

"Yes, as you can see, there's a waterfall shower, and it has LED lighting as well," I pointed out, turning on the light switch to demonstrate.

"Impressive. And this bathtub is massive. It can definitely fit two people comfortably. These jets are probably nice as hell." He sat on the side of the tub and eyed me.

I shifted, slightly uncomfortable with his flirtation, mostly because I was enjoying it. I redirected the conversation to bring the temperature down. "Are you ready to put in an offer?"

Aries stood. "Not yet."

"No?" I blinked. "I thought you liked the property."

"I do like it, a lot. But I'd also like to see something beachfront."

"I see. There aren't very many for sale. Only two. And you should know that both have a price tag of more than eight million," I warned him.

"That's to be expected. Like I said, I do like this house, but I don't love it. So, if I have to pay more for something I love, then so be it."

"And what's your budget?"

"I don't have one. The sky is the limit."

"Well," I said, "looks like I need to find you a house that you want." Dollar signs were dancing in my head.

"How about we go and discuss it over drinks? I can explain exactly what I'm looking for."

I looked at my watch, estimating how much time I had before I needed to be at my aunt and uncle's house. "I do have another appointment in less than an hour."

"I guess we need to hurry." Aries gestured toward the door.

"Excuse me. What's going on?"

The voice startled us. I turned to see a middle-aged white couple standing in the hallway, staring at us. It took a moment to register, but I realized the woman was Inez Seymour, another local real estate agent, and the man with her was Eli Bradshaw, one of the few white residents of the Black Hamptons and my least favorite neighbor.

"Oh, hello, Inez. I was just showing my client, Mr. Cora, the house," I explained.

"I take it you didn't see the updated MLS. This house is sold." Inez looked Aries up and down before glancing back at me.

I matched the energy that she was giving. "You mean there's a contract on it."

Eli took it upon himself to push past Inez. "No, she was correct. I purchased it this morning."

I wanted to slap the smirk right off his face. "How? That's not even enough time to close or get a title processed."

"We did a twenty-four-hour close, no title," Inez said.

"That's impossible."

"Not when you own a title company," Eli said arrogantly.

My body tensed as I stared at their united front.

I'd totally forgotten that Aries was with me until I felt his presence behind me. He stepped closer, placing his hand on my shoulder as he whispered, "You good?"

"I'm fine." I nodded, my eyes remaining on Eli. "As a current resident, you do understand a home can't be purchased without the HOA application being filed and the fees paid."

"I'm aware. That money has been placed in escrow as well," Eli answered.

"Why are you doing this?" Aries stepped up beside me, and Eli turned his attention to him. "Why do you need two homes here, of all places? You do realize it's called the Black Hamptons for a reason, right?"

"Mr. Coral, is it?"

"Cora," Aries corrected him.

"Over the next few days, Bradshaw LLC will own three more, including this one, and I plan on purchasing plenty more."

"You can't do that," Aries said.

"I can and I will. Although we aren't familiar with one another, let me explain something about me. The only color I see here is green. Homes like these are hidden gems. They're actually worth four or five times the asking price. We're in a recession right now, but my company will triple the money in years to come. Even the smaller houses are an amazing investment. The land they're sitting on is worth double. Imagine what will happen when I tear them down and make mini mansions."

"I'll be damned," I snapped. "That's not going to happen, Eli."

"You don't think so, huh?" He seemed amused by my statement, agitating me even more.

I turned to Aries. "Let's go. There's another home around the corner I can show you."

"I wouldn't bother wasting your time. Bradshaw LLC bought that one as well," Eli announced.

"Come on, Mr. Cora." I pushed my way past them.

Eli grinned. "I look forward to seeing you at the HOA meeting, Madame President."

The smugness in his tone made me want to smack the white off his face. I was fuming, but I didn't want to scare off a potential buyer, so I tried to suck it up.

Aries and I both remained silent as we walked out of the house to the driveway. When we were by our cars, Aries said to me, "That guy is a total asshole, and that plan of his is dangerous. He's about to be a problem for you."

"He has no idea what he's about to be up against," I said.

My efforts to keep my anger at bay were failing. I was so upset I was almost shaking.

"I take it you'll need a raincheck for drinks," he said.

"Thanks for understanding. But don't worry. I'm going to get you the house of your dreams."

"After the way you handled that guy up there, I have no worries at all, Madame President. Isn't that what he called you?" Aries winked at me. "I may be new here, but where I come from, *we* stick together."

"Thank you, Aries." A small smile came to my lips. "When it comes to the Black Hamptons, we are truly all we got."

"Let me know if you need my help. I'm sure I can be of some kind of assistance."

There was something about his confidence that mesmerized me, and there was no denying the attraction between us. I was no fool. I knew what that twinkle in his eyes meant. I wondered if mine mirrored his while I looked up at him. For a moment, I forgot that I had a husband I was supposed to be meeting for a family dinner.

"Thanks for that. We'll speak tomorrow," I said when I snapped out of my fantasy and went to unlock my car.

"I look forward to that. *And* working with you," Aries told me as he opened the door so that I could get in.

My mind raced as I headed to Aunt Carolyn's house. As much as I would have loved to continue my daydream about the things I'd do to Aries Cora if I were single, there was a more pressing issue to consider. The Black Hamptons had a new enemy to face, and his name was Eli Bradshaw.

19

Tania Reynolds

The sunroom was my grandmother's favorite room in the house. It was where she spent the most time reading, writing, and putting together her scrapbooks. Outside of church, that room was her sanctuary. Hearing her favorite music coming from the room was something I'd grown accustomed to, especially when she was in her zone. This day was no different. I followed the sounds of CeCe Winans to the sunroom, where I found her sitting in her chair, reading some papers. A sad smile came to my face as I stood in the entrance of the room.

"What are we gonna do, Grandma?" I asked softly as I took a few steps toward her.

"What? Did you say something, baby?" My grandmother glanced up. I could see the worry and stress on her face before her expression quickly changed to a look of soft concern.

"I just asked what we were going to do." I sat beside her and stared at the city tax office logo on the top of one of her pages.

"We'll be fine. I don't want you to worry about this." She folded the letter and stuffed it into the certified envelope it had arrived in. "This is my problem, not yours, and I got faith that God's going to take care of it and us."

"I'm not saying that he's not, Grandma, but this *is* my problem." I snuggled closer. "You mortgaged this house to pay my college tuition."

"That was my decision, and I will always be glad that I was able to do so." She touched the side of my face. "Your mother did her part when your daddy left her, and she did a fine job raising you. Paying your tuition was my way of supporting both of you."

Hearing the pride in her voice made me feel even worse about the financial situation she was in. It also made me pissed at my father, who, after fifteen years of marriage, had decided to divorce my mother and run off with a twenty-something-year-old yoga instructor. He unwillingly paid child support until the day before I turned eighteen, but he paid no spousal support, despite the fact that he had forced my mom to leave her job in marketing to become a stay-at-home mother. Mom somehow managed to make ends meet, but there was nowhere near enough left over to afford my college tuition. That's why Grandma had stepped in to help. Grandpa had died a year ago, and now, my grandmother was on the verge of losing the house she'd lived in for over forty years. I was sick about it.

"But Mom told me Carolyn Britton refused—"

Grandma interrupted me. "That woman did exactly what I anticipated she would. Carolyn Britton is the most self-serving creature on the planet and doesn't offer any assistance to anyone unless it benefits her in some way. But she was just one option I tried. I haven't exhausted them all. Carolyn isn't the end all, be all, even though she tends to think it."

"Ain't that the truth," I agreed. "I guess it didn't help that I was with Jesse on his mother's boat when Peter attacked him. Again, this is my fault."

"It's not, and don't beat yourself up about what happened. Peter was the one who attacked Jesse, not you," Grandma insisted. "But I do need you to stay away from him."

"I don't have a choice. The restraining order Chief Harrington brought to the house insures that."

"And stay away from Peter, too."

"Yes, ma'am." I sighed.

My cell phone rang. "It's work," I told her.

"Go ahead and take your call. I need to get dinner started." Grandma stood and kissed my forehead then left.

I answered the phone.

"Hey, Tania, it's Maggie."

Maggie was the dining manager of the American Hotel, where I'd worked for the past year. It was my day off, but if they needed me to come in, I wouldn't be mad about it. I would have loved to pick up an extra shift.

"Hi, Maggie. Do you need me to come in tonight?" I asked in a hopeful tone.

"No. Actually, the opposite," she said. "We're gonna need you to take some time off."

"Time off? What do you mean?"

"Well, Chief Harrington came in to speak to us about the incident that happened and a restraining order. We just think it's best that you don't come in for a few days, maybe a couple of weeks," Maggie told me.

"But why? I didn't do anything—"

"I know you didn't, but we don't need any negative attention or any distractions for the other staff. It's just a lot right now, and corporate made the decision, Tania."

"Please don't do this. My family is going through a financial crisis, and I need my job," I told her, on the verge of tears.

"I'm sorry, Tania. My hands are tied. You're not fired, and we'll hold your spot, but for now, you just can't come in."

I hung up without saying anything else. Corporate getting involved was mind blowing. I wasn't some high-level executive. I was just a server in the dining room. As I sat back and tried to process, I realized exactly what was going on. Corporate didn't randomly make the decision. Someone had called them, and I knew who it was: Carolyn Britton, or at least someone who worked for her. I was screwed.

As I was lamenting my situation, my phone rang again. The name on the screen was unexpected.

"What do you want?" I answered.

"Tania." Peter sounded relieved to hear my voice. "I want to say sorry, T. You gotta know that I didn't mean to do what I did. I just . . . I mean, when I saw you with—"

"Peter, stop. I don't want to—no, I don't *need* to hear this shit right now. My life has gone from sugar to shit, and I'm fucked up right now."

"You don't think I'm not fucked up too?" Peter asked. "That's why I need you to know that I'm sorry, baby. I know you're mad at me—"

"Mad at you? Are you serious?" I scoffed. "I'm too distraught to be mad. The Brittons took out a restraining order, I just lost my job, and my grandmother is about to lose her house. Please save your fucking apology."

"God, Tania, I never wanted any of this to happen." Peter sounded like he was about to cry, and for a moment, I felt compassion.

Deep down, I knew he wasn't some monster, despite the damage he'd caused. As strong as he was physically, he was tender emotionally. One of the reasons we had connected was because we were both "locals" in Sag Harbor. Unlike most of the other, wealthier families in the Black Hamptons, my family lived there all year long. Peter was a fish out of water when he and his father moved into Sag Harbor, in a part of town most Black Hamptons residents would never even step foot in. Befriending me had helped give him a sense of comfort.

"I know you didn't, Peter." I leaned my head against the back of the sofa.

"I want to see you. Can you come over?"

"No, I can't. I get that you're in a bad situation, and I played a part in it . . ."

"I don't care about that, Tania. Please come so we can talk," Peter pleaded.

"I can't. Goodbye, Peter."

The moment I hung up with him, the phone rang yet *again,* and I groaned. I just wanted a few moments to myself to process the recent events. I assumed it was Peter calling back, but then I saw the name on the screen. My heart started racing.

"Jesse?"

"Tania," he said quietly.

"Baby, I've been calling to check on you, but no one will tell me anything. How are you?"

"In a lot of pain, but I'm okay," he said. "I know you've been calling. I just got my phone back from my mom. They're pissed."

"I know."

"I need to see you. Can you come now?"

"Jesse, I can't. I'll get in trouble."

"You won't. Everyone just left the hospital for the night. They're having dinner at my house for my grandfather. I . . . I need to talk, please."

"Talk?"

"Yeah. They said the police are coming to take my statement in the morning."

"Jesse, I—"

"Please. I don't know what the hell happened. My head is all fucked up. I don't remember anything," he said.

"Shit." My first instinct was to jump into my car and rush to the hospital to hug him, but the restraining order and the damage that Carolyn Britton had already caused made that too risky. "I'm sorry. I can't. I just can't."

I'd already broken enough hearts with my actions. I couldn't do it another time. Hot tears trickled down my cheeks as I hung up the phone.

20

Sergeant Tom Lane

It had only been a few days since Peter's release, but we were both starting to experience cabin fever. Hanging out at home together was something we did often, but the fact that it was mandatory made it different. Peter's ankle monitor kept him at home, but in some ways he was lucky. The one time I ventured outside to go to the grocery store, I was approached by a local news team asking questions about the fight with Jesse Britton.

"I don't have any comments," I'd shouted toward the reporter while I shielded myself from the cameraman.

What made matters even worse was that I'd driven my department-issued cruiser. I prayed that wasn't caught on camera as I sped out of the parking lot. The last thing I needed was for our only form of transportation to be taken away.

"Dad, I can't do this," Peter announced as he walked into the den where I was binge watching one of several crime dramas I'd discovered. There seemed to be hundreds of them, so the selection was endless. I might not have been at work, but at this rate I would become a true crime detective from the comfort of my recliner.

"Do what?" I asked, glancing from the TV screen.

"This. Being stuck in here. I need some fresh air, some sunshine."

"I mean, you can always go do some calisthenics in the back yard," I offered.

"I'm sick of the back yard too. I wanna hit the beach for a run."

I shook my head. "I can't let you do that."

"I'm allowed to leave the house. I just have to stay within a certain range and be home by a certain time."

"This isn't just about the monitor, son. It's also a safety issue."

Peter looked at me like I was crazy. "Safety? You don't think I'm safe?"

"You're safe in this house."

"I'm safe wherever I go, Dad. If I don't know how to do anything else, I know how to protect myself." Peter tensed. "I'm not scared to go anywhere."

Knowing his temper was one of the reasons for our current situation, I immediately shifted my demeanor to de-escalate the conversation. "Nah, that's not what I'm saying. I'm more concerned with the safety of the trial and your future. People out there really think you're a monster. They're waiting to provoke you and get you to do or say something in retaliation."

I could see Peter thinking about what I said and was relieved when he nodded in agreement. "Yeah, I could see that. But Dad—"

The ringing of the doorbell stopped him. We looked at each other.

"You expecting somebody?" I asked.

"Nah." Peter shrugged.

"You stay here. I'll get it." I headed for the front door.

"Hello, Sergeant Lane." Inez Seymour, our property manager, greeted me when I opened the door.

"Hello, Inez."

"I hope I didn't catch you at a bad time."

"No, but this is kind of unexpected," I told her. I made sure our rent was paid on time every month, sometimes even early, so it was unusual for her to stop by like this.

"I know, and I apologize for the intrusion, but I did want to come by and share some news about your house."

"What about it?" I asked warily. Considering the way things had been going lately, I assumed she was here to deliver news I wouldn't like.

She reached into the designer messenger bag on her shoulder and took out an envelope that she handed to me.

"What the hell is this?" I stared at it for a moment before reaching to take it from her hand.

"It's a letter informing you that your house has been sold." Her tone was bland, as if she were telling me that our mailbox was being painted instead of that we might soon be out on the street.

"What do you mean it's been sold? I have a two-year lease, Inez." My loud voice made her flinch a little, but I didn't care.

"Dad, what's going on?" Peter asked over my shoulder.

"Nothing. Go back inside, Peter." I didn't take my eyes off Inez as I spoke. "The owner promised me first dibs when he was ready to sell. Now you're telling me this? This is some bullshit."

"The owner got an offer far above market value. It happens sometimes in business."

"Like I said. Bullshit."

"Sergeant Lane, I'd be more than happy to help you find a new place for you and your son."

"Nah, that won't be necessary. You've helped enough," I snapped, stepping back inside and shutting the door.

"Dad, what are we gonna do?"

Peter's voice seemed like background noise as I looked down at the letter in my hand. My shoulders felt more weighed down than ever. I finally looked into Peter's worried eyes and once again put on a brave face.

"What we're not going to do is panic. This is just another one of life's curveballs, and even though I wasn't a championship boxer, I was an all-star—"

"I know, I know. You were an all-star baseball player with the highest batting average in the state."

His wise-ass grin gave me a slight bit of relief because it meant my son trusted me. He was dealing with enough, and the last thing I wanted was for him to think we were about to be homeless.

"Damn right, I was. Which means it doesn't matter what life throws at us," I told him.

"We don't ever strike out. Even if it ain't a home run, we'll still get a base hit." Peter completed the statement that I'd taught him. I only hoped that those words would ring true this time, because so much seemed to be hitting us all at once.

The doorbell rang again.

"You think she forgot something?" Peter asked.

"I have no idea. Go get changed while I deal with her."

"Changed?"

"Yeah, we're gonna go for a swim."

"For real, Dad?" He lit up.

"Yeah, we both need it."

Peter rushed down the hallway toward his room while I returned to the front door to deal with whatever Inez had returned to say. To my surprise, it wasn't her at the front door. It was Christopher Johnson.

"Mr. Johnson," I said.

"How you doing, Sergeant Lane? You got a minute to chat?"

"I do. Come on in." I opened the door for him to enter, and he followed me into the living room.

"I have an update for you and Peter."

"What's going on?" I tried reading the look on his face, but he was expressionless.

"Jesse Britton has regained consciousness."

"He did. That's good, right? That means his injuries aren't as severe as they said in court," I said.

"It's a sign of improvement, for sure, but it's still serious. What it really means is that the investigation is going to continue. The investigating officer and DA are going to meet with him tomorrow and get an official statement from him. That statement is going to determine whether additional charges will be filed against Peter."

I felt the air slowly leave my body. "Damn it."

"We knew this was going to happen. This is going to be a lengthy endeavor for all of us, and we're still in the preliminary stages." Christopher gave me a confident smile. "We'll get through it, though, and I'll keep you informed every step of the way. I'm doing everything I can so that we're prepared."

"I appreciate that, Mr. Johnson."

"Christopher," he corrected, reaching into his pocket to remove a business card. "I'm gonna need you to call this office first thing in the morning and make an appointment for Peter."

"Who is this?" I took the card and read it.

"It's the office of Dr. Tabitha Wells, the top psychotherapist in the state."

"Psychotherapist?"

"Yes, she's going to do an evaluation and create a plan of action to treat Peter," Christopher explained.

"Hold on. My son doesn't need psychiatric treatment. Nah, I'm not going to make him do this." I handed the card back to him.

"He's not some psychopath, and I'm not gonna let anybody label him as one."

"Sergeant Lane, this isn't about labeling Peter." Christopher stared at me. "This is about getting him the diagnosis he needs and the help—"

"Help? Help for what?" I demanded.

Christopher took a moment before he answered. "The reality is Peter's anger was what led him to assault that young man. We need to be able to show the courts why he got so angry and assure them that it won't happen again."

"Are you saying you want Peter to use some type of insanity plea?"

"I'm saying I'm gonna do whatever needs to be done to keep your son out of jail," Christopher answered. "This psych eval is just the first step."

"Psych eval?" Peter asked as he entered the living room. He had changed into a pair of swimming trunks, tank top, and flip flops, and had a towel tossed across his shoulder. His ankle monitor seemed even more prominent on his bare legs.

"It's just a formality, Peter," Christopher told him. "I got you set up with the best psychotherapist I know, and she's going to be very helpful."

"I'm not crazy," Peter responded.

"I know you aren't, and that's not what Christopher is saying," I told him. "We're just covering all our bases, that's all. No strikes, remember?"

"But Dad—"

"Son, we can talk about this later. I think we need some time to think about it anyway."

"I'll leave you two and follow up tomorrow." Christopher said.

"I'll walk you to the door," I told him.

At the front door, I reached out to shake his hand. "Thanks for stopping by," I said.

"Not a problem. I want you to know I have your son's best interests in mind with everything I do," he said.

"I know you do," I said with a heavy sigh. "Listen, can I ask you a question about something else?"

"What's that?"

"Seems like my landlord sold our house. He never even told us it was on the market. Can he do that, and can the new owner kick us out?"

"The owner can sell anytime without telling you, but the new owner does have to give ample notice before you're forced to vacate," Christoper replied.

"How long is ample notice?"

"I'd say at least ninety days, sometimes more. It depends on the new owner, really. Have you talked to whoever that is?"

"Not yet. I don't even know who it is. I just found out."

"Well, finding out who that is would definitely be the first step." Christopher shook my hand. "We'll talk tomorrow."

Neither of my visitors had delivered good news. My house was sold, and my son was facing criminal charges. Now it was looking like a psych eval and possibly an insanity plea might be his only defense, and I wasn't happy about it at all. I looked at the business card I was still holding. Based on the level of stress I felt, I wondered if Peter wasn't the only one who needed therapy because I felt like I was on the verge of losing my mind.

21

Moses Britton

"Home sweet home, and it feels good." I smiled at myself in the mirror as I adjusted my tie. My eyes traveled to Carolyn, who was pretending not to look at me from across the room. "Don't you think so?"

"What I think is that we need to get downstairs and greet our guests for this impromptu dinner party you planned without discussing with me." Carolyn cut her eyes at me and went back to putting on the diamond and emerald necklace that I'd purchased one Valentine's Day.

"Now, Carolyn, don't act like you don't enjoy hosting. You've thrown dinner parties at the last minute all the time for no reason." I walked over and assisted her with the clasp. "My return calls for a celebration, don't you agree?"

She sighed. "I wish you'd stop asking questions you already know the answer to."

I softly kissed her collarbone. "You're right. I know that you're glad to have me home."

Carolyn gasped slightly, surprised by my affectionate gesture. "Moses . . . please."

I turned her around so that we faced one another. Before she could say anything, I kissed her with so much passion it left her breathless. Just as I expected, her arms instinctively wrapped around my neck, and she pressed her body against mine, the same way she'd done for decades. It might've been years since we'd been together, but there was no denying the connection we had. My hands slipped under her green silk dress and found their way between her legs. Her wetness let me know that she wanted me as much as I wanted her.

"Moses," she moaned.

"That's the welcome home I've been waiting for," I whispered into her ear. "I don't know why you always have to be such a hard nose."

"I'm not the only hard one," she said, rubbing the bulge in my pants.

"Mother, we have guests."

Our moment of lust was interrupted by a knock on the bedroom door and Malcolm's voice on the other side. Carolyn quickly stepped back, adjusting her dress and regaining her composure.

"I'll be right down," she called out.

"That boy always did have the worst timing." I laughed and pulled her back toward me.

"I disagree." Carolyn, back to her usual self, smirked and patted my chest before opening the door to leave. "His timing has always been perfect."

I waited a few minutes before leaving our bedroom, giving her enough to time to instruct the staff and act as if we hadn't been seconds from re-consummating our marriage. Instead of taking the main staircase, I slipped down the back stairwell and entered the kitchen, where I was surprised to see Alyssa preparing food.

"Alyssa, you're cooking?" I asked.

"I am." She smiled, looking up from the tray of hors d'oeuvres she was plating. "Vanessa made the suggestion to Carolyn, who seemed to think it was a marvelous idea, so here I am."

"It was a fantastic idea," I agreed. "What's the point of having an award-winning chef in the family if we can't enjoy her?"

Alyssa picked up a stuffed shrimp and handed it to me. "Well, I hope you're hungry because there's plenty."

I popped it into my mouth and savored the burst of flavor. "This is delicious, and knowing that you're cooking makes me even hungrier than I already was."

"Good. Now get out of here before your wife catches you picking at the food. You know she hates that, and neither one of us is trying to get cussed out." Alyssa pushed me toward the kitchen door.

"True," I said, grabbing one more shrimp before I walked out.

I'd barely made it into the great room, where guests had begun to gather, when I was accosted by Carolyn.

"Where the hell have you been?" she hissed as she pulled me to the side. "And why didn't you tell me about your personal guest list?"

I frowned. "What are you talking about?"

"I'm talking about Anthony Johnson and David Michaels. You didn't mention inviting them. This is supposed to be a small, family gathering for God's sake."

"No, this is supposed to be a dinner party celebrating my homecoming," I said, "Which wouldn't have happened if it weren't for Anthony. It's not as if you were trying to help me get back here."

"That's not true, Moses," Carolyn insisted boldly. "I had a plan in place. Besides, I was busy focusing on regaining ownership of the property that was misappropriated from my family."

"Yeah, that's what I heard," I said. She had always blamed me for the loss of the adjacent lot that had once belonged to her family. "Well, the good thing is now we've both gotten what we wanted. You got your land, and I'm back home by your side."

Carolyn glanced over at Anthony, who was talking to Jeffrey on the other side of the room. "You don't know the trouble that man gave me over the past few months. And don't get me started on his disrespectful-ass wife. She's a bitch."

I raised an eyebrow. "Is that right?"

"Damn right, it is," Carolyn said with a frustrated nod. "For God's sake, don't tell me she's coming too. That woman is not welcome in our home."

"I don't know if she's coming or not, but she was invited."

Carolyn opened her mouth to respond, but I stopped her.

"I am glad you understand that this is our house, not just yours. That means that anyone I deem worthy of a dinner invite is welcome, including Anthony Johnson and his wife. You're going to have to get over it."

"And why the hell should I do that?" Carolyn's eyes were like daggers, indicative of the anger she was feeling.

"Because it's business, not personal," I told her. "And we both know when it comes to business, we don't allow emotions to interfere with what we're trying to build. Hell, you were the one who taught me that. You're the smartest businesswoman I know. That's why you playing games with the Singh loan surprised me so much."

Carolyn's face softened slightly, and though she didn't say anything, I knew my words had made an impact as she walked away.

"You okay, Dad?" Malcom's voice came from behind.

"I'm great, son," I said, turning to face him. "Tonight's going to be a good night. We've got a lot to celebrate. Jesse's awake and coming home in a couple of days, and I'm back home with the family and ready for things to get back to business as usual."

"That is a lot to celebrate," Malcolm agreed. "I'm just worried about you and Mother."

"There's nothing for you to worry about," I reassured him. "Your mother and I just have to get reacquainted and reconnect. I'm sure you understand, considering you're a newlywed."

He chuckled. "Yeah. Weird, isn't it?"

"I still can't believe you and Vanessa are remarried. I'm happy about it, though. I thought for sure that would only happen over Carolyn's dead body."

"I'm glad we didn't have to resort to that option," Vanessa said with a laugh as she joined us.

Malcolm put his arm around her and kissed her cheek. "Me too."

"Well, I need to go and greet some of our other guests," I told them.

"It's good to have you back in the house, Moses," Vanessa said.

"It's good to be back."

I glanced over at my wife, who was speaking with Kimberly. I was sure Kimberly would check in later to let me know if it was anything I should know about. Grabbing a glass of wine from one of the servers, I moved around the room and chatted briefly with a few of our guests. Everyone seemed to be enjoying the party. As good as the food was, they'd better have been in a good mood.

"Everyone please make your way to the dining room to be seated for dinner," Carolyn announced.

As we were making our way to the dining room, the doorbell rang.

"I'll get it," Martin volunteered.

The dining room table was beautifully set with expensive linens, fresh floral arrangements, and fine china. Wine had already been poured, and fresh bread was waiting in the center of the table. Carolyn truly had a knack for creating luxurious events.

"This is beautiful. Thank you, Carolyn," I whispered into her ear as I pulled her chair out.

"You're welcome," she sneered, her voice dripping with sarcasm. Clearly, she was still smarting over my comment about the Singh loan and my choice of dinner guests.

"It's been a while since I've sat at the head of the table. Thank you for keeping my seat warm, darling." I winked.

Malcolm started tapping the side of his glass, and the guests turned their attention to him. "I'd like to propose a toast," he said.

"Malcolm, not yet," Vanessa said. "Martin's not here."

"Where is he?" Carolyn asked.

"He went to get the door," I told her. "He'll be—"

"Good evening, everyone. Pardon our tardiness," Everett announced as he entered the dining room with another man on his arm that I didn't recognize. He seemed to have a new plaything every year, but I was surprised to learn that this man might be sticking around longer than the others had.

"My fiancé, Morgan, took forever to get dressed," Everett said. The man next to him rolled his eyes dramatically.

When Everett first came out, it was the talk of the neighborhood, but he was so loud and proud about it that it became old news quickly. As for me, I didn't really care who he slept with. When I needed help, his money was just as green as anyone else's.

"You're right on time," I said. "We're just getting started, and Malcolm was just about to propose a toast."

I looked around the table, and I couldn't understand the troubled looks on my family's faces. Malcolm was doing everything in his power not to look at our new guests. Vanessa and Martin shot each other uncomfortable looks, then they both glanced toward Malcolm with concern in their expressions. Carolyn was communicating something to Kimberly with her eyes that I couldn't quite interpret. Everyone was uneasy. Something was brewing that I wasn't aware of.

22

Martin Britton

It was like all the air had been sucked out of the room when Everett walked in with Morgan, but I hadn't expected anything less. The moment I opened the front door and saw them standing there, I knew there would be tension. After all, Morgan had been Malcolm's lover before he remarried Vanessa. Hell, they probably would have still been together if Mother hadn't pulled some strings to end it. So, what was I supposed to do? Turn them away at the door?

They sat down, and nobody dared to say a word at first. I watched Malcolm for any signs that he might break. I was ready to pull him out of there if need be.

Dad saw me watching Malcolm and gave me a quizzical look. I averted my eyes and tried to act normal.

"Malcolm, you can proceed with your toast," Dad said, but Malcom remained silent, staring at the table in front of him.

Vanessa tugged at the sleeve of his shirt and whispered, "Baby?"

Malcolm still didn't respond, and I felt like I was going to have to step in. Mother beat me to the punch before the silence became even more awkward for the guests. She stood to her feet and raised her glass with a forced smile.

"I'd like to thank each of you for being here tonight. This is an unexpected occasion but a delightful one, to say the least. Our family is once again complete. To Moses."

"To Moses," everyone repeated, including Malcolm, who'd come back to reality and finally sat down.

I leaned toward him. "You good?"

I knew he wasn't, but I couldn't force him to talk about something he wasn't ready or willing to talk about.

"Yeah, I'm fine," Malcolm lied. "I need a drink and something stronger than this damn wine, though."

Kimberly, who was seated on the other side of me, motioned for the bartender. "Can you please bring three glasses of Scotch please, no ice."

"Right away." The bartender nodded before scurrying away.

"You probably should've made his a double," I told her.

"If I'm being honest, all three are for him," Kimberly whispered. "I just wanted to be discreet about it. So, don't drink yours."

"Hell, I need a drink too," I said. "This shit is just as stressful for me."

"Not as stressful as it is for him, I'm sure." She shook her head. "Stop it."

I sat back in my seat and redirected my attention to the salads that were being placed in front of us. "These look amazing, Alyssa."

"Thank you." Alyssa smiled. "Our first course for the evening is a mixed Asian salad with shrimp and a sesame vinaigrette."

"Jeffrey, where is Leslie?" Mother asked as we began eating.

Jeffrey looked up from his plate. "She sent a text and said she'd be here shortly."

"I hope so," Mother said. "Missing cocktail hour is one thing, but missing the first course is unacceptable."

"Relax, Carolyn," Dad told her. "I'm sure Leslie will be here momentarily, and we will make sure her salad is waiting."

"And if she doesn't make it, I'll definitely eat hers, because this is delicious," Anthony said with a laugh.

"You're right about that," Everett agreed. "The dressing is exquisite. Morgan loves Asian cuisine. Don't you, sweetie?"

Morgan glanced up and cleared his throat. "I do, and the salad *is* really good." He looked a little uneasy, unlike Everett, who didn't seem to be able to shut his mouth.

"We're thinking about traveling to Thailand for our honeymoon," Everett boasted.

I could feel Malcolm's body tense beside mine. Luckily, the bartender returned with our drinks and placed them in front of us. He quickly drank his in one gulp.

"Thailand is beautiful. It's one of the many places Malcolm and I visited the year before Jesse was born," Vanessa said, trying to one-up Everett in her husband's defense.

Malcolm understood what she was doing. "We did," he said, brightening a little. "We damn near went on a world tour. Not many places we didn't visit."

Not to be outdone, Everett lifted Morgan's hand and kissed it, looking directly at Vanessa and Malcolm as he did it. "I look forward to enjoying the world with Morgan by my side."

I eased my drink over to Malcolm, and he snatched it up. I nudged him and murmured, "Slow down a little, bro." I understood he needed to calm his nerves, but I didn't want him getting a careless buzz before dinner—the kind that could make him spew words that didn't need to be said in front of everyone. He heeded my advice and sipped the drink instead of throwing it back.

"One of the things I'm looking forward to is taking the yacht and seeing a few foreign places of my own with my beautiful wife," Dad added.

"As tight as my schedule is, I don't know if that's possible right now, Moses." Mother smirked. "I still have a bank to run."

"Touché, darling. *We* do have a bank to run," Dad replied.

Knowing that, too, was a sensitive topic for my brother, I glanced in his direction. He was concerned about whether his position as CEO of Amistad would be secure now. After all, he'd given up his relationship with Morgan to get that appointment, so it would be a shame for him to lose it now after that sacrifice. His eyes were on our father, and it looked like he wanted to say something.

"I'm sure you're also looking forward to hitting the golf course, Moses." David spoke from the opposite end of the table.

"Oh, most definitely."

"Did you play while you were in Venezuela?" Everett asked.

Dad shifted slightly at the reminder of his fugitive days. "I did occasionally when—"

Leslie rushed into the room, interrupting everyone with a loud announcement. "I'm sorry that I'm late, but we have a problem. A big one."

She wasn't alone. Reverend Chauncey was by her side, and they wore matching expressions of panic.

Jeffrey stood up and rushed over to his wife. "What's going on?"

"I was showing a property to a potential client when we were interrupted by the new owner," Leslie explained.

"Houses get sold all the time. Why is that a problem?" Mother asked with a frown.

Reverend Chauncey spoke up. "Because the house was purchased by Eli Bradshaw."

"Eli Bradshaw? But he already owns a house. Why would he be purchasing another one in the same neighborhood?" Malcolm asked.

"It's not just one. He bought the Sheffield house, too," Leslie answered.

"And he paid me a visit earlier today on the pier," Reverend Chauncey added. "That slick Rick has determined that the Black Hamptons is a prime spot. He said that our beachfront community is vastly undervalued compared to other communities in the Hamptons. He's positioning himself to make a huge profit."

"Damn it." Mother sounded weary. "I've been dreading this for years, and now it's happening."

"He's probably been planning this for a while, since it's moving so quickly," Kimberly suggested.

"Then we've got to make our move just as quickly," Dad said. He looked at Jeffrey. "We need you to amend the bylaws for the HOA so we can put a stop to this."

"Unfortunately, I'm not going to be able to do that," Jeffrey answered. "We're not allowed to amend them without validation. It would be considered bias, and we'd open the HOA up for a lawsuit."

Mother sat up in her chair. "Well, we can't allow that to happen, but we aren't just going to sit back and do nothing."

"We need a strategy," I said.

"I've already called in the reinforcements." Reverend Chauncey looked at me. "The Hudsons will be here first thing in the morning."

Mother balked. "Hudsons? Why?"

I was surprised by her reaction considering that Bradley Hudson, a highly successful attorney, was one of her closest friends. She consulted him for legal advice quite often herself.

"Who are the Hudsons?" Anthony asked.

"Bradley Hudson and his son, Lamont, of Hudson and Hudson, the law firm," Malcolm answered.

"Oh, *those* Hudsons."

"And to answer your question, Carolyn, they're coming because I called them," Reverend Chauncey explained. "He's one of the attorneys representing the plaintiffs in the class action suit against the City of New York and its partnering developers who illegally seized property from Blacks and Latinos in Brooklyn."

"We already have an attorney," Mother volunteered, looking over at Jeffrey.

"I appreciate the vote of confidence, Carolyn," Jeffrey responded. "But I'm no Bradley Hudson."

Dad turned his attention to Leslie. "How many houses are for sale in the area? We have to get to the owners before Eli does."

"Two more that I know of. My client is anxious to purchase Lisa Pruitt's home, though," Leslie told him. "Very anxious."

"Good, then you need to make sure to get that damn sale," Mother said. "I don't care what it takes. What's the other home?"

"The Sinclair home. It's listed, but right now it's a short-term rental that's occupied."

I felt Kimberly's leg hitting against mine just as I looked over and saw Malcolm staring at me. They both knew that I was quite familiar with the owner. A profoundly gifted artist, Jade Sinclair served as the curator for Creatif Noir, the only Black art gallery in Sag Harbor. She also happened to be a woman I had shared a brief entanglement with not long ago. Since that time, she let it be known that she was no longer fond of me. Her exact words whenever my name was mentioned were, "I don't fuck with Martin Britton, period."

"Martin, isn't she a friend of yours?" Mother asked.

"Uh, former friend," I said. "We haven't spoken in quite a while."

"Then you need to become reacquainted and make sure she doesn't sell to Eli."

As much as I didn't want to do it, I knew I had no choice. Mother had spoken, and the Black Hamptons mattered a great deal to me and my family. If this could help save the community, I would take one for the team.

"It's not just the homes on the market that Eli is going after. He's also targeting the homeowners under financial strain as well," Reverend Chauncey said. "He's gotten a list from the tax office."

Morgan spoke up and joined the conversation. "Sounds like he's determined to take over the Black Hamptons by any means. Like a lion ready to pounce on his prey."

"Which is why we've got to be ready to fight with everything we've got and turn the hunter into the hunted." Mother's voice was as stern as the look on her face. "Leslie, Reverend Chauncey, go ahead and sit. Dinner is getting cold, and we've got to start strategizing."

23

Malcolm Britton

After what had to be the most uncomfortable dinner party I'd ever attended, I decided to return to the hospital and spend the night with my son. My mind was all over the place, and what I really needed was some time and space to myself. Being by Jesse's bedside wasn't the ideal spot, but it was the only excuse I could think of to tell my wife.

"Malcolm, the doctors said Jesse is well enough to stay by himself. He's alert and resting comfortably." Vanessa sat on the side of the bed, watching me as I put my charger and iPad into my backpack. "And I can't believe you're riding your bike to the hospital. It's dark and late."

"I'll be fine. I've done late night rides before," I said, zipping my bag.

I'd already changed into my riding gear and packed a change of clothes. Like everyone else in Sag Harbor, I enjoyed golfing, tennis, and boating, but biking was the one sport that brought me unspeakable joy. There was something about pedaling against the wind, my lungs filling with fresh air as I covered various terrains on my customized, carbon fiber Fuji high-end road bike. It was one of my most prized possessions.

"I know you have, but I'd feel better if I went with you and we drove." Vanessa stood. "We can take my car, and I'll drive."

"No, sweetheart. You've spent enough nights at the hospital already. Tonight, you can finally get some rest. Take a hot bath, have some wine, and get into that comfortable bed of ours."

Vanessa put her arms around my neck. "I want you in the bed with me, and the bathtub too."

"As much as I like the sound of that, it's gonna have to wait until tomorrow night." I kissed her forehead. "Tonight, I'm gonna be with Jesse."

Vanessa gave me a concerned look. "Malcolm, I know what this is about. Tonight was a bit much, and it's bothering you, which means it's bothering me too. You don't have to leave. Stay so we can talk this out."

"There's nothing to talk out. The Hudsons will be here tomorrow, and we're going to come up with a plan to take on Eli Bradshaw."

"That's not what the fuck I'm talking about, and you know it," Vanessa snapped. "This has nothing to do with Eli Bradshaw. I'm talking about the guests at the other end of the table. I'm talking about Morgan and Everett."

I stepped back, tossing my hands in the air. "What about them? I'm not thinking about either one. I got way more important shit I'm dealing with right now. Case in point, my son, who I'm about to go and be with."

"Malcolm, please." Vanessa sighed.

"I'll see you in the morning when you get to the hospital." I grabbed my backpack and tossed it over my shoulder. "I love you."

"I love you too."

I rushed out, needing to escape the house. Vanessa was right; I was vexed. It wasn't just the fact that I had to sit through that awkward dinner, but it was also the interaction between Everett and my father. Thinking back, they seemed to be best buddies, even stepping into the backyard with Anthony Johnson and Jeffrey to smoke cigars and have a private conversation.

"What the hell is that about?" Martin, who also noticed the new boys' club that seemed to have formed, had asked me.

"I have no idea, but I don't like it one bit," I replied. "I'm sure Mother doesn't either."

My brother and I walked into the foyer, where my mother and Kimberly were standing after escorting Reverend Chauncey and Leslie to the door.

"Leslie is calling an emergency HOA meeting tomorrow afternoon at the church. I expect both of you to be there," Mother said. Then she looked at me. "I know Vanessa said there's a good chance Jesse is coming home soon, but . . ."

"I'll be there."

"So will I," Martin added. "But, Mother, we do have a question about something else."

"And what's that?"

"This newly formed camaraderie that Dad has with Everett, Anthony, and David." I nodded toward the rear of the house.

"What about it?"

"You don't think it's odd?" Martin frowned. "It wasn't too long ago that Everett played hardball over property that he knew was rightfully yours."

Everett's family had owned the property that Mother and the Johnsons were fighting over. Before that, the property had been in my mother's family, so there was a longstanding agreement that whenever the Simpsons were ready to sell, my mother would be allowed to purchase it at fair market value. The Johnsons were newcomers to the community with little interest in honoring the unwritten contract between neighbors, so they announced their interest in purchasing it at an HOA meeting. This humiliated my mother and infuriated her, and it lit the spark for the mutual hatred that burned between her and Sydney Johnson to this day. Everett only cared about dollar signs, so he welcomed the bidding war that took place. Our father's new alliance with Everett was like a slap in the face.

"A property for which we overpaid," I reminded her. "And now all of a sudden, both greedy-ass Everett and Anthony Johnson are our dinner guests."

"Both of those gentlemen were instrumental in assisting with your father's legal vindication, so he feels indebted, I suppose," she said. "Right now, the three of us have more important things to deal with than who he wants to invite to dinner. We're in for the fight of our life against Eli Bradshaw, and that's what we're focusing on. Understood?"

Martin and I exchanges confused glances. Mother wasn't usually one to acquiesce so easily. Maybe she had some underlying plan that she wasn't ready to share with us yet. I sure hoped so, because I for one did not want to keep seeing Everett around the house.

"Understood," Martin and I both agreed.

I turned around to leave.

"Malcolm, a moment." Mother stopped me and gave Kimberly and Martin a look to let them know that they were dismissed.

She stepped closer and spoke quietly. "I know Everett is a thorn in your side for several reasons . . ."

"I don't trust that guy. He's been a pest his entire life, Mother." I shook my head. "There's a reason he hops between the Black Hamptons and the Vineyard. He constantly runs from trouble. Dad has no idea—"

"That's not your problem, Malcolm, and whatever your father has going on with that man is on him. Honestly, the less we know about it, the better," she told me. "There's a reason Moses isn't hell bent on resuming his position as CEO of Amistad."

"Why is that?"

"I don't know why, and I don't care. My only concern is that the the bank, you, your brother, and I are protected from anyone or anything that puts us in jeopardy, including your father and his new associates." Mother touched my shoulder. "Stay focused."

"I will," I promised.

The conversation played in my head as I pedaled through the streets of our neighborhood toward the main road. The weather was perfect for a ride. Not too humid, and a slight breeze. Had I not had a pre-planned destination, I would've ventured off road and enjoyed an endless two-wheeled journey, processing my thoughts until sunrise. But knowing that Vanessa was most likely tracking my location, I stayed on the road.

I was midway there when I spotted the reflectors of another cyclist heading in my direction. As we got closer, I recognized not just the bicycle but the rider.

"What the hell?" I slowed to a stop and stared as he crossed the street and parked his bike beside mine.

"Hey." Morgan panted slightly as he removed his helmet.

"What the hell are you doing out here?" I asked, taking off my own helmet.

"I figured you'd be out for a ride to clear your head," he answered. "So, I decided to take one too."

"Yeah, well, I'm headed to spend the night with my son."

"Oh, okay," Morgan said simply. He stared at me for a moment before he said, "We really didn't get the chance to talk at your house."

"What the hell do we have to talk about, Morgan? You damn sure ain't talk to me about getting engaged, or the fact that your fiancé was helping my father, did you?"

"No, I didn't," Morgan admitted. "The thing with your father was so fast that I didn't even realize it was happening until he was home."

"Yeah, okay." I gave him a doubtful look.

"And as far as my engagement was concerned, I guess I didn't feel obligated to tell you. Especially since you got married on me, Malcolm, without a phone call or a damn explanation. Do you have any idea how much that hurt? I had to read about it on Page Six."

"I know, I know. I was wrong and terribly insensitive, but—"

"Save your apology, please. What's done is done." He shook his head. "I guess we're even as far as that's concerned."

"Everett Simpson, though? Of all people," I sneered. "I understand you wanting to move on, but Everett is a first-class asshole who uses anyone he can to get ahead."

"Wow, so you think he's only using me? Damn, I knew you didn't think I was good enough for you, but that doesn't mean I'm not good enough for anybody else." Morgan's face filled with anger. He lifted his helmet to place it back on his head.

"Morgan, no." I grabbed his hand to stop him. "That's not what I meant at all. You were one of the best things to ever happen to me, and I will forever be grateful for the time we shared."

Morgan lowered the helmet and looked at me.

"You deserve to be loved, cared for, and spoiled rotten. I want that for you, but from someone who's genuine." My fingers gently ran along his wrist. "Someone who will appreciate how fucking amazing you are."

"Someone like you?" Morgan asked.

"No, someone better than me," I admitted. "And more importantly, someone better than Everett Simpson."

"You really don't like him, do you?" Morgan raised an eyebrow. "Even after what he did for Moses? You do know that was a big deal, Malcolm, and it cost him a lot of fucking money."

"I don't trust him. I know he helped my father. I'll give him that, but I've known Everett a very long time, and although he may come from money and still has some, he's as corrupt as they come."

"I'm telling you, you're wrong," Morgan insisted. "He's working with your father, Jeffrey, and Anthony Johnson on something."

"Something like what?" I asked.

"I don't know, but whatever it is, it's going to be huge. It's going to not only pay for my destination dream wedding, but also fund our surrogate and set us up for life."

Hearing Morgan's plans of a dream wedding and starting a family with someone else was heartbreaking. In a perfect world, we'd be planning those things together, but I'd made another choice, so now I had to deal with the consequences. I meant what I said when I told him I wanted him to be happy.

My watch vibrated on my wrist with a text from Vanessa checking on me.

Are you okay?

I sent a quick reply to let her know I was fine and she didn't need to worry about me. I looked back at Morgan and shook my head.

"Look, Morgan, I hope you're right and I'm wrong. But I need you to do me a favor."

"What's that?"

"Find out what the hell they've got going on and let me know."

"Everett doesn't really talk to me about the details. He just says they have a plan, that's it," Morgan said. "I do know he and Jeffrey have some big meetings coming up about it, though. That's about it."

"That's a start. Just find out what you can and keep me posted, okay? For both of our sakes. I'd rather us be safe than sorry. I do still love you." I surprised myself with my confession.

Morgan smiled sadly. "I still love you too. I'll see what I can find out, but it probably won't be much."

"Any information will help." I put my helmet on. "I gotta get to the hospital."

"And I gotta get back home before Everett comes looking for me."

We stared at one another for a long moment, as if neither one of us wanted to be the first to leave. Finally, after a quick hug, we left in opposite directions.

24

Kimberly

It didn't come as a surprise that the fellowship hall at Easthaven **Church** was already full when I arrived. With less than twenty-four hours' notice, the entire community had shown up for the emergency HOA meeting. In addition to Leslie sending a formal announcement, Carolyn had taken it upon herself to make personal calls to members, informing them of the situation with Eli Bradshaw.

I stood outside the doorway, watching the crowd inside.

"Looks like a good turnout. That's a good thing," a strong voice stated.

I turned around to see Lamont Hudson smiling at me. "It is. It's also good to see you, Mr. Hudson."

"Mr. Hudson? Are we being formal because we're in a church?" Lamont teased as he put his arms around my waist and pulled me in for a hug. "I thought we were better than that."

"I figured I should address you as such because of your fancy suit and tie." I laughed, playfully tugging at the silk tie around his neck. "And is that a briefcase?"

"Don't get me wrong. I am here in a professional capacity, but you don't have to act funny," he said. "How have you been, Kim?"

"I'm good." I tried not to blush at the way he was smiling at me.

Not only was he a handsome piece of chocolate, but he checked every box I desired in a potential partner. He was intellectual, successful, laid back, and he made me laugh. Not only that, but he was a great conversationalist. Who cared that he was a bit nerdy? The vibe between us was obvious, and I'd secretly been feeling him for a while. I'd patiently waited for him to make a move, but he still hadn't.

"Done anything fun lately?" I asked.

"I went to jazz in the park the other night. Robert Glasper was amazing. I thought I'd see you there in VIP."

"No, I got stuck at the office and didn't make it. I'm sure it was phenomenal."

"It was. You were definitely missed, though. The only reason I got a season pass was because you suggested it."

"Is that right?" Lamont grinned.

"It is," I said, looking him in the eye. "Hopefully you won't miss the next one."

"I'll definitely try not to."

Something about the way he said it made me anxious in a good way, so much so that I no longer felt the need to wait for him to ask me out.

"Great. We can grab dinner before, or drinks after. Your choice," I said, taking matters into my own hands.

Lamont looked slightly shocked. "Just like that, huh?"

"I'm just saying, I'm game if you are, Mr. Hudson."

"I guess we'll have to make plans soon." He nodded. "Let's chat later after the meeting."

I watched him as he walked into the room and took a seat beside Carolyn and Malcolm.

"I see you cheesing at your boo," Martin said with a laugh as he walked up to me.

"First of all, lower your voice." I gave him an annoyed look. "And second, he's not my boo."

"You want him to be, though. I saw the way you were looking at him while you were talking. It's cute."

"How about you stop worrying about who I'm talking to and worry about who you need to talk to, sir?" I responded. "You call Jade yet?"

Martin's demeanor changed. This time, he lowered his tone without me having to suggest it. "Hell no, not yet. I'm going to, though."

"You'd better do it soon. Eli Bradshaw is moving fast, and we can't risk him talking to her first."

"I know, and I will." Martin sighed. "But maybe someone else should go and talk to her instead."

"Stop being a little—avoidant. And that's not the word I wanted to use, but we are in church."

"I'm not. I'm going to go by the spa as soon as the meeting is over," Martin said. "Speaking of which, here comes the cavalry. We need to get inside."

I glanced over and spotted Leslie approaching with Reverend Chauncey, Moses, and Jeffrey. I rushed into the fellowship hall behind Martin and took my seat.

After Leslie called the meeting to order, she gave the details about what had transpired regarding Eli Bradshaw and the obstacles we were facing. As expected, the association members' reactions were a myriad of confusion, anger, and angst. Voices escalated with various questions, and everyone began speaking at once. Leslie tapped the microphone in an effort to get everyone's attention but was unsuccessful.

I could see from Carolyn's expression that the disorderliness irritated her. She stood up to take control. "I'd like to take the floor, Leslie."

"Certainly." Leslie stepped away from the podium and scurried to sit beside her husband.

"Good afternoon," Carolyn said into the mic. Upon hearing her voice, the room finally quieted down. "It's understandable that we are all concerned and must address this problem head on as a collective. I feel that the first step as members of the HOA, we need to be a little more selective about who we allow into our community. Clearly, our vetting process isn't working."

"Here she goes again," Sydney Johnson, who was seated across the aisle from me with her husband, murmured.

"Carolyn, the only vetting that needs to be done is confirming that whoever purchases the home has the funds to cover the mortgage," Jeffrey responded.

"I disagree," Carolyn told him. "And that's where our problem lies. This isn't just about money. When the Black Hamptons was created, it wasn't just a place for those who were financially able to reside. There were also other standards adhered to."

"Yeah, bourgeois." Sydney snickered.

Carolyn stiffened and stared at Sydney, clearly agitated. I knew the prior history between the two women and prayed they weren't about to get into yet another verbal scrimmage.

"Syd, please," Anthony whispered, and Sydney rolled her eyes.

Carolyn continued. "If we don't get a rein on it now, we are going to lose what little strength we have left. The last thing we need is for unwanted outsiders to inhabit the place that we all call home."

While a few nodded in agreement, some, including Sydney, seemed doubtful. She voiced her opinion loudly. "Well, I feel that what you're saying screams of prejudice. Who are we to judge anyone wanting to live here? I don't understand."

"First, I wouldn't expect you to understand any of this," Carolyn responded arrogantly. "As a newcomer, you don't have the pedigree to appreciate our history here. Second, it's not prejudicial, it's preferential. There's a difference."

The tension between the two women stirred people up, and the audience started chattering again.

Lamont leaned over and asked, "Who is that woman?"

"Carolyn's next-door neighbor," I answered.

"I take it they don't like each other."

"Oh, they hate one another equally."

After Sydney sat back down in her seat, her husband stood up and spoke out.

"I think what Carolyn is trying to say is that there is a need to protect and preserve the Black Hamptons as much as possible. I get it. I'm all for people living where they want to live, that's their right. However, we recognize the need to make sure the culture, history, and affordability of this area is guarded, or *all* of us are going to be driven out, especially by the corporate buyers."

Several people, including me, applauded. From the corner of my eye, I saw the disgusted look Sydney gave him as he returned to his seat.

"Thank you, Anthony." Carolyn gave him a pleased look. "That's exactly what I'm saying. If any of you thinks Eli Bradshaw will maintain the character of this community, you are sorely mistaken. He will tear down these homes, build larger homes on the lots, and surround them with fences. He has no interest in mingling with any of us."

"I have to admit, I agree with that. One of the reasons why our community has been able to thrive for so long is because of the sanctity with which we've held onto the hopes and dreams of our ancestors. Our dedication to each other matters, and we must be selective about who comes into this community," Reverend Chauncey said.

"But is that fair? Like Jeffrey said, as long as they can afford to live here, shouldn't they be able to?" Everett asked from the back row.

Malcolm took it upon himself to turn around and answer his question. "You're not as smart as you pretend to be, Everett. These corporate guys aren't buying homes because they want to live here. All their rich, white country club friends will buy those homes from them at triple the value."

"What's the problem with that? I'm all for my property value going up," Sydney snapped back at him.

"The problem," Carolyn said, rolling her eyes, "is they'll create a value so high that Black people won't be able to afford the homes. And the ones that are living here may not be able to afford to stay."

"They're trying to drive us out of what we've created. And it wouldn't be the first time in history they've done so. We have to take this very seriously," Moses said.

"There has to be something we can do to stop them," a woman yelled out from the back row. "We have association rules for everything else—where we can park, what color paint we can have on our trim. I know we can't say no outsiders, but we've gotta be able to say something."

"We're trying," Leslie answered, looking over at Jeffrey.

"We can't have the bylaws reflect bias to any race, color, creed, nationality, or sexual identification, if that's what you're asking," Jeffrey explained.

"But there is a possibility that the bylaws can be amended to state that purchases by any LLCs or other business entities isn't allowed. This is a residential dwelling," Bradley Hudson announced as he entered the room, causing everyone to turn around to look at him.

"Bradley, you made it." Reverend Chauncey stood and shook his hand.

"I apologize for my tardiness." Bradley continued to the podium and stood beside Carolyn.

"Better late than never. Now that you're here, hopefully we can put a stop to whatever it is they're trying to do and keep the vultures out," Carolyn said.

"There are no guarantees, but we can damn well try," he said. "But we've got to start now."

Once the meeting was adjourned, I was discreetly lingering and making small talk while I waited for Lamont.

Moses motioned for me.

"What's up?" I asked when I approached him in the corner of the room.

"I spoke with Jeffrey. He and Everett are scheduled to go into the city to meet with Everett's contact. Is everything in place for the transfer?" he asked.

I nodded. "It's been set up."

"And it's not traceable, correct?"

"Not at all," I assured him. "As far as accounts go, it's nonexistent."

"Good. That's exactly what I want to hear. The sooner this gets done, the sooner we can move on to the next phase."

I looked past him toward the rear door at Lamont, who was walking out.

"Kimberly?"

"Huh? Oh, yeah, we'll be ready when it's time," I said. "Hey, I need to catch someone before they leave."

"Sure, go ahead." He stepped to the side.

"Thank you." I rushed past him and out the door.

I made it up the stairs and to the parking lot of the church just in time to see Lamont opening the door of his Tesla. Although I was tempted, I had too much pride to call out to him, so I just stood and stared. He must have felt my gaze because he looked up and saw me on the sidewalk.

He closed the door and walked over to me. "Hey, you."

"I guess you forgot that quick, huh?"

"I did. Carolyn and Rev. hemmed me up and gave me an assignment list that I gotta get handled ASAP," he explained. "Don't worry. They have a list for you too."

"I'm sure they do," I said.

"But listen. I gotta get back to the city and beat this traffic. I'll give you a call soon so we can figure this plan for dinner and drinks that you're treating me to."

"Whoa, whoa, whoa." I laughed. "Who said anything about me treating?"

"If memory serves me correctly, you did. You said dinner before or drinks after, your treat."

"Your memory sucks, sir," I told him. "I said your choice, not my treat."

"Doesn't that imply the same thing?"

"No, it doesn't. Don't be trying your legal hocus pocus on me."

"I'll call you later. And for the record, I got something else to try on you," he whispered as he hugged me goodbye. I was left speechless and wanting to chase after him as he walked to his car.

25

Sydney Johnson

“How long do you plan on not talking to me?” Anthony asked as we drove out of the church parking lot.

I responded by turning my head and staring out of the passenger side window. Why he was even attempting to hold a conversation was beyond me.

“You do realize you’re being ridiculous, right? I wasn’t trying to embarrass you in the meeting. I just needed you to chill so that you didn’t end up getting into it with Carolyn Britton again, that’s all,” he explained as if I cared. “Syd?”

I remained silent, like I’d been arrested for a crime I didn’t commit and was waiting on my lawyer to show up. I wasn’t just angry about Anthony and his actions at the meeting. Truth be told, I was still fuming over his decision to go to dinner with the Brittons the night before. We used to be a rock-solid team, but lately, his decisions made me feel like he was choosing sides, and he wasn’t choosing mine.

When he asked me to go with him to the dinner with the Brittons, I shrieked my response. “Have you lost your motherfucking mind, Anthony?”

“No, I haven’t,” he told me as he got dressed. “I don’t know what the problem is. Moses invited us, not Carolyn, and it’s just dinner.”

“I don’t care if Barack Obama gave us a personal invitation. There’s no way on God’s green earth I’d ever have dinner with that witch, especially at her house.” I stood in the center of our bedroom floor with my hands on my hips. “And I know that you and Moses are becoming acquainted, but I’m telling you right now, Anthony Britton, do not invite them to our house. I don’t want them here, and they’re not welcome.”

Anthony turned around from the mirror and frowned at me. "You're really being ridiculous. The business with the property is over and done with. Everyone has moved past this except you."

"And I'm not moving past shit. I have no desire to become cool or even cordial with anybody whose last name is Britton. All of them can go to hell as far as I'm concerned." I stormed out of the room.

By the time Anthony had returned home, I was fast asleep in bed, courtesy of the two bottles of wine I drank while watching reality TV. When he told me about the emergency HOA meeting, I was inclined not to attend, but then I remembered how much we paid in association fees.

Now I wished I hadn't gone. Once again, Carolyn Britton had taken it upon herself to disrespect me for no reason, and my husband was not backing me up the way I felt he should.

"I know you don't feel like cooking," Anthony said when we arrived home and he pulled into the driveway. "I'll run to the store and grab some stuff to throw on the grill."

I was certain he was using a store run as an excuse to leave, but I didn't care. I didn't feel like cooking and hadn't planned to do so anyway. I opened the car door and got out without saying a word. Before I got into the house, he'd pulled off and was halfway down the street. I made a mental note to curse him out when he returned for not making sure I was safely inside before leaving.

"Gabby! Tyler!" I yelled as I walked into the kitchen. Neither one answered, but I heard music, male voices, and laughter coming from the back yard. I went to the window and looked out, expecting to see Tyler and his buddies. "What the fuck?"

There was Tyler, standing with a shovel in his hand, digging into the ground. Rashid stood nearby with a tape measure. Rashid said something to Tyler, who stopped digging and listened intently. They seemed to be enjoying whatever they were doing. My heart began racing so hard and fast that I could hear it. Consumed with anger, I yanked the back door open so hard that it rattled the glass.

"Tyler! What the hell are you doing?" I bolted at him, snatching the shovel fom him and throwing it toward Rashid.

"Mom, yo, chill!" Tyler tried to block the shovel as it left my hands, but it was too late.

"Shit." Rashid caught it just in time.

"Are you crazy?" I screamed at Rashid. "How dare you have my son out here with you?"

"Mom, please. You're the one acting crazy." Tyler tried to stop me as I stormed across the yard.

"Move, Ty!" I pushed past him toward Rashid.

"Sydney, calm down," Rashid said. "We weren't doing anything wrong."

"How dare you have my son out here like he's some kind of slave worker doing manual labor," I spat at him.

"Yo, you're tripping, Sydney." Rashid stuck the shovel into the ground. "Tyler saw me out here working, and he came out to chat about what I was doing."

"Rashid told me that he was an architectural engineering major in college, and I told him I'm an engineering major too. We were talking about designs and measurements. He was showing me some structural dynamics when it comes to landscaping," Tyler tried to explain, but it didn't defuse my anger one bit.

"That's all." The look Rashid gave me resembled the disgusted look Carolyn had given me earlier, and my anger burned even hotter. I couldn't believe the nerve of him. There he was, a lowly landscaper, looking at me as if the house wasn't mine.

"Leave, now!" I shouted. I was aware that my behavior was over the top, but after the morning I'd had, I truly did not give a shit.

"What?" Tyler and Rashid said at the same time.

"Get your shit and get out. You're fired.

"Whoa, Mom—"

"Tyler, take your ass into the house." I glared at him. "And go take a shower. You stink."

"Sorry, man," he said to Rashid before storming off toward the house.

"Sydney, don't do this. I'm telling you, you're—"

"Don't!" I held my hand up to stop Rashid. "Pack it all up and get the fuck off my property before I call the police and have your ass hauled off. And I'm warning you, don't ever come back here again, Rashid."

Rashid shook his head. "I always knew you were a spiteful, hateful bitch, and I had no idea Anthony was your husband when he hired me. Believe it or not, I was just as shocked as you were, but hell, he was cool, and I was excited about the job. Then here you go with the bullshit. But you know what, Sydney? I'm glad you fired me. It tells me everything I've wondered over the past twenty years."

Something about the way he said it made my stomach clench. "What the fuck is that supposed to mean?"

Rashid snatched up the shovel. "Every buried secret don't always remain safe."

"Go to hell, Rashid." I went back inside, slamming the door shut behind me.

"Mom, why did you do that?"

I was startled by Tyler, who was standing in the kitchen. "I told you to go upstairs and shower."

"I will once you tell me why you snapped on Mr. Rashid like that. He didn't do anything wrong. I was the one asking him questions."

"I have my reasons. Truth be told, your father had no business hiring him in the first place. Now, go," I said.

"I don't understand."

"And I don't have to explain shit to you," I shouted. "Go take a shower."

Tyler sulked off. I could hear him mumbling as he went up the stairs but decided not to respond. Just as I was about to pour myself a glass of much-needed wine, the doorbell rang. I slammed the bottle on the counter, and by the time I reached the front door, I was prepared to cuss Rashid out even worse than I already had.

I snatched the door open. "Go the fuck away!"

"Excuse me?"

I blinked a few seconds, too stunned and embarrassed to reply to Moses Britton, who stood in the doorway, looking perplexed by my outburst.

"Is this a bad time?" he asked, then quickly followed up with another question. "Are you okay?"

"Yes, I . . . I'm fine." I felt my cheeks growing warm from embarrassment.

"Are you sure?" He looked genuinely concerned.

"Yes. I . . . I'm sorry, Mr. Britton. Uh, please come in," I offered, surprising myself.

"Thank you, Mrs. Johnson, and please, call me Moses." He stepped into the foyer.

"Moses, please call me Sydney," I told him as I closed the door.

"Sydney it is." He extended his hand, and I shook it. "Are you sure this isn't a bad time?"

"No, it's not. I'm sorry about that. I thought you were the landscaper that I just fired." I sighed.

"The shirtless man cursing and tossing tools into the back of the truck parked out front? I assume that's who you're talking about."

I turned and peeked out the front window, realizing that I'd been so upset with Anthony that I hadn't even noticed the truck when I got home. But there it was, and there was Rashid, throwing tools into the back.

"Yes, that's him," I said, turning back to Moses.

"Sorry that happened."

"I'm not. He needed to go," I said. "But what brings you here?"

"I'm so sorry. I stopped by to talk to Anthony, actually. Is he home?"

"He's not. He ran to the store but should be back in a little while," I answered. "I'm sorry."

"No need for you to apologize, sweetheart. I am the one who stopped by unannounced. That's not something I normally do, by the way."

Moses walked over to the door and opened it to leave, then turned around. "Sydney, I'd feel more comfortable waiting with you until Anthony returns, if it's okay with you. Just in case that guy out there decides to do something stupid."

"You don't have to do that," I said, flattered by his offer. To be married to such a horrible woman, he was surprisingly charming.

"I know I don't, but I want to make sure you're safe."

"My son is home too. I'm not alone."

"Then I'll make sure both of you are safe." He closed the door.

"Would you like some wine while you wait?" I offered, recognizing that I had lost that argument.

"I'd love a glass."

Moses followed me into the kitchen, and I motioned toward the table before reaching into the cabinet and taking out another glass. "Please have a seat."

"Thank you."

I poured two glasses and handed him one, then sat across from him at the table. "I hope you like sweet red."

"Cabernet Sauvignon. My favorite," Moses said.

"Mine too," I said, tapping my glass against his. "This one is from Napa. Kathryn Hall 2019."

"Nice." Moses tasted his drink. "I like it. I'll have to pick up a bottle. Have you tried Merus?"

"Oh my God, yes. I love Merus as well. But my fave has to be Freemark Abbey."

"Freemark's Cabernet Bosch is my personal choice," Moses said. "Have you been to their winery? It's beautiful."

"No, I haven't. Napa is on my bucket list, though."

Moses raised his eyebrows. "You've never been to Napa? A wine connoisseur such as yourself?"

"No, but hopefully soon," I said. "We've just been waiting for the right time."

His compliments were unexpected and made me feel special. He really was charming. Anthony was more into whiskey than wine, so he usually had no opinion. I was pleasantly surprised by how much I was enjoying the conversation. The frustration I'd felt moments before seemed to just fade away.

"Sometimes you have to make time to enjoy life's pleasures," Moses said.

"True. I'll have to remember that."

"I thought that I'd get to meet you last night at the dinner party." He leaned back in his chair. "I'm sorry you weren't feeling well and couldn't make it."

"Oh, uh yeah, the dinner party. I'm sorry too. I think I had some kind of stomach bug."

Moses looked amused. "Funny, Anthony said you had a migraine."

"That too." I stood to get the bottle of wine to refill our glasses.

"Come on now, Sydney." Moses laughed. "We both know there was nothing wrong with you. Honestly, I don't blame you."

"You don't?" I asked as I returned to the table and began to pour.

"Not at all. My wife can be quite intolerable and I'm sure the last person you wanted to share a meal with."

His hand touched mine as he reached for his glass. I stopped, and our eyes met. I held his stare, intrigued.

"It would've been nice to have someone as beautiful and engaging as you at the table, though, that's for certain. After meeting you tonight, I can honestly say that you were missed."

"Oh, well . . . thank you?" It came out as a question because I didn't know what else to say.

Thankfully, I didn't have to think of anything else because I heard the garage door opening. My husband was home.

26

Martin Britton

At one point in time, Creatif Noir had been one of my favorite places. I'd always loved art, so much so that I wanted to major in art in college. My parents had vetoed that decision, however, and I was only allowed to choose it as a minor after I convinced them that understanding art could be good for investment purposes. Even then, they were doubtful until I put my skills to use. As a result, we had acquired one of the most valuable collections on the East Coast, including several pieces by Black artists that were purchased from Creatif Noir.

When the media had announced the opening of a local gallery specifically for African American artists, I insisted that Amistad Bank be a major sponsor and supporter. That was how I got to know Jade Sinclair, the curator of the gallery. Her family had roots in the Black Hamptons community, and she had returned to open the gallery. She and I hit it off, and we quickly entered into a pretty steamy entanglement. Unfortunately, I had a short attention span when it came to my love life, so it didn't take long for me to become distracted by some other beautiful plaything. I'd had to avoid the gallery and Jade ever since.

"Here goes nothing," I said to myself as I stepped out of my car in front of the gallery.

The entrance was only a few feet away from where I parked, but it felt like I was walking the last mile on death row. Inside the gallery, I was immediately reminded of why I had loved the space at one point. The colorful paintings, abstracts and oils, were incredible. Sculptures of historical figures and portraits of Black faces surrounded me, each one inviting me for an up close and personal look that I wanted to accept. I took my time, soaking in the creative magic.

"Can I help you?" A young lady approached me. Young, energetic, and polite, I presumed she was an intern for the gallery.

"Uh, hello, Chloe." I read the name tag on her shirt. "I'm here to see Ms. Sinclair. Is she available?"

"Yes, she's in her office. I can grab her for you."

"I know where it is." I smiled. "We're old friends, and I'd love to surprise her, if it's okay."

Chloe looked doubtful.

I reached into my pocket and took out one of my business cards to give to her. "This is me. My family is a major donor for the gallery."

"Oh, Amistad Bank." Chloe read the card, then looked back at me. "Okay, Mr. Britton, go on back."

Moments later, I'd made my way down the corridor, past the archive rooms and studios, until I was outside the door of Jade's office. Classic jazz was coming from inside, and I listened until the last note of John Coltrane's "A Love Supreme" drifted away. It was only then that I tapped on the door.

"Enter."

I took a deep breath as I slowly opened the door and stepped inside. Jade was seated at her desk, typing into the computer. In front of her was a pile of folders and paperwork. Her braids were pulled into a high bun, and she had on a pair of stylish glasses that might have looked nerdy on anyone else. On her, they were sexy. She was so focused on her work that she didn't realize it was me in her office until I spoke.

"How are you, Jade? Long time, no see."

She stopped typing instantly. Her eyes remained on the screen for a few more seconds before she looked up at me. Her mouth opened slightly, confirming how shocked she was to see me standing there. She even removed her glasses, as if wanting to make sure her vision wasn't failing.

"Oh, hell no," she said, shaking her head. "Not today, Satan."

"Come on, Jade. Don't be like that. I come to you in peace."

"You shouldn't be coming anywhere near me, fool." Jade turned off the music and sat back in her chair. "What the hell do you want, Martin? You know what? I don't even care what you want."

"Jade, I know we ended on unpleasant terms." I took a step toward her desk.

"Unpleasant terms? Is that what you call it when you pretty much ghost someone you've dated for almost half a year? Then, not only do you go MIA, but you pretend you don't see them when you're in the same vicinity, and on occasion, turn and go in the other direction?" Jade was making me feel worse than I already did.

"You're right. The way I behaved was immature and disrespectful, and I owe you an apology. I was young and dumb, but I've grown since then, hence why I came to see you," I said with sincerity.

"Martin, I just saw you two months ago window-shopping outside the gallery with some chick in a bikini. When I motioned for you to come inside, you hauled ass."

I'd forgotten about the day Karrin and I happened to walk by the gallery. When she asked if we could go in, I quickly pulled her away from the window, giving her the excuse that we weren't properly dressed for the gallery.

"You've matured over the last sixty days?" Jade asked.

"I have," I told her. "I'm a better man now. And I'm truly sorry about everything. You didn't deserve any of the bullshit I gave you."

"Do you know how embarrassing it was to have one of the gallery's biggest supporters and advocates just vanish? I thought we were better than that."

"Hold on. Amistad and the Britton Foundation still supported you."

"Yeah, with a check. And don't get me wrong, I appreciated the fiscal donation, but you were a physical presence in this place. You attending the events and shows made a difference, Martin, and when you stopped, others did too." Jade's voice cracked, and she sounded like she was about to cry. "Creatif Noir took a hit, not just me."

"Damn, Jade. I know what I did was a coward's move, but I really thought that it would be easier to go away. I fucked up, big time." I nervously scratched behind my neck, wondering if showing up there had been a bad idea. It was obvious Jade still harbored resentment and hurt, rightfully so. As much as I wanted to resolve things and move on, I didn't know how. "I don't know what else to say."

"That's all you need to say, Martin."

"Huh?"

"I would have preferred you being honest instead of being a bitch ass, that's for sure." She sighed. "But at least you are finally acknowledging it."

"I really do apologize."

"I accept your apology. Now, sit and tell me why the hell you're really here. And please don't start with some bullshit lie like it's because you miss me, either."

"I mean, I do miss you, but I came by to talk to you about something important." I sat in one of the chairs in front of her desk.

"What is it?"

"It's about your family's house, the one on Sandpiper Lane. I know you're considering selling it."

"I am, and I have some offers. Good offers, actually. I heard about the HOA meeting and what's going on. Yes, that house has been in my family for years, and I know the history of it and the Black Hamptons. My great grandparents bought it at the same time as yours. That's why it's so valuable."

"That's also why you have to keep it, especially now."

"Martin, did you hear anything I said about the gallery taking a hit? I need money. That's why I'm using the house as a short-term rental and living in the loft here. It's additional income," Jade explained. "I'm trying to expand this place."

"I can help you do that. We can figure it out together." I leaned forward and grabbed her hand, staring deeply into her eyes. "I got you—and Creatif Noir."

And then, I saw it. There was a spark, and it was all I needed to know that she didn't hate me entirely. But just as quickly as it came, it was gone, replaced with a look of uncertainty.

"I love my grandparents and that house, but let's be honest. I don't need it. That place is enormous. I am single, no kids. Hell, I don't even have a man. Why do I need five bedrooms and a pool?"

Determined to recapture her trust, I stood and walked behind her desk, pulling her to her feet. "We can figure that out together too."

"Don't." Jade's voice was barely above a whisper.

“Don’t what?” I put my arms around her.

“Don’t do this. We’ve only been cordial five minutes.” She tried to lower her head, but I caught her chin with my finger.

“All I’m trying to do is ask you out to dinner tonight, that’s all. So we can talk and catch up,” I said, forcing her to look into my eyes. “Like you said, we are cordial now, right?”

“Just dinner?” Jade gave me a doubtful look.

“Just dinner.” I leaned in, giving her the kiss I knew she was waiting on. Her mouth was warm and inviting, just as I remembered, and the chemistry between us was still intense. Before I got there, I’d had no intention of sleeping with Jade or rekindling our affair, and I had promised myself that I wouldn’t cross any lines. But not having Karrin had left a void in my life, and I was tired of pining away for her. Jade could be exactly what I needed to get over my recent heartache.

27

Alyssa Winters

Growing up, my mother taught Vanessa and me to discover the thing we were good at, master the skill, and use it to make money. While my sister perfected her skill of marrying rich men, divorcing them, and collecting alimony checks, I pursued my love of cooking. I graduated from culinary school at the top of my class, and instead of going straight into a kitchen, I developed my career by traveling the world. I became a gourmet sponge, open to new tastes, and gained knowledge about the preparation of a variety of delicacies: French, Italian, Caribbean, and Asian. When I was ready to put my hard-earned talents to use, I applied for countless open positions. Although I was a master of ingredient sourcing, knife, and presentation skills, no one felt inclined to hire me as an executive chef in their kitchen.

I finally landed a gig as a manager at a Michelin-starred restaurant in Manhattan, mainly because the owner said I had the "look" they needed to greet their high-end clientele. Instead of wallowing in the insult, I tucked my pride, telling myself it was the stepping-stone I needed to develop time management, business acumen, and accounting skills. Then COVID hit, and I, like many in the rest of the world, pivoted. A decent camera, a ring light, and my dazzling personality were my saving grace. "Alyssa Eats at Home" was birthed in the kitchen of my apartment, launching my success as a social media cooking sensation. My online following was massive, but it was time to take my brand to the next level, starting in Sag Harbor.

"Maybe I should create a spice line," I said, talking out loud to myself as I stared at the limited selection on the shelf in front of me.

One of my favorite things to do was to go grocery shopping with just me and my ideas about what meal I wanted to invent. It was a great way for me to decompress. So many thoughts consumed me daily, and strolling through the grocery aisles gave me time to sort them out. I grabbed some seasonings from the meager offerings. They would have to do. Lost in thought about how I would put them to use, I turned around a little too quickly and bumped right into the chest of a man who was standing way too close to me. I looked up to say something smart but stopped when I saw Anthony Johnson smiling down at me.

"I'm sorry. I wasn't paying attention." I finally found my voice.

"Oh, sorry," he said in his deep, manly voice. "I didn't even see you standing there."

"No, that was my fault," I told him. "Like I said, moving too fast."

"Sounds like we were both distracted."

I looked down into the basket he was pushing and took inventory of the items inside: processed cheese slices, canned baked beans, frozen corn on the cob, and burgers. The only fresh ingredients he had were a package of steaks and a bag of leg quarters. "Yes, I guess your attention was on the cookout you're having."

Anthony laughed. "Nah, not a cookout, but I am putting a little something on the grill for dinner."

"Little something is right," I teased. "You're definitely not working hard."

"Wow, really?" He pretended to be offended. "Not everyone can be a fancy gourmet chef like you, Ms. Winters."

I was surprised that he remembered my name. We'd never been formally introduced. The night of Moses's dinner party, Carolyn introduced me as the chef once dinner was served, but I'd spent most of the night in the kitchen.

"You don't have to be a chef to use clean ingredients, Mr. Johnson," I told him. "That's basic Home Ec knowledge we learned in high school."

"I didn't take Home Ec."

"Don't tell me. You were an athlete, right?" I said, trying not to admire his muscular arms too hard. I had to admit, Sydney Johnson was one lucky woman.

"No, I was a nerd. I took computer science."

"That makes sense." I said, then pointed to the basket. "But this stuff right here doesn't."

"How about this? You give me the ingredients I need to make those stuffed shrimp we had last night. Oh, and those feta Brussels sprouts. I don't even like Brussels sprouts, but those were incredible. I told my wife she missed out on some amazing food."

"You liked those, huh?" I beamed with pride.

"Liked? I loved them. As my daughter would say,"—he kissed his fingertips—"chef's kiss. As a matter of fact, can you give a brother the recipes for the whole meal?"

"Unfortunately, a magician never tells her secrets. But I do teach private cooking classes, and you can learn to make your own. Everybody's taste buds are different. You might come up with something you like better than my recipes."

Okay, in all honesty, I'd never actually taught a private class, but how hard could it be? It was something I had been trying to orchestrate ever since I saw a commercial kitchen space in town available for hourly rent. Now, it seemed like more than an idea. As an added bonus, I could get to know Anthony Johnson to see if there was some way I could help out my sister and her little problem.

"Come on, a whole class? I can't just pay you for the recipes?"

"No, sir." I shook my head and reached into my purse. "Here's my card."

"A cooking class, huh?" He stared at the card.

"I'm just saying. You wouldn't have to tell your wife about how good everything was. You can make it for her yourself," I suggested. "You'd gain all types of cool points, not that you need them. But nothing is more romantic than a man cooking for his woman."

"That *would* be something I've never done for her."

"Think about it and let me know." I looked into his basket. "And at least get some fresh corn to go with those steaks. Maybe some salad, too. No meal is complete without something green."

Anthony laughed, giving me another glimpse of his dimpled smile and perfect teeth.

A part of me didn't think that he would call, but I found out the next morning I was wrong. My phone rang as I was making a veggie omelet for breakfast. I looked at the caller ID and saw a local number appear on the screen that I didn't know. I answered the unknown call and smiled when I heard Anthony's voice.

"Good morning. I hope I didn't wake you."

"No, I was actually up fixing something to eat."

"Good. I was calling to take you up on your offer. About the cooking class?"

"Well, that didn't take long," I said, grabbing my plate and going to sit on my sofa in the living room. I muted the cooking show I'd been watching so there would be no background noise.

"I know. My wedding anniversary is coming up, and I need to earn some cool points, as you called them," he said.

There was a hint of sadness, or maybe it was desperation. Either way, it was quite different from his demeanor yesterday at the store. Was there trouble in paradise?

"I see. When is your anniversary?" I asked, resisting the urge to pry into his business.

"In three weeks. Is that going to be enough time, you think?"

Hoping to make him laugh, I said, "I mean, I'm not a miracle worker, Mr. Johnson, but I can definitely teach you a dish or two."

"I'm a tech guru, Ms. Winters. If you're a good teacher, I can learn pretty fast."

"Great. When do you want to start?" I asked, grabbing my iPad next to me on the couch to create a list of tasks.

"Today."

"To–today?" I stammered.

"You said we don't have a lot of time. Does this afternoon work?"

"Sure," I said as if I hadn't just created a mental timeline of two days to prepare. "I'll text you the address and time."

"See you this afternoon."

As soon as the call ended, my first instinct was to call Vanessa. I reminded myself that not only did I not have time to chit chat, but neither did she. Her hands were full taking care of Jesse. Instead, I ate a couple bites of my food before hopping up to get my very busy day started. I had to come up with meal ideas, get supplies, rent the kitchen space, and lastly, make sure I was fine as hell the next time Anthony saw me. I knew he was a married man, but who didn't like eye candy?

28

Anthony Johnson

"You're late," David said when I arrived at the office. "You left for lunch over two hours ago."

Selena, the office receptionist who was eavesdropping from her desk, gave us an amused look.

"Okay," I said. "Who's gonna fire me?"

"It's the principle. You're the boss and should be setting a good example for the staff."

"Says the company VP who arrived late to work for the past three days." I smirked.

"Touché," Selena chimed in.

"Fine, point made." David followed me into my office and took his usual seat in the recliner near the window. He called it his thinking spot. "So, it's official. Singh sent the final paperwork, and we are officially in business."

"That's great," I said weakly.

"Hold up. What the hell is going on? What's up, Anthony?" David frowned. "Did you hear what I just said?"

"Nothing's up, and yeah, I heard you. We finally got the paperwork, and the Singh deal is official."

"Something's up. I just told you we finalized the twenty-five-million-dollar deal that we worked for over a year to put into place, damn near lost, and retrieved. And all you can say is that's great?" He threw his hands in the air. "I ain't expect you to pop bottles and do backflips, but damn. I expected at least a little more enthusiasm."

I knew my reaction to the news we'd been waiting for was a bit disappointing to my best friend and right-hand man, but I was too distracted by the troubles in my personal life to enjoy my monumental business success.

"I'm excited, man, I really am," I told him, staring out of my office window at the Manhattan skyline. The view was one of the reasons I had splurged on the thirtieth-floor office space in the heart of the city. "And I promise, we're gonna pop bottles and celebrate. Come to think of it, remind me to have Selena send Singh a champagne basket and a thank you card."

"Anthony, I know you. What's going on?" David pressed.

"I don't know. It's something going on with Syd." Usually, I kept my marital woes to myself, but David had been married just as long as I had and was a great listener.

"Oh my God, what else is new?" David sat back in the chair. "Don't tell me y'all are arguing about Karrin again. She ain't leaving, and Syd ain't kicking her out. Get over it, man. You know how Black women are when it comes to their sisters. You've got a permanent squatter."

"Nah, it ain't about her. That's not why Syd is tripping," I said. "As a matter of fact, Karrin hasn't even been home in a couple of days. She's been hanging out with Bobby Boyd."

"The Beast? Damn, that was fast. She doesn't waste any time, does she?" David looked impressed.

"No, she doesn't."

"That's one hell of a come up, that's for sure." He laughed. "So, why is Syd tripping?"

"I don't know. She's just been mad for a minute. I mean, when the Singh deal almost fell through, we were both stressed. I thought she'd be happier now, but she has a problem because we had to rely on Moses Britton to help us out. Then, I hired this dope-ass landscape architect to design the back yard and install a small pool, and she's still trippin'."

"What's the problem?"

"That's what I wanna know," I said. "I got home from the grocery store last night, and she tells me she fired him."

"Why?"

"She didn't say, but Tyler said she lost her shit and cussed him out because they were talking in the yard. I feel bad for the dude. He seemed legit, and he was a really nice guy."

"I don't know, Anthony. Sounds like she might be hormonal," David suggested.

I frowned.

"Yeah, you know, women of a certain age start going through the change," he explained. "Their emotions be all over the place, crying one minute, screaming the next. They're hot and sweating, then cold and shivering. That's probably what's happening."

I shook my head. "That's not what's going on, David. She's not menopausal."

David snapped his fingers. "Menopausal. That's the word I was trying to think of. Well, if it's not that, then what do you think it could be? You already do everything and give her everything she could ever want."

"Funny you should say that," I said. "I think I've been missing something very important that we need."

"What's that?"

"Romance. I haven't been woo'ing her."

"So what, you're gonna send her some flowers? You think that's gonna fix everything?"

"No, not flowers, man. I'm going to do something even better than that." I took out my phone and pulled up an Instagram page to show him.

David scrolled through the photos of the various candlelit tables with plates of food for a few moments. "This is nice. You're gonna hire a chef to come in and cook?"

"Nah, I'm going to cook for her."

David burst out laughing. I snatched my phone from him and sat down, waiting for him to stop.

"What's so damn funny?"

"I'm saying, you can grill with the best of them, but your inside cooking skills aren't even sub-par, Ant." David dabbed at the tears in his eyes.

"I know that. That's why I'm going to learn how. I'm taking a gourmet cooking class."

"A gourmet cooking class?" David looked like he wanted to laugh again, but he held it back.

"So, check this out. I went to the grocery store yesterday, and guess who I ran into?"

"I don't know. Gordon Ramsay?"

"No, fool. Alyssa Winters, the chef who cooked the meal at the Brittons' the other night."

"Oh, yeah. I know Alyssa. Vanessa Britton is her sister. I've known her for a while," David said.

"I signed up for her private cooking class."

"Anthony, I get what you're trying to do and why you want to do it, but this ain't a good idea. At all." David shook his head. "Think of something else romantic, man. Hire a violinist, take her on a tropical vacation, a couples' day at the spa, anything but this."

"What's wrong with this?" I frowned. "This is pure effort."

"And your wife is pure crazy."

"David, it's a cooking class."

"It's not about the class. It's about the teacher," he explained. "We both know Sydney has a jealous streak. That's why she doesn't have any friends. She doesn't want any other females around you. Sometimes I wonder if she even likes me hanging out with you."

"She doesn't have friends because she's a loner, David. She's introverted," I told him. "Besides, she won't even know I'm taking the classes. It's a surprise."

David groaned. "That makes it even worse."

"You're wrong, man. This is going to be great, and by the time our anniversary is here in a couple of weeks, I'll have mastered the perfect meal." I was excited about the romantic gesture I was preparing for.

"I wanna root for you, Anthony, but this isn't going to end well."

"Whatever, man. Anyways, on another note," I said, changing the subject. "Moses came by the house last night."

"Why?"

"Apparently, he's going to be able to make good on his end of the agreement sooner rather than later. Says Everett and Jeffrey are putting things into place. We do need to have an account set up and ready."

"He's moving as fast as Karrin, ain't he?"

"I told him it was no pressure. Especially now that we have the Singh deal."

I watched David push the lounger back, and he stared at the ceiling. It was his thinking position.

"What's on your mind?"

"I don't know, man. It just seems so rushed. He already made good on helping get the Singh loan approved. Why is he so inclined to do this so fast?" David asked.

"You and Jeffrey said he's always been a smart businessman who makes moves. Maybe that's what he's doing," I suggested.

"Maybe, but something feels off. You'd think after being exonerated, he'd be laying low for a while, especially when it comes to money."

"You don't think Moses is doing anything illegal, do you?" I asked.

David sat back up in the chair and looked at me. "No, that's not what I'm saying at all. But there's something going on. I can sense it. We just need to make sure we're on high alert. We're just getting back on solid ground, and the last thing we need right now is for anything to shake it up."

29

Vanessa Britton

There weren't enough words to describe how happy I was to have Jesse back at home, but playing nursemaid was not my strong suit. He wasn't a baby anymore; he was a grown man with grown man weight on him. Helping him get around was not an easy feat, especially since he was still so fragile. Sometimes, I wasn't delicate enough while helping him get from point A to point B. Like this morning, I felt like I was dragging him while assisting him from the bathroom to his bed.

"Ouch!" Jesse shouted when he hit the mattress a little harder than either of us intended.

"I'm sorry, honey," I apologized and gently put his feet on the bed.

Once he eased into a comfortable position, I pulled the fresh sheets over him and fluffed his pillow. I paused to catch my breath. I didn't want my frustration to show on my face, but I couldn't help but to harbor even more resentment toward Peter Lane for changing our lives so drastically.

"Can you close those curtains? It's too bright in here," Jesse whined.

"Baby, sunlight is good for you. It'll keep you in high spirits," I told him.

"Mom, please. I can't sleep with them open." Jesse covered his eyes with his hands.

"You don't need to sleep. It's almost noon, and you need to get up. Or at least, sit up."

"But I'm tired, and the brightness makes my head hurt. Can't you please just close them?"

"Fine." I pulled the curtains closed, and the blackout fabric darkened the room. "But I'm turning the lights on."

"I'm supposed to be resting, remember," Jesse huffed.

"You've been getting plenty of rest. What you need to do is stop moping."

"Moping? Is that what you think I'm doing?"

"A little," I told him. "Can you at least sit up so you can eat?"

"I'm in pain." Jesse cut his eyes at me and held up the sling holding his injured arm. "And in a cast."

"You won't sit up even for some of your auntie's food?" Alyssa asked as she walked into Jesse's bedroom carrying a covered tray.

I had no idea what was under it, but the room was instantly filled with the aroma of warm Italian spices. My son instantly eased up, careful not to hit his arm on anything. His eyes stared hungrily at the tray in Alyssa's hands.

She took the tray over to the bed, and Jesse reached for it. I quickly went to grab him a towel and the lap desk we'd gotten for him. The last thing I needed was Carolyn fussing about Jesse making a mess in the bed. She'd wanted him to stay downstairs in the guest suite until he was better, but he declined. Jesse didn't think he would have much privacy being on the main floor.

"Lasagna." Alyssa beamed when she took the top off the tray and displayed a plate of lasagna and breadsticks with a side of Alfredo sauce, all homemade.

"Damn, that looks good." My mouth watered.

"Don't worry. There's some downstairs for you too." She nudged me as she put the plate in front of Jesse on his lap desk.

"Now, you know I can't have all of those carbs, girl." I shook my head. "But Jesse can indulge."

"And I will." Jesse picked up his fork and dug in.

"Oh, and I made you this too." Alyssa unzipped a cooler bag on her shoulder, revealing plastic bottles filled with colorful juice. "Strawberry lemonade, and there's plenty of it."

Jesse's mouth was too full to speak, but the way his eyes lit up paired with his enthusiastic nod showed his gratitude. I was happy to see that he had an appetite, although I knew all that cheese would soon send him back to the bathroom. As long as I got a few hours' break from heavy lifting, I would be all right.

"You need anything else right now?" I asked, and he shook his head. "All right, I'll be right downstairs."

Alyssa and I exited the room together. When we got to the kitchen, I leaned on the large island and let out an exhausted breath.

"How's he really doing?" Alyssa asked, standing on the opposite side of the island.

"He's still in some pain, but it's not as bad as it was." I watched while she began packing the plastic containers with leftover food.

"What about his head injury?"

"As you can see, no change." I grabbed one of the breadsticks before she put them in the Ziploc bag.

Jesse's broken wrist, nose, and fractured ribs were one thing, but the head trauma was another. It was the toughest battle he was facing, with multiple headaches, sensitivity to light, and worst of all, some memory loss.

"What are they saying?" Alyssa asked.

"The MRI and CT scan are normal. He has an appointment with a neurologist at the end of the week. But typically, when this does happen, it heals over time. We're just taking it one day at a time at this point." I told her exactly what Jesse's doctor had told Malcolm and me when he was released.

"Girl, I can see how tiring this is for you. Are you sure you don't want to hire a nurse or someone to help out?"

"Nope, especially since I have to monitor who comes and goes. That boy has been secretly calling Tania and asking her to come see him."

"So, his mind really is messed up."

"Girl! I don't know what kind of crack that girl has between her legs, but he doesn't want to let her go. She doesn't have a choice but to stay away from him, though. Carolyn had a restraining order placed against her."

"Good. She should've been in a jail cell with Peter."

"That's another thing. The DA keeps asking us to bring Jesse in to give his statement. Malcolm refuses to let him until he's better. This entire ordeal is a shit show."

I looked at the counter and realized just how much food Alyssa was packing away. "When the hell did you cook all of this food?"

"Funny you should ask." Alyssa grinned. "I have some interesting news to share."

"Oh, really?" I saw the excited twinkle in her eye. "Did you meet a guy?"

"Something even better than that." She did a playful dance in the middle of the kitchen floor. "I got a new client for my personal cooking classes."

"Okay, why are you so hyped about it? Is it someone famous?"

"It's someone you know, that's for sure," she hinted and continued to body roll.

"Really? Who?"

"Anthony Johnson."

My mouth fell open. "Shut the hell up. Are you for real?"

"I am. Actually, he already had his first class. Who do you think helped me cook all of this?"

"Well, I'll be damned."

"Oh, but there's more," Alyssa said with a devious grin. "Mr. Johnson is quite chatty, especially while cooking. The whole reason he's taking the class is to learn how to cook for his angry wife. He's trying to get out of the doghouse."

"What? Why is he in the doghouse?" I was intrigued. Anthony Johnson was such a straight-up guy. I couldn't imagine him doing anything bad enough to deserve punishment. Then again, his wife was a real piece of work, so it could have been something ridiculously minor.

"Remember the fine-ass landscape guy I told you about who came by the house and left his card?" Alyssa reminded me. "Rashid Logan, owns Logan Landscape Design."

"Yeah, vaguely."

"Well, apparently, Mrs. Johnson took an issue with him. So much so that she fired his ass."

"Why? What did he do?"

"I don't know, and neither does Anthony. But I'm damn sure gonna find out," Alyssa said with a look of determination.

"How are you gonna do that?"

Alyssa gave me a devilish grin. "I hired him. He starts tomorrow, and I plan on asking him. Trust me, he'll be talking just as much as Anthony before he's trimmed the hedges."

30

Moses Britton

I rang the doorbell at Jeffrey's house and stood back. As I waited for someone to come to the door, I breathed a deep breath of fresh air. Since I'd been home, there had been no room or time to really relax and enjoy the fact that I was back. Business first, personal life later. I heard the door lock click, and then I was greeted by Leslie, dressed in a frilly button-up blouse and a pair of checkered pants.

"Hey, Uncle Moses." She moved aside so I could come in.

"How's my favorite niece?" I hugged her.

"I'm your only niece, but I'm fine," she said, leading me through the foyer to a sitting room. "Jeffrey's on a call, but he'll be finished in a minute. Can I get you anything?"

"No, I'm fine." I sat on one of the sofas. The space exuded an understated elegance, adorned with a mix of contemporary and vintage furniture, much like the decor in my home. I could see that Carolyn's taste had rubbed off on her. "Any progress on the other two buyers while we figure this injunction thing out?"

The fight against Eli Bradshaw was in full swing. While Bradley Hudson was in the process of filing the injunction against Bradshaw, LLC, the company Eli owned that was listed on the newly purchased deeds, Carolyn and Reverend Chauncey were reviewing the charter for the Black Hamptons and discovering any bylaws that needed to be revised to be voted on at the next HOA meeting. Despite having a solid plan in place, we couldn't run the risk of Eli buying any other available properties.

"I'm actually on my way to meet my client and Lisa Pruitt at the property. Both are excited about the offer that's been put in,"

Leslie said, grabbing her leather messenger bag. "And from what I've been told, Jade Sinclair is being persuaded not to sell."

"That's good. Sounds like our community is safe for now."

"Not quite." Leslie sighed. "There's one situation involving Aunt Carolyn that I was made aware of while I was at the country club playing tennis this morning."

"What's that?"

Leslie sat beside me and explained the dilemma she was facing that needed to be dealt with. By the time she finished, I realized why she was concerned.

"I haven't talked to Aunt Carolyn or anybody else about this. Like I said, I just found out this morning." Leslie's phone chimed, and she looked at it. "It's my client. I have to go."

"You go and make sure your client buys that house. I'll take care of that other issue." I kissed Leslie on the cheek.

"What other issue?" Jeffrey asked as he walked in.

"Just a situation with an HOA member," I told him. "Nothing major."

"Baby, I'm gone for the day," Leslie said. "Don't forget we have dinner reservations for six thirty tonight."

"I know, I know. I'll be ready." Jeffrey kissed her. "Have a good day."

"You too." Leslie waved as she rushed out of the room. "Bye, Uncle Moses."

Jeffrey stared at the place she had been standing in for a couple of seconds before turning to face me. He took a few steps toward me with his hands casually in his pockets.

"Do you have the paperwork for me?" I asked.

"I do, Moses, but I still don't know how I feel about this. You do realize this will impact your entire family, right, and not just Carolyn?" He gave me a worried look. "Are you sure you want to do this?"

"I know the potential consequences."

"Don't you think you should at least talk about this with Malcolm and Martin first?"

"No, I don't want anyone to know, especially them. I'm doing this to protect my family."

"I don't see how. Maybe I'm confused. Even before you came home, I asked if you were going to retaliate for what you went through, and you insisted that you had no desire to do so. Now, here we are." Jeffrey shook his head. "You had the perfect opportunity to resume your position as head of Amistad during the board meeting, but you chose not to. You allowed Carolyn to retain her power."

"This isn't retaliation, Jeffrey. This is security. And there may come a time when my wife loses everything she thinks she has. If and when that time comes, everything I've worked hard to build will be safe."

"Moses, this is a huge risk," he insisted.

"You of all people should know—no risk, no reward. Now, I have some other business to attend. Bring me the documents to sign and make sure they're filed by the end of business today," I said.

31

Sergeant Tom Lane

Peter's anxiety about his appointment with the psychiatrist was understandable. Initially, I was uncomfortable with it too, but after speaking with Dr. Wells, I felt a bit better about what was going to take place. Not only was her voice warm and reassuring, but so were her words.

"Sergeant, you're going to see that this will be beneficial for both you and Peter," she had told me over the phone. "As his father, I'm sure this ordeal has you questioning a lot of things as it pertains to your son's actions and behaviors that you may have missed."

"It has," I admitted.

"There's a lot at stake, and psychiatric treatment could be the key," she continued. "The first step is having him come in to complete the evaluation."

"I just don't want Peter to be misunderstood, or worse, misdiagnosed, and all of a sudden he's locked away in some nuthouse." Realizing how uncouth I may have sounded, I quickly apologized. "I'm sorry. I didn't mean to say nuthouse. I just want my son to be protected, that's all."

"And I'm going to do my best to protect him in every way. He's in good hands."

I was choosing to trust her, at least for the time being. When we arrived in the parking lot of her office, the look on Peter's face said it all. He'd rather be anywhere but there. I parked the car and prepared to get out, but he hadn't even made a move to take off his seatbelt.

"I don't understand why I have to do this," Peter grumbled. He crossed his arms over his chest like he had when he was a kid and didn't want to eat his vegetables. We'd already had the discussion multiple times, and maybe he thought that by asking again, I'd miraculously change my mind and tell him that he didn't have to go.

"Because it's not only going to help you, but it'll help your case," I explained once again. "Now, come on."

He groaned and finally took off his seatbelt. We got out of the car together and walked to the entrance. With each step, guilt began to trickle through my veins. I thought I'd been protecting my son by not telling him about Tania and Jesse. What if that decision had been the thing that led Peter down such a treacherous path? It wasn't just Peter's behavior and actions I was questioning. I was also questioning my own.

In Dr. Wells's office, there was paperwork for Peter to complete. We were the only people in the waiting area, which I preferred. I didn't want anyone trying to sneak photos of my son in a psych office or post them on social media.

"Peter, you can come on back," the receptionist finally called. When I stood up to go back with him, she shook her head at me. "I'm sorry, Mr. Lane, but you can't go with him."

"I don't have to stay, but I at least want to meet Dr. Wells."

"You will," she told me. "She'll speak with you after his appointment."

"Dad?" Peter looked at me, his eyes full of worry.

Once again, I had flashes of him as a boy. He wanted his protector by his side, but this time, he'd have to ride through the wind by himself.

"It's okay, Peter." I put my hand on his shoulder and gave him a reassuring nod. "I'll be right out here."

Peter straightened his shoulders and followed the receptionist through the door. I checked my watch and sat back down. My stomach began rumbling, most likely because I hadn't had anything but a cup of coffee. However, I wasn't going to leave to get food and risk missing anything important. Spotting a sports magazine on the nearby table, I distracted myself by sifting through it. As luck would have it, the feature story centered around the one person I couldn't seem to get away from: Bobby "The Beast" Boyd.

"You've got to be fucking kidding," I grumbled, tossing the magazine back on the table and picking up the only other choice, a women's health magazine. Normally, I wouldn't have been excited to read about the latest trends for fall fashion or healthier options for late-night snacks, but anything was better than reading about Bobby Boyd and Team BTB.

Two hours later, Peter returned. I didn't even realize I'd nodded off until I felt the tap on my leg.

"Dad."

"Huh?" I looked up and saw him standing in front of me. "You done?"

"Yeah. It was cool."

I searched his face for any signs of distress that I should have been concerned about. He not only looked fine, but his demeaner was almost pleasant. It was a complete switch from when we had arrived.

"Sergeant Lane, you can head on back to see Dr. Wells," the receptionist said.

"Can I wait in the car?" Peter asked.

"Sure." I gave him my keys, then followed the receptionist to the back.

She took me through a short hallway that led to an open door at the end. There was an aroma of jasmine in the air as I got closer to the door. I felt my anxiety calming with each step.

The office was a large one and looked exactly how I would have pictured it. There was a mahogany desk and across from it, a comfortable-looking chaise. The blinds were open, and sunlight streamed into the space.

"Sergeant Lane, I'm Tabitha Wells. Nice to meet you."

Her voice was even more soothing in person. I stood in silence for a moment, captivated, not just by the tone, but by the woman it belonged to. Dr. Tabitha Wells was one of the most beautiful women I'd ever seen. Her brown eyes were expressive, with a gaze that exuded confidence and wisdom. There was something elegant about her features, and she gave me a smile that lit up the entire room.

"Uh, pleased to meet you." My ability to speak returned, and I managed to shake her extended hand. "And please, call me Tom."

"Okay, Tom, please sit." She motioned toward the cozy seating area that was the focal point of the room, featuring a plush sofa with throw pillows and a soft blanket.

I sat down, taking notice of how the space evoked a sense of calm and comfort. Instead of sitting at her desk facing the seating area, Dr. Wells sat in the comfortable armchair near me.

"How was Peter? Did you find anything out?" I asked, anxious to hear her findings.

"Your son is a delightful young man with a lovely spirit. I really enjoyed talking with him and look forward to getting to know him better," she told me, sounding as if we were at a parent teacher conference and not in a psychiatric office.

"You don't have to sugar coat anything, doc. Just tell me the real deal. I want to know," I said. "Are there concerns about Peter's mental status?"

"Because of doctor-patient confidentiality, I can't tell you any details, but Peter does have some mental health challenges that he's dealing with that need to be addressed," she answered. "Let me ask you something. Did Peter get any kind of counseling after his mother left?"

"No. He was so little, and he seemed to be okay after a while. Things became kind of normal until he was a teen and started getting into fights. That's why I put him into boxing, and he excelled."

"And you didn't do any family counseling together?"

"I didn't even think about doing that. My only focus was getting back to normal. Our new normal, I guess." I sighed.

"I understand. Well, I'm going to schedule Peter for one-on-one counseling with me, in addition to some group therapy for his anger management. But I think family counseling would benefit both of you as well."

"I think we should focus on Peter for right now. We really don't need family counseling. Peter and I get along fine."

"It's not about getting along, Tom. It's about healing and having a safe space to strengthen the lines of communication."

She shifted in the chair, leaning forward slightly. It took everything for me not to become lost in her eyes.

"Trust me, Peter talks to me about everything. I'm the safest space he has," I told her.

"Well then, thank you for bringing him and speaking with me." Dr. Wells stood. "Peter's next appointment is in two days, here with me. In the meantime, I'll reach out to Christopher to discuss the case."

The mention of Peter's lawyer broke the soothing spell I had been under.

"Look, I know you were hired to help Peter, but I need you to know that an insanity plea is out of the question. I don't want that for him," I said as she opened the door to her office.

"Tom, we've got a long way to go before we even get to that decision. But in the meantime, please think about family counseling. It'll do you both some good."

"I'll think about it" I agreed, catching a whiff of her floral perfume as I turned and walked out.

"You've gotta be kidding." I stopped in my tracks as I walked out of the medical building and stared at the Bugatti parked beside my cruiser. Bobby and Cornelius were standing in front of the expensive car, talking to Peter. I mentally counted backward from ten before I approached them—a trick I'd learned to manage my own anger.

"Listen, don't worry about it, Pete. I'll have my man Christopher check into it and handle whatever needs to be done," Bobby was saying.

"Thanks, Bobby. I appreciate you taking care of this for me," Peter replied.

"Taking care of what?" I asked.

Peter looked over at me. He opened and closed his mouth a few times, but nothing came out. I waited for him to find some words. I wanted to know every little detail about any dealings he had with Bobby.

"How you doing, Sergeant Lane?" Bobby stood with his hands crossed in front of him.

"I'm fine, Bobby. What are you doing here?" I asked, trying to remain cordial.

"Christopher told me about Pete's appointment today. Thought I'd swing by and make sure everything was good."

"Everything went fine," I told him. I wanted to follow up with "Now please fuck off," but I controlled myself.

"Yeah, yeah, that's what Pete said." Bobby nodded. "I'm glad. Since y'all are leaving, how about we head over to Dowling's and grab some steaks for lunch, my treat?"

"Yeah, I'm down," Peter answered excitedly.

A perfectly cooked porterhouse at one of the best restaurants in town was almost enough to make me accept the invitation, but going to lunch with Bobby and watching my son act like a starstruck fan was more than I could stomach.

"No, thanks. We need to get back to the house. Peter still has the monitor on."

"Dad, come on. I can go and have lunch. What's the problem?" Peter protested.

"The last thing you need right now is attention, and as soon as you step foot in that restaurant with the champ here, that's exactly what you're going to get. Right, Bobby?" I glanced over at him. "Folks are gonna wanna take pictures, sign autographs, and ask questions."

"This is true. People do love me," Bobby agreed.

"They do. But I know that you wanna do whatever's best for Peter. And right now, what's best is for us to keep a low profile." I looked Bobby in the eye to let him know I could not be manipulated.

"Your dad is right about this one, Pete." Bobby dropped his arms. "Go on home, and I promise, as soon as they take that damn ankle monitor off your leg, we gonna eat steak and lobster and anything else you want, man."

Peter looked disappointed, but he knew there was nothing he could do. "A'ight, cool."

"I'll holler at you later." Bobby dapped Peter, and I heard him whisper something but couldn't make out what he said. Cornelius opened the door of the Bugatti, and we waited for them to drive off before we got into the car.

"What was Bobby whispering about?" I asked Peter as we sat in the parking lot.

"Nothing," Peter mumbled, looking out the window.

"It had to be something. Did it have to do with what y'all were talking about when I walked to the car?" I pressed.

"It's nothing, Dad," Peter snapped. "He just wants me to keep my head up and know that he's got my back. That's all. I'm dealing with a lot, and Bobby is someone I trust and can talk to."

"You don't need to talk to him, Peter. I'm your father, and I'm right here to help."

"I get that. But you aren't Bobby Boyd. Some things you can't fix, and he can."

His words wounded me. "Like what?"

"Nothing, Dad. Let's just go. I'm hungry."

I started the ignition and pulled off, feeling the hairs on the back of my neck stand up. It was ironic that I'd just boasted to Dr. Wells about Peter talking to me about everything. Apparently, that wasn't the truth.

32

Malcolm Britton

I was determined to find out what the hell my father had going on, and since he wasn't willing to share any information, I decided to ask the next best person. I sat in my car parked across the street from his house and watched my father as he left Jeffrey's house. Once the coast was clear, I got out of my car, but before I could even start toward the house, another car whipped into Jeffrey's driveway.

"You've gotta be fucking kidding." I watched Everett get out of his late model Benz. I took quick, long strides toward him. "Everett!"

He turned, and our eyes locked momentarily, then he smirked. "Hello to you, Malcolm."

"Don't fucking 'hello' me," I snarled at him. We were close enough that I could knock him out if I'd wanted to try, but I didn't want to get his blood on my tailored suit or my silk tie.

"Is there a problem? Because I don't recall doing anything that would cause you to have an issue with me," he said.

Everett was dressed in a pair of slacks that barely touched his ankles, and a collared polo shirt with a sweater tied around his shoulders as if he were heading off for a day of boating. Unlike me, he didn't own a boat. He was just a pretentious prick who liked to look the part.

"What the hell do you have going on with my father?" I barked.

"Your father and I are business acquaintances, that's all. I'd think you'd be a little more respectful to one of the people responsible for helping your daddy finally come home," Everett said.

"Was that supposed to hurt my feelings? Because it didn't. You aren't responsible for shit. My father was always coming home, with or without you," I declared, even though I wasn't sure if that was true. In reality, my father had shared almost no information with me or my brother ever since he came home.

"I hate to tell you this, Malcolm, but Moses has been quite thankful for my assistance. Why do you think we've been spending so much time together?" Everett smirked. "Wait, is that why you're so upset? Because Moses and I have been hanging out?"

"No, I'm not upset. You're wrong."

"Oh my God, you're *jealous*. That's what it is. Malcolm Britton is jealous." He let out a self-satisfied chuckle.

"I think it's the other way around. You're jealous of me," I told him. Ever since we were young kids, Everett had always been a tag-along. He was annoying, like a gnat buzzing around the cool kids, and he'd never had the social status I enjoyed among the elite members of the Black Hamptons.

"No, not at all jealous," he said. "I do feel sorry for you, though."

His words confused me. In all my years, I'd never had anyone tell me they felt sorry for me. "I'm one of the most respected men in this town. Highly educated, a successful banking professional, proud father, and husband. Plus, I'm a Britton. Why the hell would you feel sorry for me?"

"Because here I am, living my best life out loud in front of the whole world, loving whoever I want. And all you are is a Britton. Have a good day, Malcolm." Everett turned to walk away, but I grabbed his arm. He glared at me and snatched it away. "What the fuck is your problem?"

"You're my problem. I swear to God—" I reached for him again.

"Malcolm, you need to calm down." Jeffrey rushed out of the house and pushed me back. "What is wrong with you?"

Everett shook his head at me. "Jeffrey, he's really bothered by my newfound friendship with Moses, as if I wouldn't want to be associated with one of the most admired, well-respected businessmen in this community."

"And that's why I'm so fucking bothered. My father is well respected, and you're not respected at all. People barely like you, mainly because you're a fraud," I said.

"Says you. Clearly someone likes me, and I'm not referring to Moses."

"Everett, enough. Let's go inside." Jeffrey put his hand on Everett's shoulder. "Malcolm, what did you need?"

"Nothing," I said. "Nothing at all."

"You sure?"

"I'm positive." I turned and headed back toward my car.

"Malcolm, wait," Everett called after me.

"What?" I spun around, waiting as he strolled swiftly toward me.

"I know that your father and I being cool is difficult for you. Maybe me telling you this well help ease some of your discombobulation." He stepped so close that he was speaking directly in my ear. "I'm well aware that Moses has no idea about your prior involvement with my fiancé. Don't worry. Your secret is safe with me, unless you do something to fuck it up. I'd stand down if I were you."

I imagined myself beating him to a pulp. It was the sly smile on his face that did it for me. However, I didn't want to be facing the same charges as my son's attacker. I clenched my fists so tightly that I could feel my nails digging into my palms.

Everett walked into the house, and Jeffrey closed the door behind them, leaving me standing there, fuming.

Instead of going into the office, my destination before I'd spotted my father leaving Jeffrey's house, I went home. There was no way I would get any work done. I was too furious.

"Malcolm, you're home," Vanessa said when she strolled into our bedroom suite and saw me there. "Is everything okay? I thought you were gone for the day."

"Everything's fine," I lied, taking off my suit jacket and snatching off my tie. "How's Jesse? Where is he?"

"He's fine. In his room playing that stupid video game." She took another good look at me. "Something's wrong, Malcolm. I see it all over your face. What is it? Is it your father?"

"No, it's not my father."

"Is it your mother? Wait, did you and Martin have another argument?"

"No, Vanessa. I told you I'm fine, damn it."

Vanessa's head snapped back. I didn't usually speak to her so harshly. She stared at me for a moment before picking up my tie from the floor and placing it on the bed.

"Vanessa, I'm sorry," I said, immediately regretting my knee-jerk response to her genuine concern. "You didn't deserve that."

"What the hell is going on?" she asked.

Lying to Vanessa was something I never did. One thing we'd always done, even after we were divorced, was keep it real with one another. She truly was my best friend, and I appreciated being able to share anything, even when it was something that could be potentially hurtful. Before we remarried, she'd even been willing to hear about my relationship with Morgan, no matter how much she disliked it.

"I just had it out with Everett," I admitted.

"Everett? Really, Malcolm?" Vanessa didn't try to hide the disappointment on her face.

"It's not what you think, baby. I swear." I put my hands on her shoulder. "It didn't have anything to do with Morgan."

"Then what was it about?"

"My father. I don't trust Everett around him."

"Have you talked to Moses abut this?" Vanessa softened a little, but not much.

"I tried, but he acts as if it's no big deal. Apparently, Everett helped with this Venezuela situation and that's it. But they've been meeting up with Jeffrey, and I know there's something going on." I sat on the edge of the bed.

Vanessa sat beside me. "Listen, I know you're trying to protect your dad, but maybe the reason your dad isn't telling you what's going on is because he's trying to protect *you*."

"What do you mean?" I turned to look at her. "You think it's foul play?"

"No, that's not what I'm saying, Malcolm. I honestly don't know. But if Moses isn't talking to you about it, there must be a valid reason. You are your father's pride and joy. He wouldn't ice you out if it wasn't warranted."

My wife's rationale made a lot of sense, but I wasn't totally convinced. There was a feeling that I couldn't shake.

"I hear you," I told her. "But . . ."

"And Malcolm, we are talking about Everett. Have you considered that maybe he's just spending time with Moses to get under your skin?"

I blinked as her words processed. I hadn't even considered that until she mentioned it. Everett's obnoxious behavior wasn't new to me, so it was quite possible that he was leveraging the current situation with my father and his engagement to my ex to provoke me.

Vanessa put her hand on the side of my face and continued. "What I do know, babe, is that Moses being home is a good thing, and you should focus on that instead of Everett. Not to mention all of the other priorities our family has going on right now. Forget about that little pest."

"You're right." I leaned over and kissed her softly. "Do you know how much I love and appreciate you?"

"I do." She smiled. "But it's nice to be reminded."

We kissed again, only separating when my cell phone vibrated in my pocket. I had no intention of answering it. Instead, I wanted to spend some alone time with my wife. To my surprise, she reached into my pocket and retrieved it for me.

"But—"

"Another time, baby. There's too much going on for you to be ignoring your phone."

She handed me the phone, which was still vibrating, and I recognized the phone number of the DA's office. I quickly swiped to answer before the call could go to voicemail.

"Hey, Mr. Griggs. How are you?"

"I'm good, Mr. Britton. Thanks for asking."

"I'm sure you're calling to update me about the case," I said.

Vanessa tapped my arm and mouthed the words, "Additional charges."

I nodded at her. "Specifically, the additional charges against Peter Lane."

"Yes, sir, that's exactly why I'm calling. There have been some developments in your son's case," DA Griggs said. "The findings in our investigation have resulted in an amendment of the charges."

"That's great," I said.

"Hold on, Mr. Britton, before you get ahead of yourself. Things have taken a drastic turn, and I wanted you to hear it from me first."

"What do you mean? What's changed?" I asked, sensing that whatever he was about to say would not be good.

"What's he saying?" Vanessa whispered, leaning closer to try to hear the call.

"Maybe you and your wife should come down to my office so I can explain in detail," Griggs said uneasily.

33

Carolyn Britton

Out of all the brunch options in town, the Sag Harbor Country Club was my favorite. The dining room exuded an air of refined elegance. The tables were covered in crisp white linen, impeccably set with polished silver, fine china, and crystal glassware. The hushed ambiance with only an occasional clink of cutlery and mellow conversations never failed to provide an atmosphere of exclusivity that I enjoyed.

"I guess it's safe to say you were wrong about Moses and his diabolical plan," Lamont said as he sat across from me, looking like money in his well-tailored suit.

We'd spent the majority of the morning discussing business, eating, and enjoying the panoramic view of the lush, manicured golf course outside as a skilled musician played a grand piano on the opposite side of the room.

"That's quite presumptive and premature for you to think," I told him. "The man hasn't even been home for a month. Trust me, just because he hasn't made his move yet doesn't mean he isn't going to. I've known Moses Britton longer than you've been alive. He's making moves in silence."

"Come on now, Carolyn." Lamont gave me a doubtful look. "You said it yourself that he's been nothing but a gentleman and devoted husband since his return. If I had to guess, I'd say he's just happy to be back home."

"And that's exactly what he wants everyone, especially me, to believe. But I know better. I'm not stupid or naive."

"You mean to tell me that there isn't some tiny part of you that's glad he's back? It's okay, you can be honest with me."

I stared at Lamont, wondering why the sudden concern about my feelings regarding my husband. We'd never discussed my marriage before, and I certainly didn't want it to be the topic of conversation now.

"Lamont, you're not jealous, are you?" I asked, both flattered and slightly amused by his sudden interest in the state of my conjugality.

"Jealous?" Lamont sat back in his seat. "No, Carolyn, I am far from jealous. Don't get me wrong, I enjoy the time that we spend together, and it's truly special to me, and so are you. But I'm well aware that it is what it is."

"Well, let me be clear about something, Mr. Hudson." I rubbed my foot softly along his leg under the table. "You are just as special to me. I appreciate you as well, and I'm not just saying that because I keep you on retainer."

"Good, then we understand each other." Lamont smiled.

"We do." I nodded. "But I'm still going to need you to keep close tabs on Moses and his business dealings. I don't trust him. He's been spending quite a lot of time with Jeffrey and that damn Everett Simpson, and we all know how much of a snake that man is."

"I have been. The people I know that are or have been business associates of Everett say the only thing he's been talking about lately is his engagement."

"Well, that's one problem he's taken off my hand. I guess I should be grateful," I mumbled as I took a sip of my coffee. Everett being engaged to Morgan was definitely an unexpected blessing.

"What do you mean?"

"Nothing," I answered quickly.

"Well, I need to get over to the church. Reverend Chauncey is expecting me." Lamont stood.

"You know you don't have to do that." I motioned toward the check that he'd picked up off the table. "I invited you to this meeting, remember?"

"You did." He nodded. "Which is why this will be a tax write off."

"How convenient for you." I laughed. "We'll speak later."

"We will," he said, giving my shoulders a gentle squeeze as he walked away.

I hadn't planned to become involved with the young, handsome attorney who happened to be the son of one of my closest friends and business associates. What started out as casual conversations at social events turned into an occasional drink at a bar after a meeting. One night, after a bit of tipsy flirting, a pleasurable sexual encounter on the rooftop of a parking garage happened. It was so . . . hot, spontaneous, and exhilarating, something I hadn't experienced since Moses left. I didn't even consider what we were doing an affair, really. It was just "spending time." Time that I really, really enjoyed.

"Carolyn, how nice to see you."

I didn't realize I was so deep in my own thoughts until I heard my name. I looked over and was shocked to see Eli Bradshaw of all people standing at the table, smiling at me. Once my shock wore off, it was quickly replaced by disgust.

"Excuse me, I'm leaving." I grabbed my purse from the back of my chair.

"My apologies. I saw you sitting here, and I was just trying to speak. It's good to see you."

"I can't say the same, Eli." I stood up so fast that I bumped into the table, nearly tipping over the drinks on top.

"Now, Carolyn, why the hostility? That's not very neighborly of you." Eli had the audacity to look hurt.

"You're not my neighbor, so I don't owe you shit," I said, looking him up and down.

"That's not true. We live in the same neighborhood."

"You own a house in the neighborhood, Eli. One that you don't even live in. Don't stand here and attempt to pander to me. You're not a neighbor to anyone around here."

"I guess this attitude of yours is because of the properties I've acquired," Eli said nonchalantly.

"Acquired? You mean poached. A pleasantry from me would be a stretch. The only thing I want to give you is my ass to kiss."

Eli shook his head. "I'm really surprised by this behavior, Carolyn. You're a businesswoman. You of all people should understand my recent property acquisitions. The economy has taken a hit over the past few years, and I'm just taking advantage of the opportunities to recover, that's all."

"Oh, you're taking advantage all right. But you're not recovering. You're raping and pillaging," I snapped at him.

Eli's jaw dropped, and I stepped closer, so he knew I wasn't intimidated by him in any shape, form, or fashion. "I'm not going to just sit back and let you do this. This little plan that you think you have going on is going to fail, and you're going to go down right along with it."

"There is no plan, Carolyn. We may not be neighbors, as you say, but there's one thing we have in common."

"And what's that?" I asked.

"We are both strategists."

"Well, let this be your notice that my strategy will be to drive your ass right out of our community, so you either leave willingly or not." Moses's voice came over my shoulder before he stepped beside me.

Eli was just as shocked to see my husband appear out of thin air as I was. The only difference was that he let his shock show on his face. He fumbled over his words before the ones he wanted finally landed on his tongue.

"That sounds like a threat, Moses."

"I don't make threats. Only promises," Moses told him, then took my hand and led me away.

I let him take me to the lobby of the country club before I stopped and removed my hand from his. I quickly regained my bearings because as much as I hated to admit it, Eli had really ruffled my feathers. I smoothed down my skirt and looked up at my husband.

"Thank you, but I had that under control," I told him. "Eli doesn't scare me."

"The last thing I'm worried about is him or anyone else intimidating you," Moses replied. "I wasn't stepping in to protect you. I just needed Eli to understand that it's not just you he's going up against. It's *us*."

"What are you doing here, Moses?" I asked, ignoring his wannabe gallant act.

"I came to talk to you," he said. "Ironically, about the situation with Eli Bradshaw. How did the meeting with Reverend Chauncey and Lamont go? I saw Lamont leaving when I pulled in."

"It went well. He, uh, they just left," I said, telling myself that it wasn't a total lie, but a half-truth.

"Good." Moses nodded as he grabbed my elbow and eased me toward the corner of the room, away from anyone that could hear us talking. "Because you might not be intimidated by Eli, but he's making a game of intimidating others. Mainly those who are on the verge of losing their homes. Unlike you, he's offering to help them."

"What the hell are you talking about?"

"I'm talking about Valencia Burnett and her tax issues."

"Oh, that." I sighed.

"*Oh, that*. Is that all you have to say, Carolyn?" he hissed. "You do realize that property sits on one of the largest pieces of land in the Black Hamptons, right? And before you tell me about the situation with Jesse and her granddaughter, I already know about it."

"Then you understand why I said no when she came to me." I folded my arms.

"I do," he said, "but all of that should've been put on the back burner once you found out about Eli snatching up homes. Personal vendettas and innuendos can be handled later. I taught you better than that."

I hated to admit it, but Moses was right. I hadn't even considered Valencia or her tax situation until he'd brought it up. Now wasn't the time for me to be contentious. "Fine. I'll go and handle it now."

"If you'd like, I can go and talk to Valen—"

"I have no problem handling it, Moses," I interrupted. "But, like you said, this is business, and the interest rate she'll have to pay will not be market value. It'll be higher."

Moses grinned. "I wouldn't expect anything less.

"I'll see you back at the house later."

"Of course." He kissed my cheek, and I adjusted his tie.

If I didn't know any better, I might have thought that Lamont was correct in his assumption that Moses was not secretly planning something devious. But I *did* know better, and more so, I knew Moses. I would have to keep an eye on him, but it was good to have him in the fight to save the Black Hamptons for Black families.

"Carolyn." Valencia stood in her doorway with her arms folded.

I was taken aback by the disdainful look on her face as she stared at me. It certainly wasn't the demeanor she'd had weeks before when she approached me for help. The warmth had been replaced with a chilly reception that was far from welcoming.

"Hello, Valencia. I came by to discuss the financial situation you're having with the house." I hoped that my statement would prompt her to invite me inside. Instead, she remained at the doorway, her expression unreadable. The air between us hung with tension as I stood outside.

"That's interesting, Carolyn. Why now?" she asked, her tone cool and detached.

"Valencia, the day we talked, it was emotional for me. Moses had just come home, and I'd just been to the bail hearing. I wasn't in the best of moods, and I probably spoke out of emotion," I explained. "Things have calmed a bit . . ."

"You being here wouldn't happen to be because of Eli Bradshaw, would it?" Valencia leaned against the doorway.

"You deserve to keep your home. I want to help."

"I don't need your help," she asserted.

"Fine. Amistad wants to help," I offered.

"Well, I appreciate that." For the first time since I'd arrived, Valencia smiled. "But I don't need Amistad's help either. It's too late. My financial situation, as you refer to it, is resolved."

Shocked by what she'd said, I stared blankly. "My God, Valencia, you sold to Eli?"

"Thanks for stopping by." Valencia closed the door in my face.

"Damn it." I rushed back toward my car that was sitting in Valencia's driveway. As soon as I got inside, I called Lamont, trying not to panic. Talking to Valencia should have been the first thing I'd done once I learned about Eli and his plans. Instead, I'd let my feelings dictate my choices.

"Hello." He answered on the first ring.

"Lamont, we've got a problem. A big one."

34

Sydney Johnson

Hiring a new landscape designer had skyrocketed to the top of my priority list, especially given the state of our backyard. It was a hot mess to say the least. Sections were taped off and areas were dug up, courtesy of Rashid, who I'd relieved of his duties. Finding a replacement, however, proved to be more challenging than I anticipated, because at the peak of summer, most professionals were already booked. There was also my insistence on securing only the best for the job. I was determined to still have a backyard space we could all genuinely enjoy. Admittedly, Rashid had planted a seed of inspiration with his suggestion of a tropical oasis featuring a spa and hot tub. The vision had grown on me so much that it had turned into a desire bordering on obsession.

Sitting in the family room with my iPad on my lap, I was scouring the web for another reputable landscape design company. I had been at it for what seemed like hours and hadn't gotten up once, not even when I felt the rumbling of my stomach. The only thing that made me look up from the screen was when I heard someone enter through the front door.

"Gabby, is that you?" I called out, expecting to hear my daughter answer back.

"No, it's me." Karrin's voice echoed through the house.

Moments later, she entered the room, dressed in a striking black floral ruffled sundress. I couldn't help but notice that it was the same dress I had in my Anthropologie online shopping cart, a luxury I doubted she could afford.

"Well, look who finally came home." I set aside the iPad and sat up on the oversized, comfortable sofa where I'd spent most of the day. Despite our daily texts and phone chats, I hadn't seen Karrin in days.

"Home?" Karrin laughed as she plopped down beside me. "Didn't your husband tell me not to get comfortable while I was here because this isn't where I live?"

"Girl, please. You know your home is wherever mine is. You'll always have a place here. Fuck him. I've always told you that."

She gasped. "Whoa, do I sense some hostility? Not Mrs. My Man, My Man, My Man."

"Whatever." I smirked. "Sounds like you're the one with the man now. I see you in your couture. Nice dress."

Karrin stretched her legs and smoothed her hands against the soft fabric of her dress. "Isn't it gorgeous? Bobby got it for me. And get this. He's treating me to a shopping spree today. I came by to grab some of my stuff, and then I'm hitting the stores in town. You should come with me."

"Wait, so you're moving in with him?"

"I wouldn't call it moving in," Karrin replied. "More like hanging out at the crib. We're still getting to know each other. So far, so good, though."

"I bet. And exactly what have you learned about Mr. Bobby 'The Beast' Boyd other than he's a big spender?" I gave her a knowing look. Karrin's dating history wasn't the greatest, mainly because she preferred money over morals. "Wait, don't tell me. Spending isn't the only big thing about him."

Karrin laughed. "I've definitely had bigger. He's a'ight, but he's better in the boxing ring than he is in bed."

"Damn, sis." I giggled. "That's not good."

"No, but everything else is. So, I'll get a rose or something and deal with it," Karrin said. "I can definitely afford one, or something even better. You know they have these ones made out of glass that are supposed to be absolutely divine."

"A glass sex toy? That doesn't sound very safe. I wouldn't want anything shattering in my my honey pot." I shuddered at the thought.

"They're made of Pyrex or something, fool. They're unbreakable." Karrin playfully pushed my arm.

"I'm just saying, you don't have to settle, Karrin. I know that Bobby has money and splurges, but you deserve more than that. You deserve someone who can—"

"Don't." Karrin stood. "I'm with Bobby now. He can provide me with everything I need, and I don't want anyone else."

"I hear you, sis. I'm just saying you deserve someone that makes you feel special, like you're made for each other."

"Bobby does make me feel special. Do you see this?" Karrin reached into the top of her dress, pulling out a diamond-encrusted *BTB* chain. "It doesn't get any more special than this."

"That is pretty special," I said, admiring the custom pendant hanging around her neck.

It was obvious that Bobby was spoiling my sister, and she was enjoying it, but the sparkle she'd had in her eyes when she was with her mystery boo was missing now. As much as I wanted her to be taken care of financially, I also wanted her to be happy, and there is no happiness like when a woman is madly in love.

"Enough about my man. Where's yours?"

"Not here, and I don't know." I picked up my glass and took a sip of my wine. "He's been making himself scarce the past few days, and I'm glad."

Karrin frowned. "Scarce? Where's he been going?"

"Like I said, I don't know. Honestly, I haven't even asked," I told her. "Now that this Singh deal is back in place, I figure he's back to the same long-ass office hours he promised he wouldn't work anymore."

"I mean, the man does run a multimillion-dollar company, Syd. You're the one who always said if you wanna be with a rich man, be ready to be with a busy one, right?" Karrin reminded me.

"Yeah, that's true."

"And what have you been doing since you're home alone?" She sat back down beside me.

I picked up my iPad and showed her the websites that I'd been looking at before her arrival. "Trying to find someone to finish the back yard."

"I still can't believe you fired the fine-ass dude Anthony hired." Karrin shook her head as she looked at the screen. "I know you said you knew each other back in the day, but you still didn't say why you didn't like him. I get that you said he couldn't be trusted, but you never said why."

I tensed, regretting that the conversation had somehow turned to the one subject I didn't want to discuss. "It doesn't matter why. I was already uncomfortable with him being at the house, Then he went too far when he started talking to my children. I did what was best."

Karrin looked over at me as if she wanted to ask more questions, then simply said, "I get that."

"I'm still mad at the fact that Anthony would even hire someone without consulting me first. If I did some shit like that, he would lose his mind."

"I think he was trying to maybe surprise you, Syd."

"Surprise me with a strange man who would be spending extended lengths of time at our home? What kind of surprise is that?" I snapped without meaning to.

"Like I said, I get it."

The doorbell rang, giving both of us a much-needed distraction from the conversation. She hopped to her feet, rushing out of the room. "I'll get it."

While she went to the door, I went into the kitchen and poured myself a glass of wine. As I sipped, I stared at the bottle and smiled, remembering the pleasant conversation that I'd shared with Moses Britton. He was so easy to talk to, and he'd crossed my mind several times over the past few days. I was eager to speak with him again, this time to ask him more in-depth questions, mainly how the hell he ended up with that bear of a wife.

"My God, Syd, did you have to order a whole damn case?" Karrin groaned as she pushed a cardboard box across the kitchen floor.

"Why are you dragging that on my floors? You do realize they're marble, don't you?"

"I'm sorry, but this thing is heavy. I just got my nails done, and I ain't trying to break them."

"What is it?"

"It's wine. You ordered it, didn't you? It's got your name on it."

"Hell no, I didn't order it," I said, walking over to get a closer look. "I love wine, but not enough to order a whole damn case. Help me put it up here."

Sydney and I stood on each side of the box and lifted it onto the kitchen island. I grabbed the utility scissors out of the nearby drawer and used them to carefully slit open the top of the box.

I pulled the flap back and gasped. "No fucking way."

"What is it?" Karrin asked, peeking inside.

I took out one of the bottles and stared at the label. "This is not just any kind of wine. This is fucking Rothschild. It's like two grand a bottle."

"Syd, it's six bottles in here." Karrin looked shocked. "You ordered twelve thousand dollars worth of wine? Are you crazy?"

"I told you I didn't order it."

"Wait, there's a card in here." Karrin went to open the card, but I snatched it from her.

"Stop it, nosey."

"Girl, please." Karrin laughed. "I'm going upstairs to get my stuff. I have a shopping spree to enjoy."

"Yeah, you do that," I told her, waiting until she was gone to open the envelope. When I was alone, I slipped out the card embossed with the Rothschild label.

The words at the bottom were simple: "*Sweet wine for the sweetest lady. Enjoy sipping.*" There was no signature, but I knew exactly who the wine was from, and it wasn't Anthony.

It had taken everything within me to gather the nerve to venture across the parcel of land that separated the Britton mansion from ours. Once Karrin was packed and out the door, I went onto the balcony of our bedroom to make sure there were no signs of Carolyn, who was usually posted up on her own balcony. I also confirmed that none of the cars that she traveled in were parked in their usual spots in the circular driveway. The coast was clear. My heart beat faster with every step I took toward my neighbor's house. Never in a million years would I have imagined that I'd be making a social visit, but there I was.

As luck would have it, I didn't even make it to the front door before Moses seemed to appear out of nowhere.

"Well, isn't this a nice surprise?"

"Where in the world did you come from?" I asked, turning toward where he stood.

"Back there." He pointed toward the side of the house as he walked toward me.

"Oh. Hello, Moses. I was actually coming to see you."

"Were you?"

"Yes, I got your amazing gift. Thank you so much," I said sincerely. "You didn't have to do that."

"You're right, I didn't. I wanted to, and the more you get to know me, the more you'll learn that I always do what I want."

"I'm sure you do," I said. "It was a lavish gift, though. And as much as I'd like to, I don't know if I can accept it."

"Of course you can," Moses said with an amused frown. "It's just a box of wine."

I shook my head. "It's more than that."

"Nonsense. Actually, I have something I'd like to show you. Come with me." He turned in the direction that he'd come from.

I glanced back at my house and hesitated for a beat before following after him. We walked along a graveled path that led to a discreet wooden door. The door didn't even look like it belonged on the massive estate. It didn't have a doorknob from what I could see, but Moses eased it open.

"Come in," he said.

The cool air hit me first, and the rich aroma of wine immediately after, when I stepped inside. I descended a tiny staircase that led to another solid, wooden door that was already opened. Behind it was a dimly lit space adorned with custom-built wine racks. The racks, crafted from dark mahogany, lined the walls, each holding meticulously arranged bottles of the finest vintages. Soft LED lighting accentuated the labels, offering a glimpse into a collection that was rare and exceptional.

"Oh my . . ." My voice trailed off as I admired what had to be the most extensive wine cellar I'd ever been in.

"Welcome to my escape room." Moses held his arms out and turned around.

"Escape room?" I continued to take in the opulence of the room. Not only was there a tasting table strategically placed in the center, but there was also a cozy sitting area nestled in the corner, with plush leather chairs and a small table. I could envision intimate gatherings where discussions about the merits of a Bordeaux or the depth of a Cabernet Sauvignon could unfold.

"Yep. Everyone needs a place to escape. Some men have man caves. I have this. It's my hideaway."

"This is one helluva place to escape," I said. "I love it. It's incredible."

"I knew you'd appreciate it. That's why I wanted you to see it. Not everyone recognizes how special it is." Moses reached onto one of the racks and selected a bottle. "My better half calls it my wine storage space."

I laughed. "Oh, it's much more than that. Is it climate controlled?"

"It is." Moses placed an aerator into the bottle after opening it, then poured two glasses. He swirled them both before passing one to me. "Salud."

"Salud." I tapped my glass against his, then held the glass to my nose to inhale the aroma. "This is incredible. Opus One."

"You're good, Sydney." He gave me a pleased smile.

"This is a wine lover's dream space," I said, taking a sip. "You're one lucky man, Moses Britton."

"Thank you. Now that you know where it is, if you ever need to escape, feel free. I don't mind sharing, especially with someone who loves it as much as I do."

"I appreciate the offer. I doubt if I'd ever be bold enough to come over and risk running into the lady of the house," I said, surprising myself with my honesty.

"Well, if you ever gather the courage," he joked, "it's all yours."

I took another sip of my wine, enjoying both the taste and the intriguing man who'd poured it.

35

Leslie Bowen

I didn't lie to Uncle Moses, but I hadn't been fully forthcoming either. I wasn't sure yet whether both parties were enthusiastic about the offer Aries made to buy Lisa Pruitt's house. Aries and I had met with her, and he was instantly captivated by the grand architectural masterpiece. The mansion boasted a symmetrical design with towering columns framing the entrance, fulfilling every aspect of Aries's desires and more. From the ample bedrooms to the lavish kitchen, formal living and dining rooms, private terrace, and pool, the property had it all. Aries wasted no time. After our tour, we rushed back to my office and promptly submitted an offer slightly above the asking price.

Lisa had seemed just as enthusiastic as Aries about closing the deal as soon as possible. However, when she hadn't responded to the bid after two days, I knew something was up. I decided to pay Lisa another visit, and Aries said he wanted to go with me.

"You think she's changed her mind about selling?" Aries asked as we walked along the winding driveway lined with meticulously manicured hedges and lush greenery.

"I don't know what to think at this point."

"You look pretty, by the way," he said, glancing at me from the corner of his eye. "Emerald is definitely your color."

"Thank you, Aries." I blushed.

I had to admit the pantsuit I wore was hitting on something that day. It hugged every curve on my body while respectfully covering it up. One thing I'd quickly learned about Aries was despite knowing that I was happily married, he had no problem complimenting me. The flattering comments were random, polite, and never disrespectful. It was the look in his eyes when he said it that made me aware of how attracted to me he was. I wasn't naïve, nor would I pretend to be, which was why I was certain he knew the attraction was mutual. And *that* was what made it inappropriate.

"You're welcome." He gently took my elbow to guide me along the sweeping staircase and led to the front entrance. "This place is incredible."

"That it is." I rang the doorbell and watched through the arched windows in the front of the home, hoping to see Lisa, but there was no sign of her. "Maybe I should've called first."

Just as I began to second-guess the impromptu visit, Lisa came to the door. "You've got some nerve showing up here, Leslie."

"Huh? What do you mean?" I was taken aback.

Lisa folded her ams tightly against her chest, looking past me to Aries, then back at me. "Why did you tell me my house is only worth two million dollars?"

"Because it is," I answered.

"Well, someone made me an offer for three."

My heart sank. "Eli Bradshaw. That's who made the offer, isn't it? You can't sell the house to him, Lisa."

"Why not? Do you know what I could do with that amount of money?" Lisa asked, her voice an octave higher.

"It's not about the money," I said, trying to remain calm. Lisa looked at me like I was crazy, and I added, "Okay, it's not just about the money."

"What the hell else is it about?"

"Lisa, you love this house," I reminded her.

"I used to love this house until I found out my husband had that tramp of a mistress all up and through here when I wasn't home," Lisa snapped. Then she lowered her voice as she glanced around. "Come in. There's no sense in y'all standing there having this conversation. The neighbors talk about my divorce enough as it is."

Lisa disappeared, leaving the door open. I looked at Aries and shrugged, then went inside the house with him following me. Lisa hadn't gone far. She stood waiting in the foyer at the bottom of the spiraling staircase. A chandelier adorned with crystal prisms hung elegantly from the high ceiling, casting a warm glow over the marble floors below.

"Lisa, what Benji did was wrong. Dead-ass wrong." I resumed the conversation. "But there's something bigger at stake here. You do realize Eli is going to tear your house down, right?"

Lisa frowned. "He didn't say that."

"And your precious garden. The one that was featured in the *Sag Harbor Gazette* last summer. If Eli Bradshaw gets his hands on this house, all of your hard work will be destroyed," I added for effect.

Lisa was unmoved by my dramatic predictions. "Leslie, I know you don't get this, but the money from this house is going to give me a fresh start. Three million dollars is a hell of a lot more than the two point one you offered me."

Aries spoke up. "Fine. I'll pay three point one. Cash."

"What?" Lisa and I asked at the same time.

"Eli offered three. I'll pay you another hundred thousand," Aries said. "You already know that I love this house. I promise I won't tear anything down, and I'll make sure that garden remains pristine. But you have to accept the offer right now."

"Are you sure about this?" I whispered to Aries.

"Very," he said, giving me a reassuring smile. "But only if you sign the paperwork within an hour."

"Well, Lisa?" I asked her.

"I . . . I mean, if he's serious . . ." She stammered, clearly just as shocked as I was. "I . . . I'll sign it. The house is yours."

"Great!" He walked over to Lisa and extended his hand.

She shook it first, then hugged him tightly. "Thank you."

"Alrighty then," I said, still in a state of disbelief. "I guess I need to get to the office and send the new offer. You'll have it within the hour, Lisa."

"How about I just come to the office now and we take care of everything?" Lisa offered.

I laughed. "That sounds great."

Lisa walked us to the door, promising to meet us at the office after she called her attorney. She hugged each of us once more before we walked out. I was happy that the impromptu meeting had gone so well, but I was still in shock.

"Uh, congratulations?" I said while we walked to our cars.

"You don't know how excited I am." Aries grinned. "This house is so dope."

"I really can't believe you just did that."

"Why not?"

"That's a lot of money, especially cash."

"It's not a problem," he said casually, as if he were paying extra for a front row concert ticket instead of a multimillion-dollar home. "You know I fell in love with this house the first time you brought me here."

"You did," I agreed.

"I told you that first day that I'm a man of action. When I want something, I do whatever I have to do to get it," he said, looking intensely in my eyes.

I loved my husband, and until recently, I had never looked at another man, but Aries's playful flirting was surely putting ideas in my head. However, I had no intention of betraying my vows. My feelings toward Aries would have to remain what they were: a girlish crush. I took the key fob out of my purse because I wanted to get out of there before he found a way to change my mind.

"Well, you certainly were successful today." I shifted from one leg to the other. "Thank you. You helped save the Black Hamptons."

"It's official now. We'll be neighbors."

"We will," I said, wondering if that might be a dangerous thing. "Well, I guess we should get going so we can get this paperwork ready."

"And then we can go celebrate, I hope." Aries smiled. "Your treat since you just made a huge commission."

I chuckled. "Really, Aries?"

"Dead ass. I'm thinking a nice lobster tail and a bottle of bubbly would be perfect to celebrate the occasion."

"As much as I'd love to do that, I already have plans this evening," I told him. The disappointed look on his face made me feel bad, and I never wanted a client to walk away unhappy. "But I am excited that you have your dream home and that we'll be neighbors. We'll celebrate another time, okay?"

"Deal," he said, holding my gaze.

"Y'all are still here?" Lisa called out to us as she walked out the front door.

"We're leaving now," I told her, then glanced once more at Aries before getting in my car. "I'll see you at my office."

An hour later, the deal was done, and parties on all sides were happy. When they stepped out of my office, I stayed behind to gather all my things. My phone rang with Jeffrey's ringtone, and I felt a tinge of excitement thinking about our upcoming night on the town. Now we had something to celebrate other than our love.

"Hey, baby." I answered my cell. "Guess what? My client bought Lisa Pruitt's house."

"What? That's great, baby!" Jeffrey responded.

"I know." I balanced the phone as I grabbed the iPad and portfolio off my desk, tossing them into my bag. "I'm just finishing up and getting out of here. I'll be home in ten minutes, and we can head to dinner."

"Les, baby, listen," he started. "I—"

I stopped him before he could say another word, knowing he was about to give me some lame-ass excuse for canceling the plans we'd made. "Jeffrey, no. We talked about these dinner reservations this morning."

"I know, and I'm sorry. I'm stuck in the city, and I'm probably going to have to stay here tonight."

"You are starting to piss me off," I said loudly, then remembered that Aries and Lisa were outside my office door.

"I promise I'm going to make it up to you."

"I'm tired of hearing that shit, Jeffrey," I said more quietly. "But you know what? Fine. Don't even worry about it. I have people waiting on me." I ended the call and threw the phone into my purse.

Once again, Jeffrey had done the great escape—no, I couldn't even call it that because we hadn't even made it to dinner before he bailed. I was livid once again about being stood up. It was becoming a trend, and I was starting to feel taken for granted.

For months, I'd been very tolerant of his unavailability, and once I learned that it was because he'd been helping Uncle Moses, I was grateful. But there came a time to draw the line. Him staying out overnight was crazy, and now my entire mood was ruined. Gone was the excitement I'd felt after helping Aries buy Lisa's house, and that was major for me. The one person I wanted to celebrate with couldn't care less because he, as he'd been doing a lot lately, put himself first.

I snatched up the rest of my belongings, turned off the lights, and closed the door behind me. I took a deep breath, suppressing my disappointment as I forced a smile on my face before I continued into the waiting area.

"Ready to go?" I asked before I noticed that Aries was standing alone. "Where's Lisa?"

"She left a few minutes ago. Said she had to get back to her garden before the sun set." He laughed. "I didn't want you walking out of here alone, so I stuck around."

"I appreciate that."

"Ready? I know you said you have plans."

"I did, but they've changed," I said not able to contain my eye roll.

"I'm sorry to hear that. You know my offer is still on the table if you didn't want to go home."

I hesitated as I stared up into his dazzling eyes. On one hand, I knew Aries liked me, so going out with him would be playing with fire. But on the other hand, it wasn't my fault that Jeffrey flaked on me again. Why rob myself of a good time with a fine man *and* some good food?

"You're on. You did say you always get what you want," I said with a laugh.

"Emphasis on 'always.' Let's get out of here."

As we walked out of the building, I set aside my guilty conscience. It was just a dinner with a client, something that I often did, and also, there was no point in wasting perfectly good dinner reservations, right?

36

Karrin Wilkes

They say that the way to a man's heart is through his stomach. Well, the fastest way to my heart was through a credit card that didn't decline, and shopping with Bobby's money filled my heart with so much joy. I loved that he was ready, willing, and able to buy me whatever I wanted. It was funny. The awkward altercation near the bathrooms during our first date had actually played in my favor. After dinner, we went back to his place and were snuggled by the firepit when he asked about Martin.

"A couple of months ago, I came to visit my sister and her family for a couple of weeks. I met Martin and we started dating, so I stayed longer," I explained. "Now that we're broken up, there's no reason for me to stay any longer."

"Like hell. You do have a reason to stay, a big one. Me," Bobby said.

I chuckled. "We just met, Bobby. How do you even know you want me to stay around?"

"I know a good thing when I see one. And looking at you, I already know that you're damn good," he said with a seductive look.

I licked my lips and smiled. "I can't argue with that. But I still can't stay. My brother-in-law gave me a time limit, and I've already been here past that deadline."

"Fuck him. You can stay with me. That makes things easier for both of us. I like having my women close to me."

"I guess I can hang out here for a few days," I lied, knowing that I planned on being there indefinitely. Bobby Boyd was the lick I'd dreamed of hitting, and there was no way I was going to mess it up.

"Good." Bobby pulled me closer, and we shared a kiss so passionate that I nearly melted.

His tongue danced in my mouth, and the moment his hands started exploring my body, I felt my skin heat up. Tingling shot from the crown of my head to my toes and back again. I knew I was about to do what I did best, and to ensure he knew what time it was, I pushed him back and straddled him. I didn't care that we were outside. If anybody could see, I hoped they enjoyed the show.

As he lay back, staring up at me in awe, I took off my top and gave him the perfect view of my perky breasts. He cupped them with his hands, allowing his fingers to slightly pinch my nipples. Anyone who loves sex the way I do knows that there is such a thin line between pleasure and pain. I hissed and felt the pleasured grimace come onto my face. I was horny, so horny that I didn't even care about foreplay. I was more interested in the hole in one.

We undressed each other, and when I went to slide his hard third leg into my slippery canal, he surprised me by flipping me over onto my back. I couldn't lie, it turned me on. Even more so when I saw and felt his muscular body on top of mine. From what seemed like thin air, he pulled out a condom and put it on, making me respect him even more.

"I don't need any little Beasts running around anytime soon," he told me, spreading my legs by my thighs and kissing me at the same moment he thrusted inside of me.

No, Bobby wasn't the biggest or the best in bed, but he satisfied me there and outside of it, and I knew I'd done the same for him. I didn't need him to tell me how good I was, but giving me his Black Amex card was a nice gesture.

I didn't use it right away because I didn't want him to think I was like most women when they dated a millionaire. Trust me, I could run up a tab, but I wanted to move differently with Bobby.

"Why haven't you used the Black card yet?" he asked a couple days later.

"Don't worry. I will when I really need something," I told him while we were cuddled in bed again. "Right now, I have everything I need. You."

Bobby looked down at me and grinned. “You really feeling The Beast, huh?”

“No.” I told him. “I’m feeling Bobby.”

“Damn, I don’t think any chick has ever said that to me.” The look in his eyes was a mixture of surprise and joy. “You really are something else. That chump Martin Britton sure did me a favor dropping your ass, because I ain’t never letting you go.”

Finally, I was being treated the way I deserved to be, and I wanted to enjoy it. Every time I found myself comparing him with Martin, I reminded myself of all that Bobby was giving me. Not only that, but he was treating me right *and* loving me out loud.

Although I was trying to play it cool with Bobby, there were a few things that I wanted and that he could afford. I wanted to work my way up to asking for them, though. As I stood in the mirror in the dressing room, trying on an expensive Versace dress, I wondered if it was what I should wear when I asked him to buy me a car. It was black, lowcut in the front, and had ties on the sides of my thighs. All eyes would be on me if I stepped out in it, but I was only worried about his gaze. I took off the dress, knowing I was going to get it, and then tried on a bathing suit.

“Baby, you like this?” I asked when I Facetimed Bobby to give him a sneak peek of what he was paying for.

My phone was angled so that he had a full view. The suit fit like a glove, and I made sure my ass cheeks were visible and my nipples were noticeably hardened. Another way to a man’s heart was through his pants, and I knew it. His reaction confirmed it.

“Hell yeah, I like it.” Bobby licked his lips. “You look good as fuck.”

“Black, gold, or blue? Which one should I get?” I posed.

“Get all three, baby. That way I can choose which one I want to take off your fine ass before we skinny dip in the pool.”

“You sure?” I asked. “The price tag is kinda high.”

“Ain’t nobody worried about no damn price tag. Get all of them. Hey, Cornelius, look at how fine her ass looks.” Bobby turned the phone toward Cornelius, who was sitting beside him.

“Bobby!” I yelled, but it was too late.

“Damn, her ass is fat. I like that,” Cornelius said.

I couldn't believe Bobby had allowed Cornelius to see me without even asking. Although I'd worn a bathing suit plenty of times at the pool in the back yard, it still felt like a violation. I didn't like it at all and planned to let him know.

"A'ight, baby, get what you want, and I'll see you back at home. Oh, and make sure you get some sexy-ass shoes to go with each one of those swimsuits," Bobby instructed.

"Okay, if that's what you want," I said, the excitement of shoe shopping now overriding my brief anger.

"Damn right that's what I want. You're the lady on Bobby 'The Beast' Boyd's arm, so you gotta look the part."

"Okay, I will. Don't worry," I promised. He had no idea what he was getting himself into.

Three hours and six thousand dollars later, Darnell had all my shopping bags loaded into the trunk of the car, and we were headed back to the house. I never thought shopping could make me so exhausted, but there I was in major need of a nap.

I was just about to lay my head back when we stopped at a red light. Darnell pulled the car up next to a white Rolls Royce Phantom. It was my brother-in-law's car, parked in front of a restaurant.

"Darnell, roll down the window," I instructed, taking out my phone. "And don't drive off yet."

"Man, the light's green, and there are people behind me," Darnell moaned, looking in the rearview mirror.

"I don't give a damn about them. Just hurry up and roll down the window."

Darnell complied, and I pointed the camera at the car, snapping a photo just as the car behind us blew the horn. I snapped some more photos, then told Darnell, "Okay, fine. You can drive."

I attached the pictures I'd taken to a text for my sister Sydney. At least we know now what he's doing while he's "getting scarce." Eating, as usual.

"Honey, I'm home!" I announced when I walked into the house carrying one of many shopping bags. Although not as impressive as the Britton mansion, the one Bobby was renting was still one hell of an estate. I didn't find Bobby in the living room, the theater room, or his favorite place in the house, the home gym, so I climbed the spiral staircase and headed into the master suite.

"Bobby, where are—" I stopped and looked around, confused by the boxes and bins that were sitting in the middle of the bedroom floor.

"Hey, baby, you're back." Bobby emerged from one of the two walk-in closets, his arms full of clothes that he placed in one of the bins.

"What the hell are you doing?" I asked.

"Starting to pack up." Bobby walked over and kissed my forehead.

"Packing? Where are you going?" My voice trembled a bit.

"*We're* heading back to my home in Vegas."

"Vegas? What? When?"

"A few days. Maybe a week at the longest." Bobby walked back toward the closet.

"Bobby, wait."

He turned around.

"You said you'd be here for a few months, maybe longer," I reminded him.

He shrugged. "That was when I was planning to be here for Peter's trial. Now things have changed, and there's no trial."

"What do you mean there's no trial? What happened?"

"Bobby 'The Beast' happened. I worked my magic and made the trial disappear." Bobby grabbed me by the waist and pulled me close. "Now we can go home. You're going to love Vegas, baby, I promise."

"Bobby, what did you do?" I asked, still confused by what he was saying, or rather not saying.

"Like I said, I worked a little magic."

"What exactly does that mean?"

"Lord, you're nosey as hell. But without going into too many details, I was given some information, then I had a couple of conversations, paid a few dollars to solve some problems, and tomorrow, Peter Lane goes back before the judge. He'll be free to travel and become the newest member of Team BTB. See? Magic." Bobby waved his hand like it was a magic wand.

There were too many missing pieces to put together a full picture, but enough for me to know that whatever Bobby had done meant Peter would not be held responsible for assaulting Jesse Britton.

"This is crazy," I said with a blank stare.

"This is how Team BTB rolls, baby." Bobby kissed me.

"I gotta talk my sister," I thought out loud, suddenly overwhelmed. My mind was swirling, and I didn't know what to do.

"You go do that, and while you're there, grab the rest of your stuff and bring it back to the crib. We gotta get this stuff shipped. Better yet, you can leave that shit there and buy everything brand new. Your choice."

"I'll be back," I told Bobby.

"I'll have Darnell drive you."

"No, I'm good. Her house isn't that far, and I need some air. I'll have her drive me back over here," I said, allowing him to kiss me before I walked out of the room. My sister would be interested to know about what was happening, but there was one person I needed to talk to first.

37

Kimberly

"Well, that's everything," Reverend Chauncey said, placing the forms he'd just signed back into the envelope. "At least I hope it is."

It had been a long day, most of which was spent in Reverend Chauncey's office, reviewing and finalizing documentation to amend the Black Hamptons Homeowners' Association bylaws and completing additional legal paperwork. Jeffrey should have been the one taking care of the task at hand, but Moses had asked me to step in and handle it because Jeffrey was tied up.

"I knew filing the injunction on behalf of the HOA would require paperwork and bureaucracy, but this was a lot. I don't think there's any ink left in my pen here," he said with a laugh.

"Carolyn said the same thing while she was signing. At one point she asked why I couldn't just use her digital signature stamp to save her some time, but it wasn't an option."

"That woman is a mess. Must be nice to even have that as an option. The only signature I have is my good ol' John Hancock." He looked at his watch. "Well, it's almost five o'clock. I don't think I'm gonna make the post office today to send them off. On second thought, maybe I should send them by messenger over to Bradley's office. I know he's expecting them."

"I'll take care of it." I held out my hand, and he gave me the manila envelope.

"Thank you, Kimberly. You've been such a help with all of this. I certainly do appreciate it, and I'm gonna make sure to let the HOA members know at our follow-up meeting next week."

"I'm just doing my part, that's all." I placed the envelope into my purse. "You don't have to mention it to anyone. I may not have grown up in the Black Hamptons or own a house out here, but it's still very special to me."

"And you're special to us, Kimberly. You're a part of this community." He gave me a brief hug. "Don't worry. One of these houses will be yours very soon. Watch what I tell you."

"From your mouth to God's ears."

"He's listening." Reverend Chauncey glanced up to the ceiling.

"Good to know."

Reverend Chauncey walked me to my car, and as I began driving home, I had an epiphany. Instead of picking up sushi and spending a quiet evening alone, I decided to go into the city to hand deliver the paperwork. Lamont was just as much of a workaholic as I was, and he rarely left the office before nine. I'd been looking for the perfect excuse to see him, and now I had one.

Two and a half hours later, I arrived in Manhattan. Instead of parking in the garage, I found a parking spot closest to the street and checked the time, hoping it wouldn't take long to convince Lamont to tear himself away from his desk and join me for dinner. I did a quick mirror check, dabbing on some lipstick and perfecting my hair before grabbing my purse and stepping out of the car. Had my time not been limited, I would've stopped by my house, showered, and changed into one of my little black dresses that left nothing to the imagination. Luckily, the peach dress I wore, along with matching Louboutin heeled sandals, was just the right combination of corporate, cute, and sexy. Besides, since I was technically there on business, my attire couldn't be too much.

The lobby of the building stretched upward, soaring twenty-two stories high, with sleek, floor-to-ceiling windows. As I walked toward the elevators, my heels echoed on the polished marble floors. I pushed the button for the twenty-second floor, and a few moments later, entered the doors of Hudson and Hudson.

The receptionist was gone, and the usually busy office was quiet and dim, but the main office door was unlocked. Hopefully, it meant Lamont was still there. I continued past a half dozen cubicles to the executive suites, and sure enough, there was a light on in his office and the door was cracked. I took the envelope from my bag, preparing to knock and announce my arrival, until a sound came from inside.

"Ohhhhhhhhhh, yessssss." A woman moaned softly. "That's it. Right there."

I thought maybe I was hearing things, but the moaning continued, louder this time.

"Please don't stop. I'm almost there. Stay. Right. There," she commanded.

Oh my God. Is he in there watching porn? I wondered, unsure of what to do. On the one hand, I wanted to see exactly what he was doing. On the other hand, I didn't want to invade Lamont's privacy. Being an attorney was a stressful job, and if he wanted to get his rocks off in the sanctity of his office, that was his business.

"Mmmmmmm." This time the voice was male.

Curiosity got the best of me, and I eased closer to the door, peeking through the crack. My jaw dropped, and I blinked several times to make sure I wasn't crazy. Lamont wasn't watching porn. He was kneeling in front of his desk, shirt open, hands gripping a pair of long legs that he had buried his face between. The woman, who was sprawled in front of him on the desk with her skirt pulled up to her waist, gripped the back of his head. Her back was arched, and her head was thrown back. Lamont was doing his damn thing.

I should've walked away, but I couldn't move, too stunned by what I was seeing.

"Yes, yes, yes." She gasped, "Ohhhhhhhh, fuuuuuuuck. I'm cominnnnng."

"Mmmmmm. Hmmmmmm." Lamont's head moved back and forth. It looked like he was enjoying everything he was tasting.

Then, he stopped and leaned back. I couldn't see it, but I could imagine the smile on his face. "Fuck, I love doing that to you. It's fun to watch you lose control for a change."

"I bet. That talented tongue of yours does it to me every time." She pulled Lamont to his feet. "You are one skilled man, Lamont Hudson."

My heart raced, and I damn near fainted as I watched the woman stand and pull her skirt down over her hips. Her face, now in full view, was even more of a shock than the act I'd witnessed moments before. With each second that passed, it became harder to breathe. I wanted to run, but I couldn't stop looking.

"And you are one sexy woman, Carolyn Britton." Lamont pulled her close and kissed her.

Finally regaining my ability to move, I scurried away. By the time I made it back to the elevator, I was sobbing. Although Lamont wasn't my man, I still felt betrayed. That witch Carolyn always got whatever she wanted, including him.

I wiped my tears away before I got off the elevator and straightened myself up. The sadness I felt gave way to anger. I stormed out of the building and went back to my car. As I stood there, I glanced around the parking lot and spotted the silver Range Rover. The tire iron in my trunk was the perfect tool for what I was about to do.

"You bastard!" I screamed, lifting it over my head and smashing it into the windshield.

The impact not only shattered the glass but caused the alarm to go off. Startled by my actions, I panicked and hurried back to my car. I peeled out of the parking lot so fast that I nearly T-boned another driver.

"Son of a bitch!" I screamed as if I weren't the cause of the near accident.

I tried to calm down, but I couldn't. Images of Lamont pleasuring Carolyn continued to flash in my head. The more I tried to forget, the more vivid the visions became. Him kneeling. Her moaning. It was too much. I felt played.

My hands trembled as I hit the screen to call Moses twice, but he didn't answer. I had to do something, tell someone, go somewhere far away. There was only one person I could turn to, and only one place I could go. I needed my mother.

38

Anthony Johnson

I wasn't a heavy drinker. When it came to vices, food was usually my drug of choice, especially when I was angry or upset. My state of mind today called for something stronger than chocolate cake, though, and the half-empty bottle of Bourbon clearly reflected my state of mind. I was dangerously distraught. David was right. Taking the cooking class was a bad idea, and it had caused more trouble than I could have ever imagined. What I thought would be an act of love caused a chain reaction of incidents and a revelation that had me so vexed I couldn't eat—hence the booze I was currently guzzling.

Alyssa Winters may not have been a miracle worker, but she was a damn good chef and one hell of a cooking instructor. It hadn't even been a week, and I was already fricasseeing, sautéing, and braising like a pro. I'd become fascinated by the different seasonings Alyssa introduced to me, and I could easily see my love of food turning into a love of cooking.

Alyssa's patience and passion for culinary art made her an ideal instructor. Being with her in the kitchen was exciting and enjoyable. Our conversation flowed naturally, oftentimes extending beyond the recipes and ingredients. I found it so refreshing to be able to talk to her about any and everything, including my wife.

"Man, Sydney is gonna love this. She's not going to believe I made it. It tastes better than the Asian fusion restaurant we go to in the city," I said proudly as we packed up the leftover kung pao chicken, pad thai noodles, and spring rolls we'd prepared for the day's lesson. "She's loves pad thai, and she's gonna think this is takeout. I'm gonna let her believe it until I reveal the truth at our anniversary dinner."

"You are funny, Anthony. Didn't you tell me you cook for her all the time? Why are you so hype about it?" Alyssa laughed.

"Because I want her to be impressed."

"Uh, you own a multimillion-dollar tech company, you are an excellent father and take good care of your family. Don't you think that's impressive?"

"No, that's effortless. Impressive is when I put effort into doing something special to make her smile. I write poetry, learned to play the guitar, took singing lessons: anything to make her smile," I explained. "Nothing else matters."

"Wow."

"And now, here I am, learning to perfectly cook her favorite dishes from a phenomenal chef." I gestured at the white chef's jacket she wore that was monogramed with her name.

"Sydney sounds like one hell of a lucky woman." Alyssa stared at me with a look of admiration. "And you're one hell of a guy, Anthony Johnson."

"Right back at ya," I said. "I mean, come on. You're gorgeous, funny, and a great teacher, plus you're fun to be around. You deserve a guy who loves you enough to want to keep impressing you too."

"That would be nice, if only I could find one." She exhaled and began clearing the dirty pots and pans from the stainless-steel countertop and putting them into the sink.

"I might be able to help you with that." I removed my apron and tossed it onto the counter.

Alyssa quickly turned around, raising an eyebrow. "Oh, really? You got some prospects for me, Mr. Johnson?"

"I know a few guys," I told her. "They happen to work at the multimillion-dollar company I own."

"Well, gainfully employed and financial stability is definitely on my list of requirements."

"What else is on your list?" I asked curiously.

"Ummmmm, let's see. Attractive, God-fearing, mentally stable, emotionally available, supportive, secure in who he is, athletic, an effective communicator, enjoys traveling, desires a family," she listed. "Oh, and funny, but not corny."

"What's wrong with corny?"

"I can't do goofy guys or cornballs."

"See, that's the problem with women. Y'all are looking for Prince Charming when he only exists in books and movies. There are real kings out there."

"Where are they?"

"All you have to do is open your eyes and open your heart to find them," I told her. "And guess what?"

"What?"

"I'm corny as hell." I laughed and patted the bag of leftovers I was holding. "But I'm also impressive."

Alyssa smiled and shook her head. "You are one of a kind, Anthony Johnson, that's for sure."

"I'll see you tomorrow," I said before I exited the kitchen.

Alyssa called out to me on the sidewalk. "Anthony, wait." I turned to see her rushing toward me with a plastic container. "You forgot the rice."

"Thanks." I took the container and placed it in my bag. "And think about what I told you. There's a king ready and waiting for you."

"I really appreciate your advice, but I have to be honest. I haven't said anything, but I've had my eyes on someone since I've been here," Alyssa said coyly.

"Oh, really. Who? Do I know him?"

"You do." She reached up and put her arms around my neck. "It's you."

Before I could stop her, she pulled me close and leaned in to kiss me. I quickly turned my head, and her lips landed on my cheek.

"Alyssa, nah." I gently pushed her away. "I'm flattered, but I'm a married man."

"Yeah, married to a woman who doesn't appreciate you, Anthony." She pulled me toward her again, this time managing to hit her target. The kiss was brief, barely a peck.

"Anthony, what the hell?"

Sydney came rushing toward us.

"Oh, shit," I mumbled as I took a step back. "Syd, hey, uh . . . this is not what it looks like."

"No? Then what the hell is it?" Sydney screamed as she pushed her way between us and stood with her hands on her hips.

"You need to relax," Alyssa said boldly. "I wouldn't be out here doing too much if I were you."

"You bitch!" Sydney lunged for Alyssa and smacked her hard across her face. "Don't you ever try to come at my husband again."

"Hey, hey, hey." I reached out to Sydney and restrained her before things truly got out of hand.

"What do you think you're doing? Let me go!" Sydney snatched away from me.

"It wasn't my fault," I tried to explain. "Syd, I'm sorry."

"Stay the fuck away from me, Anthony!" She turned and stormed off, jumping into the car and peeling away from the curb.

"This is bad. I gotta go."

"Anthony, wait." Alyssa grabbed my arm. "There's something you should know before you go chasing after her."

"What?"

"I meant what I said when I told you Sydney didn't deserve you."

"I don't have time for this bullshit," I barked. "I gotta go after my wife."

"I know why she fired Rashid," Alyssa blurted out.

"Rashid? How the hell do you know him?" I'd never mentioned his name to her. Hell, I hadn't even talked to him since Syd fired him. I had tried reaching out to apologize and refund his money, but he never responded.

"He's my landscaper. I hired him after Sydney fired him, and he told me everything."

"Everything like what?"

Alyssa opened her mouth to say something, then stopped and looked at me like she pitied me.

"Alyssa, tell me what the fuck is going on."

"I think you need to talk to Rashid and let him explain." She reached out and placed her hand on my arm. "I'm sorry, Anthony."

I went home hoping to find Sydney, but she wasn't there. She wouldn't answer any of my calls or respond to any of the text messages that I sent. Confused and desperate for an explanation, I called Rashid. He answered this time.

"Yeah, Alyssa told me you might be calling me soon," he'd told me.

"She says there's something I should know about my wife, and that you're the person to ask," I said, getting straight to the point.

He was quiet for a moment before finally answering, "Uh-huh."

"We need to talk." I felt a ball of lead form in the pit of my stomach.

The conversation took place in the parking lot of a local bar. He was just as pleasant and cool as the first time we'd met, at least until I asked about Sydney and the firing. As he began to explain the entire ordeal and how my wife was involved, it felt as if the life we'd built began to crumble one brick at a time with each word he spoke. By the time he finished, I was in a state of disbelief.

"I'm sorry, Anthony," Rashid said. "You didn't deserve to find out like this, but you do deserve to know the truth."

"Is that what this is?" I stared at him. "I think that has yet to be determined."

"It's as close to the truth as we can get right now."

I left without saying another word.

Sydney still wasn't home when I returned. This time, I didn't bother trying to reach her. It was best that she was still gone because I needed time to process. The bag of chips I tried eating didn't soothe me at all. I went into the kitchen looking for something else to devour, but nothing in the cabinets appealed to me. My search led me to the pantry, and that's where I found the bottle of Bourbon sitting on the top shelf, waiting for me.

By the time Sydney arrived home, the Bourbon bottle was empty. Although my body was intoxicated, my mind was still very sober. She walked into the bedroom, where I sat on the side of the bed, wearing a pair of sweatpants and an old, tattered T-shirt instead of my usual silk pajamas.

"Where are the kids?" she asked, still sounding angry.

"I told them to spend the night at David's. They won't be back until the morning."

"Good. They don't need to be here right now."

"I agree."

Sydney flew off the handle. "I can't believe you, Anthony! What the fuck were you doing with that bitch?"

"I was taking a cooking class to surprise you for our anniversary," I answered, remaining calm.

"It looked more like you were tasting each other," she snapped.

"I wasn't doing anything, Sydney. She tried to kiss me, and I pushed her away, then you came running up."

"Bullshit!"

"What's bullshit?"

"What you just sat there and said," Sydney replied. "Are you fucking her?"

"What?" I raised my voice for the first time during the conversation.

"You heard me. I asked, are you fucking her?"

"I'm not even going to justify that with an answer."

"I knew it. You are fucking her!" Sydney reached out to hit me, but I deflected it. "That's why you won't answer."

I grabbed her wrist and forced her hand away from me. I got up from the bed and stood over her, staring her right in the eye. "Listen to me and listen to me good, Sydney. I haven't been with, had sex with, or even touched another woman since the day I told you I was in love and asked you to be my woman. You are the only woman I've even thought about fucking."

"And I'm just supposed to believe that?"

"Damn right you are, because it's the truth. I've never lied to you about anything, Sydney." I stated. "Can you say the same?"

She froze for a second. "What do you mean?"

"I mean, can you look me in the eye and say that you've never been with another man and that you've never lied about anything?" I made sure my question was as clear as possible.

"Yes," she insisted.

I tossed my hands in the air. "Ain't this some shit? You're really gonna look me in the eye and lie about lying."

"I'm not lying about shit. And why the hell are you upset with me when you're the one kissing another woman and lying about it?"

"I didn't lie about it. I told you Alyssa kissed me," I retorted. "Don't get it twisted. I'm not the liar here, Sydney."

"I told you I've never lied about anything."

Unable to contain myself any longer, I got right in her face. "Then why the hell does Rashid Logan believe there's a possibility that Tyler is his son?"

My question stunned Sydney. In that moment, I could see the fear in her eyes as her jaw dropped and she covered her mouth with her hand. In that moment, I knew that everything Rashid had told me was the truth. One thing about Sydney, she hated being lied on as much as being lied to. Had there not been any legitimacy to it, she would have immediately denied it. She didn't.

"Anthony, no. Tyler is yours." She reached out to touch me, but I stepped back. "I can explain."

"I don't want you to explain shit!" I wiped away the tears that I'd been holding back all night. "You lied to me, but you know who told me the truth? Rashid. I know all about what happened when you went down to Black Bike Week in Myrtle Beach our senior year of college. And now it all makes sense, why you didn't want to wait to get married before graduation. You were knocked up!"

"Yes, I was pregnant . . . by *you*, Anthony. And no, I didn't want to wait because I was in love with *you*." Sydney sobbed.

I laughed ruefully. "So much in love that you fucked Rashid in Myrtle Beach without a condom. If that's what you consider love, then I don't want that shit. I'm gone."

"Anthony, wait, please."

It was too late. I was gone in more ways than one.

39

Martin Britton

That evening, the air was cool and refreshing, with the unmistakable scent of fallen leaves and salt water blending in perfect harmony. I loved this time of year in the Hamptons. The sunset was especially gorgeous, the perfect backdrop for sipping cocktails. I couldn't think of a better time or place for Jade and me to continue our conversation about her selling, or rather not selling, her family's home. We'd gone to dinner twice and talked on the phone a couple of times, but her decision still hadn't been made. Time was of the essence, so I invited her to the yacht. Her immediate acceptance came as no surprise.

While waiting for her to arrive on the pier, I reminded myself that there was nothing wrong with what I was doing. I was merely reconnecting with an old friend while pointing out the value of keeping the property that had been in her family for generations. I wasn't making any promises or leading her on in any way. We were just enjoying each other's company with no expectations of anything else. I had to admit, though, that Jade being attracted to me did work to my advantage.

As I stood on the deck of the yacht watching her walk toward me, I couldn't help but admire her beauty. Her skin glowed in the warm evening light, and her features were illuminated with a soft radiance that seemed to exude from within. Her braids, no longer held hostage in a bun, fell long and loose. Her flowing jumpsuit couldn't hide her curves.

"Hey, you." I greeted her with an embrace as warm as the air surrounding us.

"Hello, Martin." She smiled and held up a bottle of champagne. "I brought us something to sip on during the sunset, as you so eloquently put it."

"Now, you know you didn't have to do that," I told her. "I already have some chilling for us."

"Well, maybe we can enjoy this one for mimosas at sunrise." She winked.

"Sunrise, really?"

Jade shrugged. "Just being proactive in case I get too tipsy to drive and have to stay for the night, that's all."

I took her by the hand and led her to the area that I'd already set up for us. A table with a chilled bottle of champagne and a charcuterie board of meats, cheeses, fruit, and chocolate sat between two cushioned lounge chairs. Soft R&B drifted through the built-in speakers.

The scenic view couldn't have been more perfect. The sky was painted in hues of soft pink and orange as the sun dipped below the horizon. After I filled our glasses with champagne, we walked to the edge of the deck to watch the wispy clouds drifting lazily across the sky, adding depth to the picturesque scene unfolding before our eyes.

"This is beautiful," Jade said.

"Yeah, there's nothing like it anywhere else in the world." I stood beside her. "One of the blessings of living here."

"It is," she agreed. "I guess I spend so much time focusing on the beauty of art inside the gallery that I forget about the magnificence of the outside."

"Guess you need to get out more."

She turned to look at me, not fooled by what I thought was a subtle lead-in to discussing the property. "I'm going to need more than a sunset on the water to make me turn down the offer I got, Martin," she said. "I told you I'm weighing all of my options to see what makes sense."

"Is this an option?" My heart pounded in my chest as I stared at her, the sexual tension between us evident. In a moment of recklessness, I threw caution to the wind and crossed the line, pulling her into my arms. Jade's mouth welcomed mine, and our tongues tangled, tasting the sweet residue of champagne. The promise I'd made myself to stay at a safe distance was easily broken as I took her by the hand and led her into my stateroom.

We hungrily devoured each other as we undressed quickly. My hands rubbed and squeezed her round bottom as my lips planted kisses all over her. Her sweet moans made the monster between my legs jump as I wrapped my lips around one of her nipples. I sucked gently, the way I would my favorite piece of candy, and allowed one of my hands to come up and fondle her other breast. When I couldn't take it anymore, I stepped back and reached for the drawer to the nightstand. My hand rummaged around until I found a condom.

Before I could rip it open, she took it from me and pushed me onto the bed. "We don't need this yet. Lay back," she instructed seductively.

I did as I was told, centering myself on the bed as she lowered her head and took my hardness into her mouth. Her braids tickled my inner thighs as her head bobbed back and forth rhythmically. I closed my eyes, enjoying her masterful skills. My toes curled, and just as I was almost to the point of no return, I stopped her.

"Get up."

Sensing what was to come, Jade retrieved the condom, opened it, and used her lips to slide it on my dick that was already on the verge of exploding. It was time for me to regain control, but Jade had other plans. Before I knew it, she straddled me, easing me into her wet center that was beyond ready to receive me. A soft moan escaped my lips as she slid down my shaft. My hands caressed her back, and she gripped my shoulders to control her ride.

"Oh, Martin." She tossed her head back while she bounced up and down.

The feeling of her body sliding against mine mixed with the pleasure below was almost too much to handle. I flipped her over on all fours so that I could take her from behind. Watching her bottom ripple with each stroke was a beautiful sight to see. I didn't know why I had ever stopped hitting that. It was amazing.

An hour and a few more positions later, I couldn't stop the volcano from erupting. I'd held on for as long as I could, and she was already two orgasms in. It was only fair that I got mine.

When it was over, I collapsed next to her as we caught our breath. She scooted closer to me and brushed her fingers gently along my chest.

"I hope that was as good for you as it was for me," I told her.

"I can confidently say that it was. Should I thank you now or later?" Jade looked up at me.

"No thanks needed at all. The pleasure was all mine."

Jade kissed my chest. "The past few days have been quite enjoyable, Martin. I hope we can continue enjoying one another's company."

I tried not to tense up, knowing she would feel it since she was lying on me. But I couldn't help the uncomfortable feeling. Reconnecting with Jade had been a slippery slope, but it had to be done to save the Black Hamptons. Sleeping with her was something I had wanted to avoid, but it was too late. It was evident she was hoping to pick things up where we left off, but that truly had never been my intention.

"Jade, you are gorgeous, talented, and incredible. I care about you, and I'm not going to lie to you. Not this time."

"Oh God, Martin, lie about what?" She sat up on her elbows, looking nervous.

"I'm just coming out of a relationship, so I'd like to keep things casual between us," I said. "Enjoy being friends for a while."

To my surprise, she nodded with a smile. "Oh, okay. Casual works for me too. I totally understand."

"Really?" I asked, overwhelmed with relief.

"Yeah. And I appreciate your honesty this time. I wish you would've had this same energy the first go around. Would've made shit a lot easier for both of us." Jade sighed. "Now that that's out of the way, can a girl get some more champagne, friend?"

"Damn right you can." I kissed her before getting out of bed and stepping into my discarded shorts. "I'll be right back."

I returned to the deck to grab the champagne and glasses. The sun was gone, now replaced by the full moon sitting high in the darkness, reflecting in the water along with the bright stars. I stayed there a moment to take it in, then went to gather the items I'd come to retrieve. As I turned around, I saw a familiar figure on the pier, staring at me.

"Karrin?" I called out.

"Hey, Martin." She waved and walked closer.

The sight of her against the backdrop of the moonlight took my breath away, and for a moment, time seemed to stand still.

"What are you doing out here in the dark?" I asked, excited to see her but concerned at the same time.

"I . . . I was just taking a walk out here, that's all. I remembered how beautiful it was at night, and I guess I wanted to see it."

"Oh, yeah." I nodded, sensing something was wrong. "Karrin, is everything okay?"

"Yeah, but I do need to tell you something important that you need to know."

"What is it?" I frowned, my eyes now landing on the *BTB* chain around her neck that was so shiny I could see it in the darkness.

"Martin, what's taking you so long?" Jade called out.

"Uh, I'll be right there," I returned, cringing at the horrible timing and praying that Karrin hadn't heard anything.

The look on Karrin's face let me know that she had. "Oh, I'm sorry."

"Nothing to be sorry for."

"I'm gonna grab the strawberries too, Martin. I'm hungry." Jade emerged onto the deck wearing just the shirt I'd worn earlier. She hugged me from behind. Karrin turned and rushed away.

"Shit," I whispered to myself. "Karrin, wait!"

It was too late. Karrin continued running down the pier into the distance.

"Oh." Jade's arms dropped from around my waist. "I didn't mean to interrupt anything."

"Nah, it's cool," I told her. "She just happened to be on the pier when I came out here, and we were just speaking. That's all."

"I see," Jade responded. "That's your ex, right?"

I turned and faced her. "Something like that, if that's what you wanna call it."

"She's pretty and must be one hell of a woman, that's for sure."

"I can't lie, she is." I sighed. "But how would you know that?"

"Okay, Martin, since we're being completely honest, I know all about your summer fling that ended in heartbreak. I didn't know that was her until I walked out here. But what I also know is she's now dating Bobby Boyd, and she got his nose wide open," Jade told me. "I don't know what kinda magic she got, but Bobby was about to give me a check—a big one—to make her happy."

"Why would Bobby want to pay you? He saw a painting or something?"

"No, fool. He made me an offer for my house that he's been renting for the summer."

"Bobby 'The Beast' Boyd is living in your house and wants to buy it?" I asked, trying to comprehend what she was telling me.

"Wanted to, but not anymore." Jade shook her head. "Can we sit and talk about this while drinking, please?"

"Sure."

"Now, explain what the fuck is going on, please," I said after we'd settled into the lounge chairs with fresh glasses of champagne.

"What's there to explain? Bobby's renting my AirBnB. He called and told me he was interested in purchasing it because he'd be in the area for a while, plus his new girl needed a spot to stay." Jade bit into one of the strawberries and sucked the juice from it. Had I not been so intrigued by what she was saying, I would've been turned on. "Honestly, I thought the reason you came into the gallery that day was because you were on some bullshit over her and Bobby. But then Eli Bradshaw popped up after you left and made an offer too. That's when I realized you were being sincere in what you were telling me. I wasn't going to sell to that gentrifying motherfucker, but I was considering selling to Bobby."

"But you said Bobby doesn't wanna buy the house anymore."

"Nope. He called and told me he changed his mind. Says he's not extending the rental time either. He's going back to Vegas, and his girl is going with him." Jade sipped her champagne.

Was that what Karrin had wanted to tell me? That she was leaving? There was a piercing pain in my chest, knowing she was leaving with Bobby. She barely knew him. I thought about how my mother had accused her of being a gold digger and wondered if there might have been some truth to it. Then, I remembered the way I felt when we were together and the way Karrin looked at me when she smiled. I knew it was love.

"Martin, are you okay?" Jade touched my arm.

"Yeah, I'm good," I lied and cleared my throat. "Anyway, so, now that Bobby doesn't want to buy the house, what are you going to do?"

Jade tilted her head and looked at me. "Is Amistad and the Britton Foundation truly interested in supporting Creatif Noir?

Because that house is the only thing I have that can fund my dreams, Martin."

"I promise you, Creatif Noir will have Amistad and the Foundation's full support. And mine," I said. "I've already discussed it with my parents, and we all agree."

"Well, I guess I can hold onto it a little longer, and while I'm at it, enjoy spending time with my friend, right?" She smiled and raised her glass. "To friendship."

"To friendship." I clinked my glass against hers, grateful that I'd completed the task I was given, but sad that what I had with the one woman I loved was really done.

40

Sergeant Tom Lane

As I entered the crowded courtroom, I was even more on edge than the first time I'd been there, mainly because I didn't know what was about to take place. The only thing Peter and I had been told by Christopher was that he needed to be in court at 9 a.m. for an emergency hearing. I pressed for more details, but Christopher got another call and said he'd explain when he saw us.

We'd arrived as scheduled and worked our way through the crowd of reporters yelling questions at us in front of the courthouse. Christopher was waiting for us at the top of the stairs.

"You go ahead inside, Sergeant Lane. Peter and I have to discuss a few things before we go in," Christopher instructed.

The courtroom was already full, and as I walked to one of the few empty seats behind the defense table, I took notice of who was in attendance. There were several officers from the department, Reverend Chauncey, and of course, the Brittons—minus Carolyn, which was slightly alarming. Although I made sure to avoid looking in their direction, I could feel the family glaring at me. I took my seat and began praying in my head.

"Hello, Sergeant."

I was so caught up in my own thoughts that I hadn't even realized Dr. Wells was in the seat beside me until she spoke. "Hey, Dr. Wells. How are you?"

"I'm well, thank you." She smiled.

I felt at ease for a brief moment, but my anxiety quickly returned. Peter's psychiatric evaluation was completed a few days ago. Could that be the reason for the emergency hearing?

"Were you petitioned to be here?" I asked Dr. Wells.

She shook her head. "I heard about Peter reappearing before the judge, so I'm just here to support, that's all. I'm sure this has to be stressful for him and for you as well."

"You have no idea," I said. "But I appreciate you being here. It means a lot."

Her presence held significance for me, particularly since I couldn't seem to shake thoughts of her ever since we left her office. Her voice, her smile, her genuine concern for Peter had lingered in my mind, occupying my thoughts more times than I could count. Having Dr. Tabitha Wells beside me was an unexpected but welcome surprise. I stole a subtle glance downward and was happy to see that her ring finger was empty. Of course, that did not necessarily mean that she was available or interested in me. Plus, there were the ethical implications of pursuing a romantic relationship with a parent of a patient, even if she were interested. Either way, I was happy to have her beside me.

"I hate to ask a question that I already know the answer to, but how are you?" she inquired.

"Very stressed." I was sure the answer was written on my face.

"That's totally understandable."

The side door opened, and Christopher, Peter, Chief Harrington, and the district attorney walked in. Peter kept his gaze focused ahead of him, looking up only once to find me for the nod of reassurance that I typically gave him right before one of his matches in the ring. Our eyes locked, and in that moment, the roles reversed and he gave me a nod. The exchange was brief, but long enough for me to notice the absence of distress in his face. I wasn't sure what was about to take place, but based on his demeanor, Peter wasn't worried.

"All rise." The bailiff called the court to order, and we stood while presiding Judge Matthew Proctor took his seat and the hearing began.

My heart pounded with a mixture of hope and anxiety. I watched intently as the proceedings unfolded. I tried to focus on each and every word spoken by the judge and the attorneys, but my mind was consumed by a whirlwind of emotions, making it difficult to concentrate.

"Your Honor, based on the new findings of the investigation and the recanting of the Prosecution's witness statement, we request that the assault charge be dropped at this time and the charge of breaking and entering be amended to criminal trespass," Christopher stated.

"DA Griggs, are you okay with that?" Judge Proctor asked.

"Yes, Your Honor," the district attorney said, then added, "For now."

Even with the comment, I felt a surge of relief.

"This is some bullshit!" Malcolm Britton's voice boomed through the courtroom, his outburst causing gasps and shock to ripple throughout. I turned to see him standing, his wife attempting to restrain him, along with Carolyn, who was now present.

"Malcolm, no!" Vanessa Britton pleaded.

"Bro, chill." Martin Britton placed his hand on Malcolm's arm, but Malcolm pulled away.

"Order in the court!" The judge struck his gavel repeatedly, attempting to restore order to the chaotic scene unfolding in the courtroom.

"You're really gonna let this bastard get away with nearly killing my son?" Malcolm continued yelling.

"Son, calm down, please," Moses Britton said.

"Bailiff, please escort Mr. Britton out of the courtroom," Judge Proctor instructed.

"That won't be necessary. We'll gladly leave this circus that's taking place," Carolyn announced. "And trust me, everyone involved in this miscarriage of justice will be dealt with on every level: county, state, and federal."

"Let's go." Moses put his arm around her as they followed their family and a few other community members out the double doors in the back of the courtroom.

"Now, let's proceed," the judge stated. "Based on the evidence presented before the court and the discretion of the Prosecution, both the assault and breaking and entering charges against Mr. Lane are dismissed. However, the defendant will still be charged with criminal trespassing."

"Your Honor, my client is ready to plead guilty to the criminal trespass charge at this time," Christopher said.

"Is that true, Mr. Lane?"

Peter stood up. "Yes, Your Honor."

"The court accepts your plea. You're hereby ordered to pay a fine of one thousand dollars, and I expect you to stay out of trouble, young man. See the clerk on your way out. Court is adjourned!" Judge Proctor struck the gavel again, and just like that, it was over.

Tears welled up in my eyes as I gazed at my son, overwhelmed with gratitude. Despite the hardships we had endured, we emerged victorious and stronger than ever before. My chest swelled with pride thinking of the courage Peter had displayed throughout the ordeal. Yet, amid the joy and relief, a sense of solemnity lingered as the gravity of the moment sank in. I knew that this was not the end of our journey, but rather a new beginning.

While I was elated about the felony charges being dropped, I couldn't shake the certainty that there would still be repercussions. My concern was torn between the Brittons and Bobby Boyd. Both were viable threats in my eyes.

"I'm so glad things worked out in Peter's favor," Dr. Wells told me.

"Yeah, me too. I've been praying for a miracle, and I'll be damned, we got one."

"Dad!" Peter yelled.

"Son." I walked over and embraced him. "Congratulations."

"I can't believe this. I'm so happy I don't know what to do." Noticing Dr. Wells beside me, he said, "Dr. Wells, you're here."

"I am, and I'm happy for you, Peter." She offered him a kind smile before Christopher approached.

"Peter, we have some paperwork for you to sign, and you gotta get that thing off your ankle, man," Christopher told him.

"Christopher, thank you." I extended my hand, and he shook it. "I appreciate everything you did to help Peter."

"Hey, I just did my job. Honestly, it was a team effort, though. Right, Peter?" Christopher nudged him.

"Yeah, it was," Peter agreed.

Something about the word "team" and the look they exchanged bothered me.

"Let's go so we can get out of here and celebrate." Christopher motioned toward the side door with his head.

"I can go with you," I said.

"No need, Sergeant," Christopher told me. "We can meet you out front when we're done. It shouldn't take long."

Peter followed Christopher out of the same door that they'd entered. I looked around and saw that Dr. Wells and I were the last ones inside.

"I guess we need to get out of here," I told her.

As we walked out, she asked, "So, what's next for Peter now that this is over?"

"He'll definitely get back to training for the Olympics."

"He told me that was one of his aspirations. I think that's amazing."

"Now that the felony charges have been dropped and he's not facing any jail time, I'm hoping that's still a possibility," I said, then stopped walking. "Listen, Dr. Wells."

"Yes?" She turned and looked at me.

I was so caught up in how beautiful she was that I nearly lost my train of thought. "Even though Peter's legal situation is over, I'd like for him to continue therapy."

"I think that's a good idea, Tom. Getting treatment for his anger will certainly be beneficial. He'll have tools in place to help in case, God forbid, a situation like the one that led up to this happens again. I'm sure he has trauma not just from the altercation, but this entire ordeal."

"He does."

She suddenly looked past me to the exit doors. "What in the world is going on out there?"

I turned and saw the crowd of people gathered on the courthouse steps.

"Oh, probably just the press. They were hanging around when we got here. Peter and I barely made it through the crowd."

"Is that Bobby 'The Beast' Boyd?" She stepped closer. "Wait, that *is* him."

Tensing, I made my way to the doors, silently praying that Dr. Wells was mistaken. Unfortunately, she was not. Bobby stood at the top of the courtroom steps stood with Cornelius by his side, posing for the cameras as if Bobby had just won a boxing match. I didn't need to ask why they were there. There could only be one reason.

Oblivious to Dr. Wells, I eased out the door farthest from the crowd and stood in a far corner, anxious to find out what the hell he had to say.

"I came out here today to show my support to my man Peter Lane, a talented athlete with a bright future. I'm glad that things played out the way they did in court because at the end of the day, Pete's a good dude," Bobby proclaimed to his captivated audience. "And what I don't want is for this to be the only thing he's known for. That powerful punch of his is going to be put to good use . . ."

Cornelius handed something to Bobby, but it wasn't until he held it up that I could see what it was. The crowd erupted into cheers as I stared at the diamond chain dangling in the air. I realized what was happening and felt a surge of panic.

"With Team BTB!" Bobby bellowed.

"What's going on?" Dr. Wells appeared by my side, craning her neck to catch a glimpse of the spectacle. "Is that Peter?"

Too stunned to answer, I watched as Peter stepped forward. Now I understood why Christopher had whisked him away and told me not to join them. The entire thing was a PR setup for Team BTB. Peter smiled as he faced Bobby, allowing the chain to be draped around his neck. I scanned the crowd and there, in the distance, I spotted Malcolm Britton, his face full of pain as he watched the young man who'd assaulted his son bask in a moment of glory. As a father, it made me feel a pang of shame.

"Pete is heading back to Vegas with me, on the private jet, of course, and he'll be joining the rest of the team so he can get ready for his first professional fight. He's going to be the next champ. I can feel it." Bobby put his arm around Peter, both of them grinning proudly as the crowd went wild again.

"Tom, are you okay?" Dr. Wells touched my arm.

"Yeah," I lied, closing my eyes to avoid witnessing my son selling his soul to the devil.

"Yeah, Peter! Team BTB, baby! Power Punch Pete!"

The crowd cheered and clapped.

"Tom." Dr. Wells repeated my name, gently touching my arm. "Come on. Let's go back inside."

"Nah," I shook my head and stormed off, nearly running to get to my son. I pushed past Cornelius and grabbed Peter by the lapel of his jacket, pulling him away.

"Yo!" Bobby yelled as he was shoved aside.

Cornelius and a few others from Bobby's entourage moved to intervene, but Bobby had the presence of mind to stop them. "Stand down. It's cool. Let him talk to Pete," I heard him say as we made it through the door.

I continued pulling Peter as I searched for somewhere private for us to talk. He'd been the center of enough attention, and I didn't want to give people anything else to discuss. The men's restroom was the first thing I came across that seemed suitable, so I dragged him inside.

"Dad, please." Peter pulled away from me.

"Boy, what the fuck is wrong with you?" I shouted, shoving Peter against the wall. He looked shocked. I'd never put my hands on him like that before.

"Nothing's wrong," Peter replied.

"Do you even realize what you've done?"

"I do. I did what was best for us." Peter straightened his suit jacket.

I grabbed the chain and told him, "No, you did what was best for you, Peter. You're the one leaving on a fucking private jet going to Vegas. Did you even think about any of this before you agreed to it?"

"Yeah, I did. It's all I've been thinking about. I thought about Bobby hiring the top attorney to represent me and how he's been nothing but supportive and helpful because despite what happened, he believed in me."

"Son, I've always believed in you and had your best interest at heart. That arrogant bastard doesn't even call you by your right name. Who the fuck is Pete? You hate that shit." I began pacing in frustration. "Leaving is the last thing you need to do right now. What about therapy and getting your anger under control? What about your Olympic future? Did you think about any of that?"

"No, I thought about a secure future. Not just for me, Dad. For us."

"What the hell does that mean? You think that couple hundred thousand dollars Bobby's gonna pay you is gonna secure your future? It's not."

Peter reached into the inside pocket of his suit and took out an envelope, handing it to me.

"What the fuck is that?" I stared at it.

"Open it," Peter insisted.

I took the envelope and opened it. Inside was a set of folded papers. "What the hell is this, Peter?"

"It's the deed to the house and a bank receipt for a deposit of fifty thousand dollars that went into your account today."

"What?" My eyes widened and I stared at him.

"I love you, Dad. I know you don't agree with my decision, but Bobby really had my back, and I owe him. He saved me, so I gotta go. Plus, I want to. I want to live my own life, Dad. I love you, and I'll always love you. You're the one that's been here. That's why I wanted to make sure you were straight before I left." Peter sniffed, and I saw the tears that were now streaming down his face. "I messed up big time when I beat up Jesse Britton, and I'm sorry. Just know that I'm still going to make you proud. Bye, Dad."

"Peter, man, listen . . ."

Peter turned and sprinted out of the bathroom before I could stop him.

"Peter!" I called as I ran after him, but he was gone. There was no sign of him in the hallway. My heart was pounding, and the sweat pouring from my temples mixed with the tears on my cheeks. With each step, it became more and more difficult to breathe, and I grabbed onto the wall for support.

"Tom."

I glanced up and saw Dr. Wells as she ran toward me. Her beautiful face was the last thing I saw before I hit the ground and my entire world went black.

41

Tania Reynolds

I sat on a bench at the end of the pier, staring into the distance, where the scenery around me blurred into a hazy backdrop for my swirling emotions. The sky above was a canvas of shifting hues, transitioning from fiery sunset to deep twilight. Despite the picturesque beauty of the evening, I couldn't enjoy it. The profound sense of heartache and confusion I felt weighed heavily on me, overshadowing any happiness I usually would've gotten from the view.

My thoughts filled my head like a turbulent storm, torn between the love I felt for one man and the guilt of betraying another. The beach, which I had hoped would offer me solace, only served to magnify my inner turmoil. The waves crashing against the shore, the salty breeze blowing against my skin—none of it could soothe the ache in my heart or the fear in my chest. Instead, it only added to my sadness, causing another wave of tears to fall down my cheeks.

"Tania, right?"

The voice coming from behind startled me, causing me to jump. I turned around to see the beautiful woman as she came and sat beside me on the sand, uninvited. She wore a flowing, sleeveless maxi dress in a vibrant shade of turquoise that complemented her mahogany skin. Hanging from around her neck was a sparkly *BTB* necklace.

"Yeah." I wiped my tear-stained face with the collar of my shirt, hoping she didn't notice. She looked familiar, but I couldn't place her. "Do I know you?"

"No," she answered, "but you know my niece and nephew, Gabby and Tyler. I'm their Aunt Karrin."

"Okay. Yeah, Tyler is smart, and Gabby is really nice. I like them both. They're cool."

"That they are. I love them." She smiled. "So, why is a pretty young lady like you sitting alone out here crying?"

"I'm not crying. I got sand in my eyes, that's all. It's kinda windy," I lied.

"Ain't that much sand in the world that can cause those tears I've been watching you shed for the past hour. I was over there." She pointed to a bench farther down the pier. "But hey, I get it. Hell, I came out here for a good cry myself but got caught up watching you instead."

"My bad." I managed a small smile.

"So, what's up? What's got you so sad?" she asked.

I thought about the answer to her question. The predicament I'd gotten myself into was so fucked up that telling my mother and grandmother wasn't an option. And there was no way in hell I could tell my friends. As crazy as it seemed, talking to a stranger made sense to me.

"My life is in shambles." My tears returned as I began to speak.

Karrin put her arm around my shoulders. "It's okay, Tania. You can talk to me. Is this about Peter Lane?"

"Yeah." I sniffed.

"You don't have to cry. He went back to court today, and he's good now," she said.

"I know. He's been calling and texting, but I haven't talked to him yet."

"Why not?"

"Because I'm the reason everything happened. It's complicated," I said, fighting feelings of guilt and regret as I began to explain, suddenly eager to confess what I'd done. "My grandmother made a huge sacrifice for me to go to college, and she was about to lose her house. I told Peter about it, and he said he'd fix it. I didn't know what he meant, and honestly, I didn't even believe him until Bobby Boyd showed up at my house saying he needed to talk to me. So, he talked, and I listened. He told me that Jesse's head trauma caused memory loss, so he couldn't give a statement about what happened. That made me the only witness, so I . . . he . . ."

Karrin found the words that I was looking for and finished what I was trying to say. "Gave you the money to save your grandmother's house. That's why you retracted your statement."

I gasped. "You know about that?"

"I know bits and pieces. Bobby's my boyfriend, so I hear things." She pointed to the chain I'd already noticed.

"Team BTB," I murmured.

"Team BTB," Karrin repeated. "Listen, I get it. You did what you had to do. I can't fault you for it, Tania."

"I feel so bad for Jesse, though," I whimpered. "He wasn't the one who did anything wrong, I did. I was the one cheating, even though I love Peter."

"You made a mistake. We all do," she said. "You learn from them, and life goes on. Believe me, this isn't the end of the world."

"It is. At least for me it is. My life is over." My lip began trembling as I pulled my knees to my chin and began rocking back and forth.

"Why do you think that?"

"Because I'm pregnant." I'd been holding onto that secret for the past two weeks.

"Shit." Karrin looked as shocked as I'd been when the pregnancy test showed a plus sign.

"And before you suggest it, I'm not having an abortion." I glanced over at her.

She shrugged. "Your body, your choice, girl."

"I know me saying that sounds dumb, because terminating the pregnancy would be a quick fix, but it won't make all of this shit I'm dealing with go away." I sighed. "Believe it or not, the only thing I'm certain of is I'm having this baby. Everything else has yet to be determined. Am I stupid?"

"No, you're not stupid. You're fine."

Hearing her say that made me feel a little better, but I was still in turmoil. "Peter wants to marry me."

"Okay, that's a good thing, isn't it? You just told me you love Peter and you're pregnant, so marriage makes sense. Obviously, he loves you too if he had Bobby help you out. Look, I know that you're young, but that man just signed a deal of a lifetime and is about to have a bank account full of more zeros than you can count. If you ask me, you hit a lick and a big one, girl. You got love, a baby, and a check for the next eighteen years even if shit doesn't work out." Karrin looked as me as if I were crazy. "And you got the nerve to be sitting over here crying? Girl, please. You don't have no problems, for real."

"Yes, I do."

"I'm listening." Karrin folded her arms.

"Because I don't know if the baby I'm carrying is Peter's or Jesse's," I said before I began sobbing.

Karrin pulled me to her chest and rubbed my back until I was finally able to pull myself together. By then, my shirt and her dress were covered in my tears.

"What am I gonna do?" I asked.

She gave me a strange look and didn't answer right away. I thought something was wrong until she finally mumbled. "Jesus Christ, this is déjà vu."

"How so?"

"Nothing." She shook her head like she was trying to clear her thoughts. "This is just weird because someone I love very dearly was in this exact same predicament once upon a time."

"What did she do?"

"The same thing you're going to do: the best thing for you and your baby. You're going to accept Peter's proposal, pack your shit, and get on that plane with us tomorrow," Karrin told me.

"I can't just leave and go to Vegas."

"You can and you will. Don't worry. You're not gonna be alone. I'll be there with you. We can shop and be rich housewives together," she said with a laugh.

"But what if it's not Peter's baby?"

"Peter asked you to marry him. Jesse didn't. And if you know like I know, you won't ever mention this again."

Karrin stood and helped me to my feet. The sun was now gone, and the sky was a shimmery, deep midnight blue. "Honestly, it wouldn't be Jesse that I'd worry about. It's that bitch of a grandmother of his that would make your life miserable."

"Oh God, you're right. She would," I said, thinking of the hell that Carolyn Britton would put me and my family through.

As much as I didn't want to, leaving was the best thing for me, my family, and especially the baby I was carrying. Everyone knew about my indiscretion with Jesse, and my pregnancy would cause speculation and conversation that I didn't want to deal with.

"Thank you, Karrin." I hugged her. "For everything."

"We're going to have a good time. You'll see. You're not the only one who needs to get the hell away from the Black Hamptons. My heart and I do, too."

"Your heart? Aren't you Bobby's girlfriend?" I asked, confused.

"I am. But just because your body is on the arm of a man doesn't always mean your heart is with him too." She put her arm around me, and we began walking, "Don't worry. Auntie Karrin has so much to teach you."

As we strolled down the pier, it dawned on me where I knew her from. I'd seen her with Jesse's uncle Martin. Karrin was his ex, which meant the heart she was leaving was his. The beautiful stranger who was now my new "auntie" was going through the same confused heartache as I was. One question lingered in my head as we walked. I wondered but I didn't ask: Was she pregnant too?

42

Malcolm Britton

"I'm sorry, Dad." Jesse apologized for what seemed like the hundredth time. I wasn't sure if his repetition was due to his short-term memory loss or his need to reinforce his remorse.

"There's nothing for you to apologize for, son. You didn't do anything wrong, and this wasn't your fault." I rubbed the top of his head affectionately.

"I tried to remember what happened. I promise. I just couldn't."

"Baby, listen." Vanessa kneeled in front of Jesse, who was sitting on the side of his bed with his head down. "You don't remember yet, that's all. But you will. It'll just take some time."

"But that asshole is free now and becoming a famous boxer, while I'm stuck here forgetting what I ate for breakfast and considering plastic surgery to have my nose reset. No wonder Tania won't talk to me," Jesse said, then repeated, "I'm sorry."

"Tania can go to hell, and so can Peter. Don't even think about them. Right now, all you need to do is focus on you." She touched the side of his face. "And your nose is fine."

The weight of disappointment and frustration hung heavy in the air. The slap on the wrist the judge gave Peter felt like a slap in the face of justice. My hands clenched into tight fists as I struggled to contain my anger. It was not just anger toward Peter, Judge Proctor, DA Griggs, and lying-ass Tania. I was also angry at myself. I'd failed to do my due diligence as a father, and now Jesse was paying for it.

"I'm sorry," Jesse repeated.

"Damn it, Jesse. Stop apologizing!" I snapped, no longer able to contain my exasperation.

"Malcolm!" Vanessa scowled at me.

It was my turn to apologize for my outburst that certainly wasn't helping the situation. "I'm sorry, Jesse. That was uncalled for. I'm just so upset."

"It's okay, Dad." Jesse looked up at me.

As I looked at my son, I saw the pain in his eyes, the confusion and disbelief that not only could someone could hurt him and get away with it, but also because the head injuries he sustained left him defenseless. I knew that the moment would leave a lasting impact on Jesse: physically, mentally, and emotionally.

"I'll be back," I murmured, then walked out of Jesse's room.

"Malcolm, you need to pull it together," Vanessa whispered, trailing after me in the hallway. "This is hard for him."

I made sure we were far enough away so our son couldn't hear us before I stopped and pivoted to face her. "Don't you think I know that? Watching him go through this is hard for me too."

"It's hard for all of us, Malcolm. Jesse being beat to the point of unconsciousness was hard enough, but Peter Lane walking away like nothing happened makes it even worse. But right now, that's what we have to deal with," Vanessa stated plainly.

"Vanessa, I'm his father, and I failed him."

"What? That's ridiculous."

As I stared at her, I realized the contrast in our attire. While I still had on the suit and tie that I had worn to court, she wore yoga pants, a tank top, and sneakers. We'd been home for hours, yet changing clothes hadn't even crossed my mind. That's how consumed I was.

"It's not ridiculous. It's the fucking truth," I retorted. "If I'd been focused on the case and not distracted by trying to find out what Everett Simpson was doing, we wouldn't have been blindsided by what happened today. Making Peter Lane pay should've been my one and only priority. I fucked up."

"You didn't fuck up, Malcolm."

"I did and you know it," I insisted. "If I—"

"What the hell are the two of you yelling about?" My mother's voice interrupted me. I turned to see her standing at the top of the staircase, hands on hips. "I can hear you all the way downstairs in my office."

"I'm sorry, Carolyn," Vanessa said, lowering her voice. "Your son feels responsible for the outcome of the case. He says it's his fault."

"Malcolm, that's ridiculous." Mother rolled her eyes. "You didn't have anything to do with the bullshit way DA Griggs handled the case, or Chief Harrington's incompetence with the investigation."

"I should've been on both of their asses about the case, though. Calling, visiting their offices, hell, hiring a private investigator. I should've done more." I shook my head. "But I didn't. And to quote my wife, this is something we have to deal with."

"To be honest, we all could've done more. I should've been making calls the State Department and following up, or at the least, demanded that Griggs have the trial moved to another jurisdiction." She approached us. "But I was too distracted by getting rid of Eli Bradshaw and making sure that little plan of his to destroy our community didn't work."

I was surprised to hear my mother's admission of her own shortcomings. Humility was not her strong suit. Although her empathy was appreciated, it didn't alleviate the heaviness of defeat I felt. The image of Peter Lane standing next to Bobby "The Beast" Boyd in front of the courthouse, both cheered by the crowd, lingered in my mind.

"And Vanessa is correct," Mother continued. "We do have to deal with it, and we will. The only way we'll get through this is the same we way get through everything else. As a family."

"That's what I was trying to tell him," Vanessa commented. "Beating himself up isn't going to help."

My wife's comment made her the next target of my frustration. "Who the hell else am I supposed to beat up, Vanessa? Peter Lane?"

"Malcolm, you need to calm down. Actually, you need to leave. Take a walk, a drive. Better yet, spend the night on the yacht," Mother instructed.

"What?" I exclaimed.

"You heard me. Spend the night on the yacht." She repeated her instruction, this time adding an explanation. "The last thing we need here in the house is you yelling at everyone. Go and clear your head. Come back in the morning when you've had time to calm down."

Mother descended the stairs, leaving my stunned wife and me in the hallway.

"You gotta be fucking kidding me. Now I'm being sent away like a grounded teenager?" I shook my head and threw my hands up in frustration.

"Malcolm, Carolyn's right. You need some distraction from all of this. A night on the yacht might do you good," Vanessa said. "I'll go with you. Just let me get Jesse settled and then pack—"

"No, you stay here," I interrupted, realizing that being alone with my own thoughts might be what I needed. "If I'm taking space, I want it from everyone. I'll be back in the morning."

"Are you sure?" Vanessa asked.

"I'm positive." I kissed her forehead and left.

The peace and solitude that the yacht was supposed to bring me was nonexistent. Depsite being alone with no interruptions, the turmoil of my thoughts prevailed. The soft rush of the water against the hull provided a momentary distraction, but my mind remained clouded with frustration. Standing at the edge of the deck, I sipped a glass of premier Scotch, hoping to find solace in the moonlit water, hoping to relax, but my tension remained. Desperate for some relief, I changed into a pair of shorts and a T-shirt and decided to go for a run on the beach instead.

Without the AirPods I usually wore when running, the rhythmic pounding of my footsteps on the sand became my soundtrack. For a half hour, I ran along the shoreline, the cool night air wrapped around me, providing the oxygen I needed to continue the impromptu personal marathon. With each breath, the storm of emotions raging within began to subside, gradually giving me a glimpse of the serenity I was looking for.

I stopped momentarily to gather my thoughts and take in the scenery. As I stared into the darkness, something floating in the distance caught my eye. The object seemed out of place. I took my shoes and socks off to walk in the water to get a closer look. As I strained to make out what it was, my heart skipped a beat. It was a body. A sense of dread came over me, sending a chill down my spine.

"Help! Help! Someone called nine one one!"

My instincts kicked into overdrive. With a surge of adrenaline, I waded into the water, my movements fueled by a desperate urgency. I reached out, grasping for the lifeless form, pulling it toward the shore with all the strength I could muster.

"Help me, please!" I screamed at the top of my lungs, gasping to catch my breath while I laid the body gently on the sand.

"They're on the way!" A passerby walking his dog rushed toward me. "Oh God, should we do CPR?"

"No, I think it's too late for that," I panted. "Help me turn him."

"Okay." The guy helped me flip the face-down corpse onto its back.

Shock and disbelief overwhelmed me at the sight of the dead man's face. I rubbed my eyes with the back of my hands, wiping away the saltwater that I hoped was making me see things. I blinked and looked down at the dead body in front of me, and a sob escaped my lips.

"Morgan."

Notes